Sins

of

Retribution

ALSO BY JAMES C. GILLEN

Tortured Skin

Crimson Madness

Sins

of

Retribution

By

James C. Gillen

ISBN: 1-942212-06-2
ISBN-13: 978-1-942212-06-5

Hydra Publications
1310 Meadowridge Trail
Goshen, KY 40026

www.hydrapublications.com

Sins
of
Retribution

CHAPTER ONE

Light had become nothing more than different shades of shadows along the hospital corridor. Moonlight found its way in through the rooms to my right casting grotesque shadows into my pathway. The chrome on a distant wheelchair glowed in the distance. No sounds other than the ever present beating of my heart. I breathed in the stale air, polluted with the copper-like hint of fresh blood. Somewhere in the distance, a killer waited on me. Ancient and powerful. A master blood sucker that had turned me into the hunted.

In almost total darkness, my mind began to play tricks on me. Hearing and seeing things that weren't there. I couldn't get my feet to move forward. My hand slick with my own sweat as it tried to gain a firm grip on the wooden stake. My mouth grew arid as I tried to swallow. Muscles cramped in the Florida heat.

Out of the distant room to my left, Asa stepped into view. Seven foot tall, maybe more. The biggest monster I had ever encountered. His black Jamaican skin shimmered with muscles as he advanced. Any source of light now gone.

I tried to run as he approached with speed. I swung the wooden stake, but hit nothing. Oversized hands slammed me to the wall. What breath I had in my lungs pushed free. Panic set in as I tried to escape. Voices started to laugh from places unseen. Taunting me, urging death.

Fangs dug deep into my throat. I heard the snap of skin, the rip of muscle. I couldn't break free. Swallow after swallow, I could hear my blood rush down his throat.

My stake pushed forward, but still those jaws locked tight. I pounded my fist against his head. Nothing.

I grew cold. I couldn't speak. A pounding echoed through the hallway, again and again. Pound. Pound. Pound.

I broke out of my nightmare fighting against the sheets. I sat up and looked around the room only to find the same empty space that had been there when I went to bed. My hands were balled into fists from holding the imaginary stake from my dream. Mark it as official. I had lost it.

It had only been six weeks, three days, two hours and forty-eight minutes since I had killed Asa, the pure blooded master roach of Orlando, but I still had no peace of mind. I staked him in self-defense and left him to die while I tracked down a few of his little friends. When I came back, Asa's body had vanished into thin air. This left me with the source of my nightmares. Dead or alive?

My name is Paul Isaac, vampire killer. Welcome to my little paradise.

Wiping away beads of sweat from my brow, I tried to clear the cobwebs in my head. The dream seemed so real. I could close my eyes and live it again. My skin on fire even though the room around me remained cold. The darkness left my sight helpless past the back of my hand. Asa's presence reached out to me from beyond the realm of death. He had to be dead. I saw the stake in his heart. No blood sucking roach could live through that.

The doorbell rang again in three quick pulses followed by synchronized knocks. My muscles tensed from the jolt. I tended to be a bit jumpy when it came to loud noises in the night. I had seen with my own two eyes things that were hell bent on eating me from flesh to bone. It would be an understatement to say I had an enemy or two. All would like nothing more than see me six feet under. Add in a ringing doorbell at three in the morning and I transformed into a recipe for a nervous casserole.

You see, by all accounts, I'm what's called a vampire executioner. I cut the heads off the corpses of fang victims before they can rise as one of the undead. I hunt down the vein sucker responsible, which should be a good thing to all those that live and breathe and call themselves human, right? But that's not the case these days. In a time and age of all political correctness, it has allowed the dregs of society to enter the game, and by that, I mean vampires, or as I prefer to call them, cockroaches.

Activist groups such as the Knights of the Night and governments from around the world now see these blood sucking bat heads as protected artifacts and members of society. They can own businesses, work in your building, even live in the house next to you. And there is nothing you or I can do about it.

To lessen the fear of these monsters, Hollywood and Washington alike have portrayed them as sparkly and beautiful, drinkers of animal or synthetic blood. It's a political stench that spreads like a disease. That stench is bullshit and I'll shout it to the roof tops until someone out there wakes up and smells the true coffee.

Some say I'm a dinosaur in this modern world. Only able to stake and kill if the victim has risen from the dead or if the bastards stray too far from the straight and narrow. Even then, human and fang laws seem to hesitate in handing me the legal papers to separate their heads from the body. Now, those laws are in place to protect them from me. I'm seen as the bad guy, vigilante. Some even call me an avenger. You can go to hell if you're one of them.

Candy coat them as historical artifacts, a misunderstood society, an irrational fear, whatever you want, but I've seen the cold hard facts. When we, as a society, start protecting the very things that try to eat us, there's a flaw in the system. These things are vicious killers, hell-bent on sucking us dry, and we've basically given them the rights to do so. To those of you that support the Knights of the Night, and you know who you are, kiss my vampire staking ass.

By the time the second round of doorbell rings and knocks happened, I had dressed in a black Harley Davidson t-shirt and well-worn blue jeans. Still in the dark, I reached into the nightstand next to my bed and reached for my Magnum, loaded with ultra violet bullets. Never underestimate bumps in the night. And without a confirmation of Asa's death, my weapons became a security blanket.

The sweat ran down my back and turned cold, sending a tingle down my spine. I fought the urge to shiver. It would make getting an accurate shot more difficult. I took a deep breath, gathered my nerves and walked out of the bedroom in methodical soft steps.

As I worked my way down the stairs, I bent low and tried to see through the thin curtains that produced a single silhouette. I listened to the silence. My eyes scanned the room below for anything that might have already found its way inside. For all I knew the shadow at the door had been nothing more than a diversion. A bit paranoid, I know, but that's how I've been able to stay alive for as long as I have.

Below me, nothing more menacing than my living room furniture, glowing in the soft light that came from the outside streetlamps.

"Who's there?" I asked as I hit the bottom step and moved close to the wall on my right in case I needed to dive for cover. Just because something knocks on the door one minute, doesn't mean it won't break it down the next.

Two more rings followed by three knocks. Further apart in time, but with the same urgency behind them.

"Paul," a familiar muffled voice called out.

I allowed myself to breathe again as I lowered the Magnum slightly. "Price, that you?"

"Paul, please help me." Shadows danced across the artificial light as it mixed with the black sky. A man paced on my porch. I knew him by the shadow alone. Large and round like Santa Claus and usually about as jolly. Price found himself at the end of a grand career and placed out to pasture in the monster district.

I brought the Magnum back up again out of instinct and started to make my way to the door. "What's wrong, Price?" My mouth went instantly dry.

"Please Paul, I need to talk to you. You gotta help me." He hated the monsters as much as I did, just in a different way. He feared them and I didn't blame him.

With my knee on the edge of the chair in front of the window, I reached for the corner of the curtain and peered out at the man at my door. I trusted Price with my life, but if he came here in the hands of monsters, they could be using him as a decoy to get to me. I planned to open the door either way. I had already made my mind up on that one. Still, I wanted to know whether I had to be ready to kill when I did.

No monster hid in the shadows behind him. Only Price.

And I could tell by the look on his face something had him in a state of shock.

I moved from the chair to the door in one giant step and opened it as quick as I could. I stared into eyes that were filled with more terror than I had ever seen. It left me with more questions than I had answers to.

Price nearly fell to the floor as he took a step forward. I grabbed him by the shoulder and helped him to the couch. His momentum did most of the work for us. Like a wadded piece of paper, he curled up and rolled to his side. He breathed hard and rocked.

I kept my eyes on him as I stepped back, shut and locked the door. I still didn't know what had brought him to my home at an ungodly hour, but I sure as hell didn't want it coming through the door.

"Price, what's going on?" I asked again. I tried to be the stable one. Nausea twisted my stomach.

He began to right himself and looked up at me. New tears fell across his cheeks. Then his big hands covered his face as his head sank in them. "They got him, Paul. They're going to kill him. I just know it." I could see him shaking.

"I need a little more to go on than that, Frank."

Again, his head lifted up to me. "Josh. They got Josh."

"Your grandson?" I knew the name from past conversations, but nothing more.

He shook his head.

"Who?" I tried not to let my frustration show, but I needed better answers from this conversation. And if this talk turned out to be as much of a life or death situation as the old man had led me to believe, pulling answers out of him one by one only wasted my time. Roaches didn't wait for you to make sense of it all.

"The vampires. Those damn blood sucking sons of bitches." I smiled. I couldn't have said it better myself.

My blood ran cold. If Price's grandson had locked horns with blood leeches, he might be in greater danger than I could help with. This, I would never say aloud to Frank. "Why would they have your grandson?"

"Seems Josh went down at one of the clubs tonight and

got into a tangle with a vampire and killed it. Or I guess I should say, someone killed it. Josh happened to be in the wrong place at the wrong time." He took in a deep breath and blew it out like steam from a kettle.

"And now you think they'll kill Josh in retaliation," I finished for him.

Price got off the couch and began to pace. His hands moved instinctively to his pockets. Sweat rings started to sprout under his arms. "You know what will happen to him if they think he did it."

"By their law, he could be put to death," I finished again. I allowed my thought process to bake, then spoke. "Don't worry, Frank, the coffin nappers have to turn him over to the police and he has to be tried in a human court before he could be tried before a Vampire Council."

Frank looked at me with a glare I had never seen in his eyes before. I saw a fear that caused the wisest of men to do irrational things. "That's just it, Paul. The vampires straight up took him from the scene. From the bits and pieces I've been told, the police didn't stop them. The damnedest thing I ever heard."

I tried to fill in all the blanks as fast as I could on two hours of sleep. My thought process was lethargic and unclear. "You've had to have heard something wrong. Since the vampire laws, a Council can't judge a human life without due process in human court first. If he's found guilty, then the Council can pass judgment. If the fang heads don't do it by the law, they can be staked."

Price stopped and stared at me. "Tell that to my grandson." He shook his head. "You've got to get him back. He didn't do it. I know it in the bottom of my heart. He's a good boy."

That's what everybody thinks about their kids and grandkids, I thought. "Who'd he kill?"

"Nobody. He's been set up. You've got to believe me." More tears began to flow from those sad eyes. "Quinn's doing it to get to me. Josh didn't kill anyone. You gotta believe me when I say Josh's innocent."

"Wrong choice of words," I said as I grabbed his shoulders and shook him slightly. Quinn happened to be another name that gave me multiple nightmares. Orlando's commercial master roach. A slang term given to the blood suckers that have risen from the dead. Commercial roaches are the ones the humans have fallen in love with. They are charismatic, beautiful, charming. They own all the businesses along Church Street's vamp district, Bat Town. Unlike the pure bloods and their anonymity, the commercial kind loved the spotlight and were nearly as addicted to money and fame as they were blood. "What's the name of the vein weasel Josh is accused of killing?"

"I don't know his name, just that it was one of Quinn's vamps. But from what I hear, Josh was taken by some other vampire clan, coven, whatever the hell they are but you know as well as I do, nothing happens in Bat Town without the consent or knowledge of Quinn. Not that it matters much."

I didn't agree. Blood suckers don't enter another's territory, much less conduct business in it. If they were responsible for the death, it could be a sign of a turf war. Something didn't add up, but that would be filed away for later. "Regardless of who has Josh, the bat heads won't risk killing him without a court order. It's too risky even for that set of pompous bastards. "

He ran his hand through his hair as he closed his eyes. "You know that and I know that, but the simple truth is still the same. They have Josh. They'll kill him before giving him back." He looked back to me. "You gotta tell Quinn he can have me, just let Josh go."

This sounded bad. I didn't want to say it to the old man, but I knew in my heart, Josh could be between a rock and a hard place. With the cockroach laws and the human sympathizers, things don't work themselves out nicely. Someone had to go down for it. Guilt, innocence, it didn't matter. The fang heads always found ways around the human laws. "Kansas working this one?"

"No one will tell me a damn thing. Probably is, but I can't get him to make eye contact with me, much less speak to me. Been drinking like a fish again, too." He swallowed hard with his hands on his hips. Truthfully, I thought he might hyperventilate and pass out. Or worse, his bad heart would explode. I watched him as though he would break. My hands ready to grab him at the first sign of cardiac arrest. I filed away the second part as exaggeration.

Being the lead detective in Bat Town had come with a price for Kansas. He had been willing to sell his soul to stay on their good side. This made him far more dangerous than the coffin crunchies. And as for his drinking problem, I didn't care. Nor did I blame him. Anyone that cashed a paycheck for working in Bat Town should be allowed to drink as much as they wanted.

I looked back at Price and thought about everything. Most, I planned to keep to myself. Already a bundle of nerves, there was no reason to tell Price his grandson might be killed if found guilty by a Vampire Council. "I'll talk with Kansas and see what he knows about this." It sounded generic, but what the hell.

"No. He's behind all of this somehow. I know it." Price began to pace harder.

"You don't know that."

He stopped and looked at me. "After what he did with the cover up with the Knights murders, you gonna stick with that?" Price waved a hand at me as if swatting a fly. "Don't matter if he's in on it or not. Josh's throat is in their mouths all the same." He turned to keep me from seeing him cry. "This isn't about a murder. It's personal against me and my family. For all I know Kansas helped Quinn set this up. He's got a wife and a kid on the way now you know. Changes the way a man looks at things."

I wanted to argue with Price, but couldn't. You normally can't when someone is right. Members of Knights of the Night had been murdered about the time Asa showed his ugly face. Kansas and the city officials did their damnedest to keep it out of the public eye and away from me. Any bad press about the vamps meant less tourism in Bat Town, and that led to less money flow for everyone from the coffin sleepers to the human city officials. If Price hadn't let me in on the cover up, it would probably still be going on now. Turns out it the cover up and murders were all about money, greed and power, but as the old saying goes, the more things change, the more they stay the same. "You know as well as I do that Kansas wouldn't do something like that. Take a deep breath and think rationally. You're jumping to wrong conclusions." Neither of us bought it.

"Given the choice between protecting his family or mine, which do you think he'd do?"

My mouth opened to speak, but I closed it just as fast. I couldn't answer.

I didn't have the right answer.

"My point exactly."

"Were there any witnesses that can help Josh?" I asked.

"I don't know. Neither Kansas nor the police department will tell me anything. Soon as I found out about it, I came over here." He looked out the window, then back to me. "We have to kill Quinn and get Josh back. You know as well as I do that with Quinn in charge, he won't even get a fair trial. Their laws are more than a little different than ours on things like this. They're looking for a reason to suck him dry. If they find Josh innocent, they've cheated themselves out of a hot meal. I say we beat them to the punch and kill them all."

"What?" I could see myself saying something to that affect, but not Price. Not a man of the department. "You can't do that. Then you'll be up on murder charges yourself. Or more bluntly, get yourself killed."

"I can't stand around here and allow them to kill him in cold blood. I won't allow Quinn and the rest of those monsters to do that. I won't." He looked out the window again. "I shouldn't have come here. It's not your place to save him." With that he began to walk to the door. "I guess I needed to talk to somebody that feels about the vampires like I do. Someone that still saw them as monsters." He stared at me. His eyes filled with more tears. "Someone that's already lost someone to them." The guilt hung thick in the air.

He was right. I had lost something to them. My mother and father were vampire victims. I became an orphan at eight years old. Price knew it would get a desired reaction. "Wait," I said as I stopped him with my hand. "You know I'll do anything I can to help you. That includes keeping you from getting yourself killed."

"I can't live with myself knowing I didn't try something. I'd rather die than live with that guilt."

The more I told myself that I shouldn't going to get involved, the more involved I got. "First things first, you need to have the department talk to Quinn about this mystery roach and his coven. I doubt they'll get a straight answer from him, but at least you can feel him out for what he might know and what you're up against."

Price began to pace again. I watched him, ready to catch him if he fell. Ready to catch him if he went down. "I don't know, Paul. I want Quinn dead for this. No matter what we do, no matter how many witnesses we find, he's going to kill Josh. Maybe I can take his place or something."

I wanted to tell him he might be wrong, but I couldn't do it in good conscience. With the coffin nappers, nothing turned out to be a sure bet other than they would be at your throat at the first opportunity. Still, I couldn't let him go into Bat Town and try to rescue his grandson, guns blazing. They'd kill him for sure. That only left one person.

Note to self: Never answer the door in the middle of the night, no matter how many times the bell rings.

"Give me some time and I'll… I'll look into it." There, I said it. No take backs.

I had barely gotten the words out of my mouth when the bear of a man had me in a hug of death. "Thank you, Paul. You don't know what this means to me and my family."

"Just promise me one thing, Price."

"Anything."

"Don't do anything stupid until I talk to Quinn. Let the police finish their investigation. Go home and get a good night's sleep. I'm sure it's all a misunderstanding." I had no proof of what I had said, but I needed to calm Price down as soon as I could. If I didn't, he would be a heart attack ready to happen. And I didn't want it to happen in my living room.

Against my better judgment I had committed to something that I wasn't sure I could do. I didn't know Price's grandson from Adam. For all I knew he might be a punk ass that had gotten what he deserved. Then again, if he killed a blood roach, he couldn't be all that bad.

CHAPTER TWO

I heard the second series of knocks at the door as I sat the Magnum on the chest of drawers in my bedroom. I rushed down and opened the door with far less caution than earlier in the night. In fact, I halfway expected Price to return with more unrealized fears or questions. He had proven to be a smart man that always covered every angle and the more time given to dwell on something, the more thought he put into it. Chances were, this wouldn't be the only return visit I would encounter from him tonight.

"What's up, Price?" I said as the door whipped open.

Pasty white fingers grabbed me by the throat. Air instantly escaped my lungs in a dry scream. Fangs only inches from my skin. Glowing eyes reflected light that bled from inside my home.

My heart came to a full and complete stop as I saw the dead face in front of me. I tried to grip those hands and break free, but the pressure remained tight "Good evening, Master," Sasha answered. A thin smile spread across his thin Slavic face. Black hair traced his pale skin in an arrangement of tiny tentacles.

Sasha had been second in command under Asa, and now as far as I knew, the new master vamp of the pure bloods in Orlando. I had tried to kill him as well on the night his master died, but things didn't work in my favor. Now I had doubt I'd get another chance.

My fingers pried at his hands but they remained tight and relentless as they lifted me from the floor and threw me further into my home. I landed squarely on the coffee table. Wood shattered in various directions. Bruises began to form around swelled skin. I gasped for air as I looked above me. The monster waited for me to make my move. His pale fingers again reached for me, this time grabbing the skin that used to be part of my chest and lifted me into the air.

He smiled. Yellow teeth and a gray tongue only inches from my face. His breath nothing short of a sewer pipe. Eyes bloodshot and unfocused. Unlike the commercial vein addicts, these bitches didn't use magic facades on the humans. They were almost proud of their ugliness. "Seems as though we have some catching up to do, Avenger." Saliva dripped from the corner of his mouth.

This time, he slammed me against the wall that led to the kitchen. I heard the painting next to me slide to the floor in a violent crash. Before coming to a stop, I planted a right hook to his face. Knuckles returned with skin missing, but the adrenalin turned the pain into a fuel for survival.

I reached for anything that I thought might help me, but other than fingernails, I didn't have any options. Chances looked good for a quick snack for this daisy pusher.

Long greasy hair slid down the sides of his long face as he peered at me. "I thought you'd be a lot more of a challenge than this." With that, he drove me to the floor and dribbled me a few times before stopping long enough to kick me in the ribs. "Do not lose too much blood on me Avenger. I plan on drinking most of it."

After being orphaned, Father Garcia and the Holy Church raised me and protected me. He had taught me to hunt and kill neck biters. One night we killed a so-called innocent fang head on the eve of the new laws going into effect. The press dubbed us the Saint Avengers, forever tarnishing who we were and what we did. I hated it. The roaches loved it.

My muscles twisted under his control. My lungs fought for air. Focus dimmed as the pain increased. I could smell the scent of death on him. Rotten and pungent. I didn't know why he had come here, but knew I had been the center of his pain's attention.

Facing certain death, I pushed off with as much force as I could, sending us both over the top of the couch. My fists pumped like pistons into his head. I wouldn't win this fight, but I didn't need to; only needed to buy enough time to get upstairs to my weapons of mass destruction.

It didn't work. The vein weasel picked me up and tossed me across the room. I fought to keep the effects of the pain inside. Blacking out would be lethal.

I found myself face down and struggled to crawl along the floor. If my memory served me right, I had a crucifix on the edge of the countertop. It would take a miracle to get to it, but at the moment, there were no other options.

I belly crawled across the floor. I looked up at the silver chain that still seemed miles away. Somehow I needed to get to my feet. I had a better shot of monkeys flying out of my ass, but when faced with certain death, you hang by your fingernails for anything that might keep you from becoming casket chow.

My shirt grew tight as Sasha elevated me. Once again, I made involuntary eye contact with Mr. Yellow Teeth. His fist traveled at light speed as it hit me squarely on the nose. Tingles of pain bombs exploded through my face. Blood instantly shot down my throat with such abundance and speed, I nearly drowned. I spit as much of it back up as I could, but a never ending supply replaced it. Thick strings of it matted down my goatee.

Gasping for air, I took a swing at the monster, only to have my fist crushed in his hand. Bones struggled against the pressure. "By the time the sun rises, I will be the new master vampire of this city. I own your blood." A lingering laugh. "After I have my fill of you that is." His voice remained dark and uncaring. Worse yet, I knew he never bluffed. He would make this as nasty and bloody as he could and then let me suffer all over again.

I shook my head. My vision closed as the swelling around my broken nose forced my eyes into slits. His grip on me lessened. I found myself upright. It allowed me to handle the biting pain without it taking my breath. "Thought I already helped you with that honor. Asa's dead."

He pondered my answer for a moment. "You don't even know what you are do you?" Another well planted kick to my ribs before picking me up again. "You know nothing of who you have become, do you?"

"The man that's going to separate your head from its shoulders." I head butted him as hard as I could, but the grip remained. I had gained nothing short of a major headache. My foot struggled to kick and cause damage.

From behind, more power move into the room. I spit more blood from my mouth and coughed it up from my throat. A shadow circled above me, waiting for its turn to attack.

Shoved backwards across one of my dining room chairs, I landed on the boot of a second blood junkie. I took in the monster dressed in black leather, mirrored sunglasses and flipped a shiny razor blade through his fingers. It appeared and disappeared with magical speed. The horror that gathered in my throat overflowed. I wanted to fight back, but couldn't.

Victor squatted down and lifted his sunglasses. He laughed as he looked at me. "Well, what do we have here, Sasha? I thought you said we were going to kill a master vampire, not some pathetic has been."

"What the fuck do you want, Victor?" I asked. I searched for the Magnum. Gone from my possession. In fact, I didn't have anything more deadly than a hang nail on me and by the smug look on the leech's face, he knew it too. Victor had a reputation as a very dangerous blood sucker. The kind that people thought of when they locked their doors at night and slept with crucifixes. We had a history. Shortly before the laws protecting neck biters went into effect, I had tortured him with holy water, leaving his face open sores that dripped blood to this day. The right side of his face looked little more attractive than raw hamburger.

Victor pulled me close. "Avenger, so good that you recognize me through such swollen eyes. Perhaps I should release some of the pressure." The razorblade cut my cheek in a motion so fast I didn't have time to react.

I gasped as I spit more blood. Most of it in Victor's face. The cut stung.

He grimaced for a second, wiped away the spit and blood with a handkerchief, then pulled my chin to meet his gaze. I closed my eyes best I could. I had no plans of going under his gaze and make things easy for him. His voice remained calm, almost soothing to the untrained ear. "Manners would gain you much. There is an old saying in your world; you can attract more bees with honey than with vinegar. Or so I think the saying goes." He placed the razor to my throat and stopped. "I think it is only fitting that I make that pretty boy face of yours a little more distinguished, do you not agree?" Again the razor separated skin along my neck. I could feel the warm blood trickle from the wound, but refused to act as though I felt the pain or fear. I'd die laughing at them if I had to. Victor's finger scooped my blood and placed it on his tongue. "He tastes like chicken."

Sasha laughed. He bent low and licked the stream of blood from my throat. I fought the urge to shiver. "I can taste the power in your blood. Dangerous and intoxicating. A fountain of youth." His fingers dug into my throat as he bit.

"Give in to your fear. Your father did," Victor added. "From what I hear, your mother helped drain him while you ran and hid that night." He studied me. "Here you are, the son of an executioner and a vampire bitch, yet you've become nothing. Odd and sad at the same time."

Oh yeah, one more thing. There is a nasty rumor amongst the cockroach community that my mother was not only a victim of a fang attack, but a neck biter herself. Story goes that she dated and married my father, a vampire executioner, in order to kill him Depending on whom you talk to, she was really in love, and sleeping with, Albert Kincaid. Kincaid was the founder of the vampire rights organization Knights of the Night as well as the owner of the world's largest necro-porn company, NecroPussy.

Worst of all, most believe Kincaid to be none other than my biological father. Kind of hard to ask him now, since he had been drained and beheaded by those he exploited. At least fate got that one right. I'll never accept any of it. Simply slanderous lies brought on by those who sleep in the dirt.

"If you think I'll give you the satisfaction of begging for my life, you've got another thing coming." I could feel my body growing cold as Sasha continued to dine on me. My ears rang louder with each passing second. I came to terms that I would bleed to death.

Sasha pulled away and grinned, showing me, yet again, those ancient tools of the trade. "Who said anything about begging to live, master?" He lifted my head close to his. His voice vibrated through my ears in eerie tones. "I assure you, Avenger, you will die. You should be thankful I found you before the others did. When you killed Asa, you left us all with an imminent threat of danger. That threat dies with you tonight."

He bit me again. My head rolled back as the room spun and bells rang. I could feel the old, lethal power running along my skin, mixing with my growing fear and anxiety like a Molotov Cocktail.

"With Sasha as the master vampire it will be a show of strength. The visitors will eventually back down. As we are now, they see us as weak and disorganized." Victor stretched my neck tight as Sasha fed. "Look at me," he said pointing to the wound on his face. "You should have killed me when you had the chance." Black hair got caught in the infected open scars, matted with dried blood. "I have waited for this night for many years. So many things I want to do to you before you die." A fist punched the side of my head. Bones reverberated the blow. Flesh swelled. Blood trickled. Claws and fangs worked in synchronicity.

My eyes caught the silver shine of the crucifix sitting on my countertop. A sliver of hope glowed out of arm's length. I started to lunge upward only to be stopped by pale hands and the weight of two monsters.

Victor followed my eyes to the cross. That demonic smile returned. "Do not attempt to grow a brain, Avenger. You know as well as I, that you will be dead before you reach it. It will make you look like a fool and ruin my fun. Killing you too soon would be most disappointing."

Sasha pulled free and rose above me, my blood dripped from his mouth. "I suppose I should tell you what will happen to you tonight. After all, you are the root of all the excitement." He slapped my face playfully and gave an evil laugh. Turning to Victor, he spoke again. "Tie him up."

Jagged edges of pain shot through me. Electrical pulses blossomed in my veins. Screams of souls rang in my ears. The room spun.

Victor wrapped a large rope around my ankles and tied a quick knot. I fought against the magic with everything in me, only to find it frustrating. I had moved far past scared as I hung upside down and dangled in front of the two cockroaches from a rafter in the ceiling.

Sasha squatted near my face. With a light touch, he stopped my swinging. "You see, Avenger, there are those in the vampire nation that see you as more than what you are. I will not waste my time going into such things, but simply know that your death will bring about a balance of things for us." With the power still wrapped around me, I bit my lip in pain. His bite marks burned as they pierced my vein. Again, I twisted against the rope only to find my efforts useless. I swung with all my might at the fang head in front of me, but even if I connected with him it would be harmless. Being tied upside down from a rope left me very little leverage, not to mention weakness had taken my strength. Even keeping my eyes open became a struggle. Sasha laughed. "Careful, Avenger. You will pull a muscle." Yellow fangs inched closer. They stung as they entered me again. I screamed in both pain and rebellion.

My ears rang as he drained me. Pain gave way to numbness. I think I continued to scream and fight, but the sounds and sensations grew distant. I came to terms with my own death.

CHAPTER THREE

I couldn't stop the shaking. Cold. Dizzy. Light pierced my eyes, forcing them closed. Pain my only jumpstart. I tried to swallow, only to find my throat so swollen and sore, the act became impossible. Nausea built as I tried to move. I heard screaming. All in my head. A thousand souls trying to escape. My ears rang, the room spun.

Cold. So very cold.

The events ran through my mind in thin shards of dreams and reality. Asa. Price. Sasha. Victor. Pain. Lots of pain. Was it real? A Dream? Was I even alive?

With the vampire blood from my mother, I had doubts as to what rules applied to me. Neither human nor vampire left me with a lot of unanswered questions. Before I came along, it had been understood that my condition was impossible. Turns out, both sides feared me for the possibilities that might arise. If the blood in my veins possessed some sort of magical power, it had failed me so far.

Again, I tried to open my eyes, only to shut them again. Disoriented I tried to dig my way to the surface from the inside out. The hollowness seemed to cover me in a cocoon. I had to find a way to distract the pain long enough to gain some sort of reality.

Cold. So cold it hurt. Muscles ached. Fatigue. Cramps. I grit my teeth as my body tried to find any remnants of life somewhere deep inside me.

I opened my eyes in tiny spurts despite the pain. I caught glimpses of my living room. Furniture now nothing more than kindling; blood everywhere.

My ears rang so loud that if there were any other source

of sound in the room, I would never hear it. Blaring and relentless. My heart beat throbbed to the pulse of the pain from the bites Sasha had made.

This time, my eyes shot open in a distinct form of horror. The thought of the monsters drinking my blood shocked my system into a form of reality. The memories of their fangs sinking into my skin sent jolts of shivers through me. Instantly, my tongue rolled across my teeth to feel for fangs.

Nothing. Only cold.

"Can you hear me?"

God? Is that you? I thought.

"Paul, wake up!"

I could hear the voice, but it seemed so far away. My mind second guessed the voice as it tried to ride above the ringing in my ears. My mind struggled between real and imagined. I wanted to answer, but ---couldn't. I felt paralyzed and in a state of confusion. I remembered the nightmare with Asa from earlier. I had slipped back into it. Thoughts pumped through my veins. Nothing made sense.

"You've gotta wake up. Don't die on me."

Familiar. Distant still, but familiar all the same.

My eyes opened. This time a little longer and a little more focused. Not much, but enough. A figure stared back at me. Death became the least of my worries. I had woken in hell. "Kansas?" With what little strength I had left, I tried to lift myself from the floor. "Sasha? Where is he?"

Kansas' hand pushed me back down. "They're gone, for now." His hands shook. His face, pale and unshaven "We've got to get out of here."

"You look like hell." Anyone that knew Kansas, knew that despite all his faults, and there were a bag of them, he dressed like a model out of a men's magazine. Ironed and starched shirts, crisp folds, shined shoes, thinning hair combed just right. But tonight, he could have easily passed as some homeless man down on his luck. Price had been right: I could smell the alcohol on his breath. I didn't address it. I didn't care.

He gave a nervous laugh. "Funny, I thought about to tell you the same thing." In quick darts, he looked around the room. He didn't seem convinced we had seen the last of our visitors.

"Hang in there. Try not to move. God, what happened here? There's blood everywhere." A deeper squint. "Jesus, your nose looks awful. Did they bite you or beat you?"

"The beat me, then they bit me. Sasha and Victor." I looked around. Life came back to me in quick fashion. Panic dug in. "You cut me down?"

He looked at me with a puzzled look. "Yeah? Wasn't I supposed to? Don't tell me you meant for all this to happen to you." I noticed a new flavor of strangeness to him and it had to do with more than just alcohol. Instead, an urgency to his body language that animated him from head to toe. I filed it away under odd. "You okay? We have to get you out of here. If we don't get you something for those bites, you'll bleed to death. They don't coagulate or whatever the word is." The detective began to pace back and forth to the window. He opened the curtains. Perhaps checking on a phantom ambulance or perhaps the return of my assailants, but each time he pulled them back, spears of street lights streaked through the room. He might as well of had a target pressed against my head.

"I won't bleed to death." I didn't want to talk about the advantages of the virus running through my veins. Kansas knew about it, but at least didn't push the issue. I placed my left arm over my eyes. "Please keep that curtain shut, Kansas. You're killing me. In fact, turn all the lights off." My throat burned, my words barely a whisper.

"Looks like Sasha tried to beat me to it." He looked at the curtain still in his hand, then back to me. I saw him jump as he caught himself and practically threw the curtain back into place. With a quick fan of his hand, he turned the room black. Kansas walked back to me. "What happened? Why'd they do this?"

"Some cryptic jargon about making the coven stronger and their vendetta against me killing Asa. Something I'm not even positive I did. Don't forget, you, me, the police, --- no one found any signs of him where I had staked his blood sucking ass." I pulled myself up against the overturned couch. I stopped as the room began to spin. Again, my eyes went shut. Even the shadows in the room were too bright.

"You think that's what this is all about? You killing Asa?"

I shrugged. "If it is, they're a lot more convinced he's dead than I am."

Kansas grabbed me by the elbow. "You lost a lot of blood. Most of it through your face, but still... God, your nose!" Again he looked around the room. "We really do need to get out of here. They're gone, but you know as well as I do, they'll be back."

I saw something odd in his behavior. I couldn't put my finger on it. I could blame it on his fear of the fang heads, but there seemed to be more to it. I'd let it go for now. He had been right. I had to get out of here. My home had been a revolving door of unwanted guests and I had a human in the hands of sadistic monsters not far from here. I probably needed to go to the hospital, but tonight's visit had left me with other distractions. "Price mentioned something about his grandson being caught up in a vampire murder. What do you know about that?"

I saw the look on his face. He let me go as if I had shocked him. "Enough, why?" he added reluctantly. He turned away from me. I could still feel the guilt.

"Why does Quinn have him? Shouldn't this be a police matter?"

Kansas started to say something then clammed up and shook his head. He began to pace in front of the window again. He purposely looked away from me. To him, I represented the coffin leeches and he didn't want to get caught in my gaze.

It didn't take a rocket scientist to see that the detective not only knew about the murder, but had helped the bat heads orchestrate it to some level. But to what level? The answer scared me. I tried to keep my cool, but the anger busted through in a volcanic tirade. "How can you consider yourself a human by feeding that slime ball Price's grandson? Have you totally lost your mind? Might as well go down to Church Street and start your own buffet line for them. You know as well as I do that the only way we will ever get him back now is in a body bag. And if that happens, it's not Quinn and his walking dead you'll have to deal with. It will be me. And I promise you Kansas, I'll make it as violent and dirty as I can."

"You wouldn't understand."

"You're right. I probably wouldn't. I have balls and

morals, something you wouldn't know about if it pricked you all night." God, I hated being too weak to put him out of his misery here and now. I didn't see a respectable man of the law in front of me. I saw a coward and a murderer. A murdering pimp to the blood suckers.

"You know I'm going down there and getting him back. Even if he's guilty as hell, he doesn't deserve to be fed to them like bait on a hook. All you've done is started a cockroach chum line." I gingerly touched the bite marks on my neck. Tender and tacky. For the first time the virus had served its purpose well. Without it, I would have probably bled to death even if the monsters had stopped sucking on me. Asa had bitten me before, but I had injected the coagulating serum to be safe. Through doctors' appointments and tests, it looked as though my virus would stop the bleeding, but up until now, I didn't have the guts to take the chance.

"What were you thinking, Zeke?" I waved off Kansas' answer. "Forget it. You weren't. That's the problem."

"Paul, trust me on this one." His answer laced with annoyance. He wiped away a tear with trembling hands. His body language left me wondering if he heard a word I had said.

"Trust you? If I trusted you, I wouldn't have known about the fang suckers that were killing the Knights of the Night. If I trusted you, I wouldn't have known about Albert Kincaid, the Necro-porn king being killed and beheaded by a twisted vamp hell-bent on cashing in on his misfortune." I shook with disgust. "What's wrong? I mean the truth."

Another glance to the window. "Paul, I didn't want you involved with Kincaid's murder because of the rumors that he might have been your true father. I thought it was best to keep you out of it as much as possible. True or not, you know, Quinn and the vampires would have had a field day with that one." He shook his head and bent next to me again. "I just need you to get down there and talk to Quinn. Tonight. You're right, you have to get that boy back." He took in a gulp of air. "You'll have to trust me on this one."

I shook my head the best I could. "No dice. Done that enough to know what it will get me. I'd make you go with me, but I can't trust you any more than I can Quinn. You're too far in bed with the coffin critters to let you go on your word. You're feeding humans to the blood suckers, Kansas. Trusting you is the last thing I'm going to do. And another thing that slime ball Kincaid is not my father. Never was, never will. It's another lie the bat heads have spread about my mother being a vamp who she slept with." We would have to settle that discrepancy at another time and place. My mother was dead. Kincaid was dead. And if I didn't act soon, Josh would be dead.

He gave me several quick glances. I could see him weighing his options. He tried to think of just enough of the truth to tell me to get me to shut up. "All I can tell you is that it's imperative that you talk to Quinn. My hands are tied." At least he had changed the subject. For that alone, I thanked him.

"Hmmm, imperative. Big word for someone like you."

He gave me the finger and I sarcastically smiled.

"Why did you let them take Josh?"

"I didn't let them take anybody." His mouth opened and closed a couple of times. "Okay, I let them take him, but it was for his own protection. They were going to kill him if I didn't."

I sat up a second time. My head spun. For now, I fought off the blackout. "What? Even you can do better than that. Putting him in the hands of things that will suck him into a raisin is not exactly called protection. It's called an appetizer."

"I'm telling you the truth." His voice grew stern with stress. A deep exhale finished it off. I could tell by the heaving of his chest, something had him wound a bit too tight. Something far deeper and darker than Sasha and Victor.

"Protection from what?" I asked as calmly as possible.

Kansas looked around and lowered his voice. "Please Paul, take my word for it. When it comes to the vampires, I only have the illusion of choice. There's nothing I could do."

I stared at him, but said nothing as I propped myself up on my elbows. Blood flowed through me and I could feel my strength come back with a vengeance. Warmth returned as the blood filled my veins once again. The leeches were right. Power did run through my veins. I healed much quicker than a human, but still remained weaker than the neck biters. I didn't have fangs, but still had a dark craving for the taste of blood. Didn't care for the sun, but I could walk in it without turning to ash.

Small victories, but victories all the same. "Are you through being dramatic?" I asked dryly. "Quit acting like someone pissed in your cornflakes. We're talking about a person's life here."

He gave me a long stare. "Quinn doesn't have the boy, Paul. It's some new vampire in town." Kansas seemed to expound before my eyes. "Please, we don't have time to talk about it now. I'll fill you in as we go. Grab everything you need to kill a vampire. You'll need it. This guy's a real bad ass." He cried. This had turned out to be a very strange night. "Believe it or not, but that's why I came here tonight. I want Josh out of this bastard's hands as much as the next guy." He broke down and started to cry. Again, odd. Kansas didn't know Josh any better than I did. The emotion didn't match the situation.

I put my hands to my head. From my talk with Price, I already knew Quinn didn't have the boy, but he knew who did and how to get him back. "Let me get this straight. You allowed this coffin muncher to take Josh, but now you want me to talk to Quinn about it, even though Quinn isn't the one that has him? Not to mention you're practically having a nervous breakdown in front of me. What do they have on you?"

He crumbled before my eyes. Question was, why? "Don't do this to me, Paul. Just go to Bat Town and talk with Quinn about it. I didn't let the vampires take him. I tried to keep him alive. No matter what you think about me when this is all over, remember I'm trying to keep everybody alive."

"My point exactly. Turning Josh Price over to the bat heads when he's accused of murder and confessing that you're trying to keep him alive, kind of contradict each other. Somehow I think he might have been a bit safer in a jail cell."

"That's just it. I'm not in a position to make demands. Right or wrong, your opinion is not anything more than that."

I watched as Kansas looked out the window again. "Why are you here?" I asked.

The detective turned with another look of worry on his face. "What do you mean?"

"In the six years I've lived here, you've never set foot inside my home. We never visit each other. You've never sent me a Christmas card. Hell, we've only gone to lunch together a handful of times. I find it a bit odd that you're here. The last time

I woke to find a 'friend' in my home, she had set me up for her killer roach boyfriend. That it, Kansas? You got a killer boyfriend coming over?"

He rolled his eyes. A smirk. "Yeah, that's it, Paul." He shook his head and began to pace. "If I wanted you dead, I'd ..." He turned from me, placed his hands on his hips and sighed.

"You'd what? Give me to your little undead buddy too?"

"Go to hell, Isaac." He turned away from me. A little more pushing and he would explode. I knew him well enough to know that parts of this visit were being conveniently left out. I'd find out sooner or later. Anyone under the duress that I saw in Kansas would melt down in a matter of time.

"How did you know?"

"What?" He began to pace again.

"You knew Sasha and Victor were coming here didn't you?"

A nervous laugh. "It's not important."

I stared him down.

"Look, I saved your life. Now, drop it. If it wasn't for me, Sasha would have killed you tonight. And if we don't get out of here now, he might come back and finish what he started. I spooked them once, but twice might be a different story."

I kept staring at him.

"God!" he shouted. "Call it luck, call it a lie, call it what you will, but dear God, Paul, please help me by talking to Quinn. Maybe he knows this vampire. He can negotiate with him better than you or me. Let's face it, I'm with the police department and you're a vampire executioner. Trust isn't going to be something this vampire thinks about when he deals with us."

I knew I wouldn't get any more out of him. Even if I did, I wouldn't understand it. I couldn't make heads or tails out of his endless rambling. Putting all three of my visits together, I had come to the conclusion; something big loomed in Bat Town and I would be involved, like it or not. "Bring everything, huh?"

Kansas shook his head and sighed in relief, but his face still showed calamity behind his eyes. "Everything."

CHAPTER FOUR

It had been nearly twenty-four hours since I had been attacked by Sasha and Victor. Even with various viruses running through my veins, still, for the most part, I remained human and needed time to heal. If I had gone to Bat Town last night as both Kansas and Price had wanted, I wouldn't have made it back in one piece. I stayed at home and got as much rest as I could. Something told me I'd need every ounce of strength I had to make it back to bed in the morning.

I drove my black 1970 hemi 'Cuda north down Church Street, heading into the heart of Bat Town, still trying to digest my nightmare. I had been on the biting end of most of it, and the thumping pain in my body remained a constant. Strength returned fast, but not fast enough for what I needed. Even at full power, I couldn't take on two master daisy pushers tonight.

I hadn't taken the time to shower or even wipe away the dried blood along my neck and face. Add in the colorful bruises and swollen flesh and I looked like hell baked over. They would all heal in time, but for now, I looked nothing short of a living jig saw puzzle. With lives hanging in the balance, I couldn't put this off another night.

Neon hugged around Bat Town in infinite colors and flashing strobes of illumination. It drew in its human prey like a giant bug zapper. Still, the humans came. The threat of the undead had been permanently removed from their normal thoughts.

Scanning the horizon, nothing looked out of place. Droves of young people moved along the sidewalks or stood in line to one of the clubs or restaurants. None of them understood the thin line between willing freak and lethal lunch.

Traffic had crawled to a stop. Ahead of me, nothing but a sea of taillights fading into a vanishing point. With my windows rolled down, I could simultaneously feel the heat of the Florida night and hear the repetitious thumping of bass reverberating from the clubs.

I pushed the clutch in, shifted to neutral and lit a cigar. None of us were going anywhere fast. I could see the Coffin Restaurant ahead of me, but knew all too well that it would take fifteen minutes to go the extra block, not to mention finding a parking spot. It gave me extra time to heal, or so I told myself. The idle time would also give me a chance to dwell on all the things that could still go wrong tonight. Each ended in a violent twist of death. A smarter man would back out and sell ships in a bottle in the Caribbean.

Quinn had gotten his position through violence and bloodshed. Most saw him as a powerful monster full of charisma and charm on the outside, but the inside I saw him as nothing more than candy coated death. Now, on the favor of a good friend I would be eye to eye with him, and that never turned out to be a good idea. It didn't matter what Kansas had said. Anyone in the custody of coffin biters is in harm's way. Period.

"Who's gonna die tonight?"

I jumped, hitting my head on the top of the car. The cigar fell between my legs. My right foot hit the accelerator and sent the huge Detroit engine into a furious growl. Lucky for me the 'Cuda was still in neutral.

"God, I've never seen you so jumpy," Angie said leaning inside the car, her assets inches from my face. Lustful distraction made me forget about Quinn and the big bad roaches. "Who's gonna die?" she repeated.

The one word that best described Angie had to be lust. A werewolf, full of girl power, and the source of so many of my problems. I considered her a friend more than a foe. I had only known her for about two years, and in that time she had bitten me in wolf form, leaving me with the furry virus as well as the coffin pathogen. She had done it to save my life, but it still carried its weight in baggage as most of the diseases down here did.

Her eyes were framed in thick black mascara; lashes

reaching out to capture me. I stared back at perfection. I brushed away the ash as I recovered the cigar with nothing damaged but my pride. "If you scare me again, it's going to be you."

She licked her deep red lips like a kitten getting the last drop of milk from her whiskers. "God, what happened to you? You look like something chewed you up and spat you out. What happened to your nose?" Her hips rested on the top of the door as she slithered further inside. I could help but imagine what the view would be like from the other side of the car.

"I disagreed with something that tried to eat me last night," I said, taking a drag from the cigar.

I could feel her warm breath hit me with each word; sensory overload. My eyes sank into her beauty, begging to never know freedom again. Emerald pupils stared back at me, while the whites of her eyes glowed with light. She let the conversation about my bruises go. "Take me for a ride." Her fingers traced the Hurst shifter as she purred.

"Unless you're seeing something I'm not, we're not going anywhere for a while." Glowing red taillights remained constant ahead of me.

"I wasn't meaning the car, baby," she said as she successfully slithered all the way in the seat. After a quick breath, she leaned over and kissed me on the cheek. "I'm glad you're here. I was about to go looking for you."

"Why's that?"

"A couple of vamps were down here last night looking for trouble. Mentioned your name. They killed another vampire, and took some kid with them. The police looked the other way which can only mean Quinn's up to something."

My head snapped from her cleavage to her face. "What vamps? I mean, the ones that took the kid. Do you know who they were?" Angie's attire tonight included a black leather dominatrix teddy, thigh high leather boots and a choke collar. Chrome studs moved along her sides stopped by black mesh lace that gave a shadowy view of the flesh underneath. Forget everything I said about dirt nappers in Bat Town. Angie was easily the most dangerous thing down here.

Her eyes sparkled as she motioned me closer with a curl of her finger. Golden locks of desire flowed around her face. I still had no idea about her natural color. In fact, I hadn't seen it the same color twice.

She had animalistic power, strength of ten semis, and the speed of lightning. And with a solitary finger, she controlled me. I leaned in to her. Her tongue traced my lips. Then her sexy demeanor changed. "I don't know who they were, but there's something about them that scares the living shit out of me. According to Asa's vamps they're here to put Orlando under new management." Her hands touched along my chest. "I've never seen them before. Their power feels different too."

"Their? Meaning more than one?" Thank God for Angie. She quickly had become the one and only occupant of the monster district that I put all my trust in. Which says something about my shrinking circle of friends.

She shook her head as she moved even closer to me. "They came down here asking about you; where they could find you. I could tell they were nothing more than trouble looking for a place to happen." Angie's fingers lightly pulled the collar of my black t-shirt away and exposed the bite mark left by Sasha. "My God, who did this?" She pulled my shirt out a little farther and then studied my face. "You look like hell."

I tried to control my shaking as much as possible, as my eyes darted to the cars in front of me again. "I had a visit from Sasha tonight. He and Victor tried to have lunch, but Kansas somehow showed up in the nick of time." I took a deep breath as I thought. "Looks like there's a power struggle brewing as to who will be the next master vampire of the pure bloods. I don't get why they want to talk to me. All I did was take out their master. They take things like that a little too personal."

"You're talking about things that would rather suck blood than fuck. Of course they're not going to make sense." She checked her lipstick in the mirror with a soft pucker, then returned to my wounds.

Who could argue with that logic?

She continued to look at the bite and grimaced, but at least she stayed on topic. "They were talking to Kasey and a few of the vampires close by. I overheard them." I started to speak when a finger gently touched my lips. Her red nail lightly move along my cheek. "Don't worry lover, I intervened. I told them that you were out of town." She smiled. "Visiting Isabella."

Isabella.

There was a name from my not so distant past. She had made off with some valuable vampire art, threatened my life, and had been caught by Angie, half nude in my home. I smiled as I thought about the underlying motive the wolf next to me had. "Would you recognize them if you saw them again?"

She pointed to her temple. "All up here." Her hands returned to me and traced along my face, dropping sparks of power. Tiny bolts of lightning sprouted from her fingers as they circled my wounds. Tingles caused my muscles to dance. Pain evaporated into strength. Goosebumps lifted the hairs on my arms. Damn, she was good.

My mind began to race as I tried to think of anyone that would be looking for me with thoughts of revenge or death. I stopped thinking about it. The list expanded in seconds. I grew cold with a different kind of fear. Afraid to ask the question, afraid not to. "You say you saw who killed the vampire?" To me the question landed in middle ground.

"It wasn't the kid, if that's what you want to know. It was one of the two vampires that were looking for you."

"That kid you're referring to is the grandson of Frank Price." I left it at that.

The fear that I once saw in her eyes snapped into anger. "Those demon bastards!" Her hand slammed the inside roof of the car. "He's just a kid. Those vamps would have eaten him for lunch before he knew what hit him." Angie's eyes were fixed on mine. Glaring with alarm. "Both the police and the damn vampires know he didn't do it."

"You're sure of that?" Now those same eyes were glaring at me. I didn't answer the question behind them. "What happened? Why didn't anybody tell the police the truth?"

"I seriously doubt any of them saw it. The vampire moved with such speed, human eyes wouldn't have seen it. The witnesses saw a vampire had been killed. Price's grandson happened to be standing next to him."

"So he was set up?" I said it more to myself than anything. "That's the easy answer. Why? That's the one that will probably come back to bite us, no pun intended."

Angie shrugged her shoulders. "The thing that doesn't make sense to me is that vampires usually don't kill each other unless it's over territory or power. With Asa dead, there will be a power struggle. But it made no sense to kill one of Quinn's coffin munchers. Unless the new vamps plan on taking over both covens. If so, things are about to get butt ugly."

I looked over to her and shook my head. "Looks like I have a lot of questions to ask Quinn. Somehow I don't think it will be all that big of a surprise when I show up tonight; even less of a surprise when I tell him he has visitors." I blew the cigar smoke from my lungs. "If it's over power or territory, you know as well as I do that he's got to be involved. I don't know how or why, but it's all a little too convenient to be coincidence. He and Sasha are playing me against one another."

Angie's eyes narrowed. "So kill him. I don't see the problem." Angie had always been black and white when it came to these things. One of the reasons we got along so well. It's also what scared me about her. We were too much alike.

I gripped the steering wheel as I ran out of patience with the traffic jam. I had more skin to save than I originally thought. I took a long drag from the cigar, allowed all the possible scenarios to percolate through my head. "Angie, I want you to do me a favor. I want you to stay out of sight tonight. We don't know what they're up to. If they're kidnapping innocent humans and killing their own, there's a lot at stake." No pun intended.

Shock filled her face as she gasped out a nervous laugh. "May I ask why? Got a hot date you don't want me finding out about again?"

"I just have a real bad feeling about all this. The commercial cockroaches know I'll be coming for Price's grandson and Sasha and the pure bloods along with this new coven want me dead. Somehow, it will all come to a head. I need you to be alive if I'm ten toes up in the morning." I checked for the Magnum in the shoulder holster. "Josh Price is nothing more than the cheese meant to bring me into the trap. What really sucks is the fact that I have no choice but to walk into their little snare. You need to get out before you get yourself tangled into shit you can't get out of."

Traffic began to move. I popped the 'Cuda into gear and

began to inch my way closer to The Coffin Restaurant. I turned to find Angie looking out the window at the crowds along the sidewalk. I knew her well enough to know wheels were turning in that beautiful head. A very bad sign, every time. In a quick jerk, she faced me again. "If you think I'm going to let some blood sucking bully make me cower and run, you're crazy. I can take care of myself." As quick as she looked at me, she looked out the window again.

I had seen her in action enough to know she could handle anything down here, but I still didn't want her life hanging over my head. "I know that." I shifted to second.

I started to say more, but Angie's hand flew out toward me, catching me in the chest. "Stop the car!" I opened my mouth to ask why, but Angie had already jumped out the window on the passenger's side. Her head popped back in. "That's them!" I hit the brakes. Horns began to instantly blow from behind. A small crowd instantly formed. "Give me the 9!"

To my right, I saw the two lanky vein weasels swim through the crowd. Both were tall, one with red hair, the other blond. Eyes searched for the weak. Pale skin shined in the neon. They made no attempt to hide what they were. Tale tell signs of pure bloods. Unlike the commercial vamps, which were able to give the illusion of beauty to the naked eye, the pure bloods embraced their ugliness.

"Have you gone insane?" I shouted back.

"Do you want to find Josh Price or not? I'm handing the bat boys that have him to you on a silver platter. Now get your ass out of the car and help me." Her hand reached back into the car.

The commotion caught the attention of our new friends. Two sets of dead eyes stared at us, then turned with blurred speed. Screams filled the sidewalk as the two began to cut their way through the sea of people, knocking several to the ground.

Before I could think, I found myself out of the car. From my hip holster I pitched the 9mm to Angie while grabbing my Magnum for myself. "Don't kill them yet, if you can keep from it. I want to know what they know."

I couldn't tell if she heard me or not. She moved along the tops of the cars ahead of me, gaining on the red head with each jump. Somewhere along the way she had kicked free of the stiletto heels. Animalistic power took over. On the other hand, I lagged further behind. I could think of only one thing to slow him down. I pulled the cartridge of ultra violet bullets out of the Magnum and replaced them with traditional. This would allow me to wound them without killing them.

Ahead of me, I could see one of the bloodsuckers run over the tops of the cars, then disappeared on the other side. Tires screeched. Horns blew. Screams filled the air.

I moved along the left hand side of the cars, most now stopped in cock-eyed positions. Drivers still tried to make out what had happened as I moved by with blurred velocity. My muscles began to strengthen and my pace quickened as the furry virus and undead blood ran through my veins gained control.

Angie moved along the opposite side of the street, 9mm sniffing the air. She gave the trigger a pull and sent a shot into the black sky. It instantly moved any straggling sightseers from her path. Blonde hair streamed behind her.

The vein weasels split as they hit Orange Avenue. I cursed under my breath as I realized they were trying to divide and conquer.

As I rounded the corner, blinding lights stole my vision. More horns blew. Shadows cut through the lights. Flashes of movement. Chaos slowly eroded in my sight. My inertia sent me into the street as I tried to make the corner. My hip met the fender of a Honda. I lost my footing momentarily. Pain burned to the bone. I lost my vamp as shadows of running people littered my view. They moved in and out of the headlights. All lost in the pockets of darkness.

Still struggling from me recent attack, each forward stride gave the wound reason to thump with sparks of pain.

An object cut through the air, whistling as it missed my head by inches. The blood lapper had picked up a car door and hurled it at me. Profanity spewed from my mouth. I knew these things were powerful, but nothing like this. Metal bent against itself as it smashed into another to my right. Glass exploded from the windows. Screams bellowed from the wreckage.

Somehow, in all the commotion, I had managed to hunch down next to one of the trapped cars, waiting for what, I hadn't made up my mind. Fear had suddenly paralyzed me. Most of me wanted to run. The bite on my neck kept beat with my heart in jabbing notes of pain. I couldn't stop the bleeding. I tried my best not to panic. If I died tonight, it wouldn't be hunkered down beside a twisted piece of metal.

The driver and his passenger were bleeding and unconscious, possibly dead. I closed my eyes for a second and tried to get the image out of my mind. Death and blood still didn't settle in my stomach all that well.

I wanted to help, but didn't have the skills needed to save a life. Stopping to help them would allow my coffin sleeper to escape in the night. I could choose to save two and sacrifice hundreds of others stranded in the roach's path. For the love of God, I couldn't let that happen.

My hands shook as I chickened out of my interrogation plan. I emptied the Magnum of the regular bullets and replaced them with the ultra violet. Since my attack the other night, I found my fear level growing out of control. I kept seeing Sasha's fangs and feeling them sink into me.

Back to my feet, I pulled the Magnum up ready to strike, but I hesitated too long. A pale hand grabbed me and slung me across the top of two cars. My back skipped along the slick metal, ending with a deadening thud.

The daisy pusher pounced on me before I slid back to the pavement. Nails dug deep. Red glowing eyes framed by white skin. Lips parted, showing fangs that glistened in the headlights with saliva.

I pushed with everything I had, keeping the monster off of me. As it began to rise, I forced my feet under its stomach to give me more leverage. It also freed the hand with the Magnum.

My wrist rotated the weapon to the chest of the monster as it bit down on my forearm, ripping tendons and slicing muscle. In an instant, my fingers went numb. Unable to pull the trigger, I cursed in his face.

The monster swallowed my blood. "So it is true. You have the virus in your veins. I can taste it. My master shall be pleased to learn of its truth. And even more pleased that I have found you."

Pain stopped me from answering, but I could hear

myself scream at the thought. I had always found a way to justify my denial. Now my worst fear looked back at me, dripping with my own secrets. My blood had the vampire virus.

The monster fell on me again, reaching for my throat. With both hands I blocked the bite as blood dripped on my face and in my eyes. Muscles burned and dying flesh filled my thoughts, but I knew if I gave into the pain, my life might be snuffed. No way I was going to be bitten again. I had met my quota for the night.

A normal human would have already been a vein weasel shake at this point, but my strength kept the bite at bay. It wouldn't for long. I tried to reach in my jacket for a stake, but in doing so, I'd have to sacrifice the one arm that pinned the maggot taxi upward.

I had no choice in the matter. I couldn't hold this thing at bay for much longer. I snapped my neck upward, breaking the thing's nose. Slimy black liquid splattered from it as though I had busted a water balloon. A deep growl filled my ears. As he lifted up, I reached for a wooden stake.

Around me I could hear the screams and horror of those leaving their cars and running for what safety they could find. Under the cars, I could see the hundreds of moving feet, all with the same idea. They scattered as though a thunderstorm had erupted. If I didn't kill this thing, some of them wouldn't make it.

Again, I tried to fire the Magnum. My strength built, but it would be too late by that time. I moved the stake toward the things chest and pulled away my wounded arm, allowing the monster to fall on top of me.

The wooden stake split through the center of the vampire's chest, piercing the heart like a ripe melon. Muscle and bone split to either side. Deep breathless gurgles filled the monster's throat.

I kicked and screamed as I moved out from under it. I shook away the chills that ran up my spine, as cockroach blood and guts spilled on me and ran into my mouth. I pointed the Magnum on the fang mouth as it now looked up at me. "Who are you?" I screamed.

The vampire smiled. "I am one of many that ushers in your death, vampire."

I wiped away a spoon-sized ball of meat from my face and swallowed hard, trying not to vomit. "Seems as though you're the one that's about to die, fang boy. Why are you looking for me?"

He laughed as his hands reached for the stake. It remained deep in his chest. I no longer worried about him going anywhere fast. In a matter of seconds, he'd be dead. My interrogation window had closed in a hurry. "To kill the human that is also a master. Judas is rising. Retribution is at hand."

"What the hell does that mean?" All life left him. I shook with anger and unused adrenalin. Dried blood painted my skin a dark red. It would take more than soap to make me feel clean again.

I kicked him hard, trying to find any life that I could. In the end he had cheated me of the answers I wanted, and planted the fear he came to sew.

As I began to catch my breath, I looked around and saw thousands of unblinking eyes staring back at me. Humans that were getting a firsthand look at what monsters really can do. I looked deeper into their eyes, and noticed that most were in fact looking past me.

I turned to follow the hollow stares and saw a leather and lace vixen as she walked toward us carrying the head of a dead cockroach. Inside, I smiled as I turned and looked down at the fallen coffin muncher at my feet. I didn't know how all of this might turn out, but I knew of two little fang heads that wouldn't be a part of it.

"Get any info out of that one?" I asked.

"Nothing worth saving his life for." The sweet scent of vanilla filled my nose as she circled in front of me. "Now what do we get to kill?"

I had to laugh. "I'm going to go see Quinn about all this. Something tells me I'll have lots to kill by the time the sun rises."

I lit another cigar in celebration, brought the Magnum down on the already dead cockroach and fired. Together we watched the body turn to ash and blow away in the light fall breeze.

CHAPTER FIVE

I descended on the Coffin Restaurant propelled by driven anger. Most of the cockroaches saw me as that. The Coffin sat at the far end of Bat Town on Church Street around the corner from where I had killed the bloodsucker. And like all the other businesses in the undead district, Quinn Rubio owned it.

Quinn spent most of his time here running the night-to-night operations of Bat Town. He had become the undead ambassador to all the tourists and locals alike. All the gullible mortals wanted to see and eat with the master vampire and live to tell about it. To most of them, it was a harmless game with no consequences, but I knew better. I found it stupid and pathetic, but that's what our world has come to. We faced global warming, war, and famine but what did we do to help humanity? Gave the vein junkies of the world citizenship and the right to live. Gag me with a bloody spoon. But I planned to rock their world with a bit of reality.

I entered the dining establishment dressed to kill in my trademark black leather and dark sunglasses. Dried cockroach blood still decorated my face and hands. The smoke from my cigar curled around my shaved head as I looked to the roach doorman, dressed in his black tux. Before I got inside, there would be the usual sparing with him about letting me in, but tonight it would be in his best interest to simply keep his trap shut and let me go unmolested.

"Where do you think you're going, vampire man?"

So much for his best interest. "I have a dinner date with Quinn, but I'm a little late, so you have time to make a very important decision. Either forget you saw me, or you will be specks of ash that I'll brush from my jacket."

He looked at me and gave a nervous smile. "I doubt that Mr. Rubio will be dining with you this evening. Besides, you can't shoot me, Avenger. We both know that. Times are different. You're nothing but outdated flesh." He looked to Angie. "And what business do you have here, wolf?"

"To eat your heart out," she purred as her fingers carved out an imaginary heart on his chest.

The doorman backed away and turned his attention back to me. "No one comes in here unless specifically ordered by Quinn, and you are not on either the guest list or menu."

I opened my leather trench coat and revealed the vampire head.

He jumped back with disgust in his face. "What the hell's that?"

Angie kissed his cheek and smiled. "Just a little head, honey. I'd be glad to do the same for you if you want."

I moved his attention back to me before he got too distracted with Angie's innuendos. "Not only can I go through those doors, but I will. Now we can discuss the laws and politics behind it as you flurry to the ground if you like, but either way, I'm through negotiating with you." I returned a sarcastic smile of my own as I pulled the cigar out of my mouth and blew the smoke in his face. I flicked the butt on the sidewalk at his feet.

The maggot taxi looked back to Angie, but said nothing. She shrugged and blew a kiss.

"I can't let you in even if I wanted to. There's a dress code, you know. The wolf is a little under dressed to say the least." His voice nothing more than air with a hint of sound as he turned to me. "And you…are a bit bloody."

"Thought that was the way you liked us."

He smirked. "You'll have to leave the weapons and religious articles at the door."

I shook my head. "Don't think so, cupcake. I plan on using them both if things go my way. Pray you won't be part of the carnage when it's all over." I moved passed him with no further problems. Lucky for him.

The Coffin was one of the most posh restaurants I had ever seen. Decadence and indulgence ruled with over the top décor, live music and top-notch food from some of the most notable undead chefs in the world. It had become a playground for the rich and famous, dress codes of tux and tails for the men and gowns for the ladies. Angie and I were easily the most underdressed in the room. No chance of us blending in.

The large room glowed with countless candles, and every chair filled with a potential victim. Waiters and waitresses hurried in a chaotic ballet, carrying dishes of the trendiest food ever to hit a human pallet.

I could smell the rich aroma of freshly cooked steaks and other smells that made my mouth water. I found it ironic that creatures that couldn't eat a bite of solid food would be running a restaurant, but go figure.

The live jazz band played an upbeat version of "Days of Wine and Roses" as I scanned the room for the most powerful cockroach in the city.

My eyes came to rest at the center table. His back faced me, long black hair cascaded down his shoulders. Light caught in its shape. A group of well-dressed guests looked to him with a gaze of wonderment. Plates of filet mignon and baked potatoes steamed with heat. Knives and forks already at work.

I checked my pockets, a second time, for all the weapons I had on me and made damn sure if things went bad, I'd at least have a fighting chance. Backing out now, wasn't an option.

Thick power radiated throughout the room, making my skin crawl. And it would suffice to say that many of them were powerful enough to snap my neck and drain me before I knew it.

As I made my walk across the vast floor, I caught the attention of many of the diners as well as the vamps, but everyone behaved themselves. Angie paced behind me and teased the gentlemen as she passed. Both music and conversation evaporated to silence as we moved deeper inside the room; forks and other utensils clanked to rest against china. The only sound filling the room were my footsteps as I crossed across the dance floor. With each step, I tried to talk myself out of why I came here.

It seemed to take me an hour to get to the center table, where Quinn still faced away from me. My heart pummeled against my chest as I approached. Fear far outweighed my hatred for his kind. I had been on the pounding side of his power before and I didn't find it at all enjoyable.

I stood and stared down at the top of his head. My hand shook as it grasped the Magnum I had hidden under the trench coat. Numb with fear, I took in his presence. Many had died for what I had just done.

"Are you going to stand there or shoot me, Mr. Isaac?" Quinn asked as he brought his glass to his mouth for a sip, followed by a touch to his lips with a napkin. He never turned around or made any movement. I still couldn't believe humans could sit at the same table as these cockroaches and eat anything while the vampires sipped on human blood. Surely they knew the goblet didn't contain chocolate milk.

"I guess there's no need for me to announce myself."

"Nor the wolf." He turned to meet me with methodical care. "Every eye in the restaurant looks as though some insane creature has entered. That only leaves you. Besides, it would be impossible for you to come here unnoticed. I have been expecting you." He smiled large enough that I could see fangs. "You are practically one of us yourself. I can feel the power off of you as easily as you can from me." He took a long look at me. "Not to mention you smell of fresh blood tonight. Perhaps you would care to clean up first."

I tried to hide my anger. He had poisoned me not long ago with the cockroach virus, leaving me with traces of it in my system for the rest of my life. For that alone I owed him a bullet to the heart. Most disagree with the story of how I got the virus, but I liked mine better. "I'm guessing you know why I'm here."

Quinn turned to the guests at the table, who looked at the undead man before them with uncertain horror written on their faces. Their eyes volleyed from the master roach to me, trying to decide whether to run or remain perfectly still. If I were them, my choice would always be to run. In fact, I wished I had that luxury. As Quinn returned his attention to me, he spoke. "With you Mr. Isaac, anything is possible. Please enlighten me with the details of your uninvited presence." There it was: the underlining tone of agitation and sarcasm. If anything, I was making his night a little more uncomfortable. Goodie.

"I'm here to retrieve the young man you have in your custody. After that you can enlighten me on why Kansas is freaking out, Sasha wants me dead and who this new daisy pusher in town is."

Every eye at the table looked at the vampire for answers. No matter how this turned out, I had slammed his credibility with doubt. Quinn turned to me. He tried to catch me with those hypnotic eyes of his, but I dropped my gaze just in time. "I know you happen to live in a world of lunacy, Mr. Isaac, but this is a little over the top, even for you. I have no one of the sorts under my protection, nor do I know of the imaginary boogiemen looking for you. As for why Kansas is, ---as you say---, freaking out, perhaps time will allow us to unravel the mystery at another time. Now if you do not mind, I wish to finish dinner with my guests," he said with a wave of his hand.

I slammed the head of the dead vampire down on the table. Blood curdling screams filled the air as maroon liquid pooled under the head. "Tell me how imaginary this looks to you? Now unless you want things to really get out of hand I suggest you take me to the young man you've taken hostage." I had everyone's attention, might as well fill them with all the dirty details I could.

The master blood leech looked at the head with a smirk. "I am sorry, Avenger, but I do not know the deceased. Now if you do not mind, you have severely worn out your welcome." His voice was as monotone as he was dead.

"Don't you lie to me tonight, Quinn. Playing stupid won't work. I'm fresh out of patience. Now either tell me what you know about all this, or I'll see to it the next head I slam on this table will belong to you."

Quinn stood and pushed me back a step with sheer power. "Perhaps we could discuss this matter at a different time. As I have announced before, I am having dinner with a few friends."

"Friends. These are your friends?" I looked to them. Eyes still stared at me waiting to see if I would kill them all where they sat. Gentlemen held their wives as if they would be able to save them if I wanted them dead. "Are you telling me you're friends with this maggot taxi? Did he tell you that he tried to poison me a few months back? Tried to keep the deaths of blood sucker supporters from the media so that those like you would keep coming down here to the clubs and restaurants? Friends? He'll be at your throats in no time if your credit cards get denied tonight. He's a predator, not a friend." An electrical force from unseen hands shoved me back, further away from the table.

"You have only a few more seconds to leave before I rip your throat out," Quinn said in my mind.

"Really? Say it out loud to your friends, Quinn. Let them hear how you've threatened me."

"When that head had a body attached to it, I heard it asking about the master vampires and Paul. Don't tell me you don't know anything about it," Angie finished. "Either you're behind it, or know who is. The vampire that died the other night is of your coven, so I find your lack of knowledge nothing more than a lie. Nothing happens down here that doesn't tie to you. Save the bullshit for the tourists, Quinn."

Quinn turned to look at the head again. He picked it up as if it was a carved pumpkin, and turned it with an inquisitive flair. "I presume this attack occurred in the vampire district?" He made a point not to acknowledge Angie or myself. His dead eyes still fixed on the head.

"At the end of my nails," Angie answered. I breathed easier at Angie's vague answer. Never tell these coffin nailers more than you have to.

Quinn's eyes refocused on me. "So am I to believe that your wolf that killed this one?"

"She killed one and I killed the other."

Quinn's focus shifted to the head again. He examined it with undead eyes that couldn't hide the hint of horror behind them. With as much grace as he could muster, Quinn turned back to the humans at the table and smiled as he handed the head back to Angie. "Please, excuse me. Mr. Isaac and I have much to discuss. Please continue with your meal."

I did my best to hold my ground as the fear under my skin threatened to explode through every orifice of my body. I had to tense my muscles simply to keep from shaking. My finger rested on the trigger to the Magnum under my coat. My body convulsed. The possibility of me shooting myself in the foot seemed greater with each passing minute.

Quinn whispered to me in a deep threatening tone as we walked further away from safety. "Do not attempt to threaten me, Mr. Isaac or the young man in question will be the least of you worries, I assure you. The pure blood vampires have many issues they find a bit unsettling and you hold the key." Pure bloods--- the name given to those born vampire rather than born again.

Quinn gave another smirk. "The vampires that hold the human are not from my coven. And they are here by illegal and uninvited means. Something I will take care of in its own due time. Chances are, you will not get the human back." He looked at the head of the vampire Angie held by the hair. It spun slowly in her hand.

"This vampire is here on behalf of a particular master vampire in this territory, but I assume Sasha and Victor have already told you this. It is this master vampire that holds Josh Price's death certificate, not I." Quinn looked around the restaurant as he continued to push me further from the main floor to the darker corners. He wanted me away from human ears. He gave a sinister smile and looked back to the table where he once sat. "Now that you have killed these vampires, negotiation might be a little tricky."

"I'm not here to negotiate, Quinn. You helped take him because of Frank Price. You're just trying to get back at him for telling me about the Knights of the Night murders." My hand remained tight around the Magnum as a precautionary measure.

"Frank Price's grandson? Really? It truly is a small world after all, is it not?" Quinn gave a throaty laugh. His face now only inches from mine. Wisps of his black hair tickled my cheek. "It is important that you listen rather than run your uncontrollable mouth. If this particular vampire I speak of does indeed come looking to negotiate this human's life, you may need to be more careful in whom and what you kill. The pure bloods are not particularly the forgiving kind."

With Quinn, you had to read between the twisted lines to find the strands of truth. He made a game of asking the right questions. "What does this blood licker want to negotiate? And why negotiate it with me instead of you?"

He gave a knowing grin. "It is not I that has what this master vampire wants. This is not about blood or revenge, but power. And if you had any intelligence to speak of, that alone would have you running away."

I put the Magnum in Quinn's face. I had committed to more than I bargained for and I knew it. Fingers stiff and unresponsive; fear settled in. "As you can see, I'm not going anywhere, so be a good little suck head and give me the name of the roach I need to kill."

"The name of the vampire sent here to kill you is Judas." A quiver ran down my spine. It had been the same name the dying coffin lover in the street gave me. Quinn looked around the room before speaking again. "He is part of an ancient coven. Killing my vampire is their way of showing power, and my cue to mind my own business. Customary for uninvited visiting covens. I would have done the same in his territory."

"You let Judas kill one of your own vampire minions and you sit here and do nothing? You're not a coward, Quinn. You're a liar." Angie said.

He shook his head. "I have nothing that this visiting vampire wants. It is not me that must find ways to negotiate for a life, and I will not go to war with Judas over one dead vampire, much less a human."

"Not that I care, but why me?" I asked.

"Avenger, in order to become the master of a pure blood coven, one must kill the previous pure blooded master vampire." I could see the humor in his eyes. He had blindsided me.

"I still don't see what that has to do with me," I answered.

"You were the one that killed Asa--- Asa was the pure blood master vampire. How can make it any clearer to you?" His voice slithered under my skin.

I shrugged. "I've killed master vampires before, I don't see what made Asa so special." I said the last part as sarcastically as I could. "So perhaps it needs to be a little clearer."

"But at that time you didn't have vampire virus in you," Angie finished.

I looked at her in shock. "Please tell me you don't mean what I think you're implying."

"In the world of vampire politics and pecking order, the one that kills the master vampire becomes the new head of the coven. Now that you have the vampire virus in you, you are seen as not only a threat to their way of life, but an authentic heir to the throne. Unclean and undeserving nonetheless, but a master all the same."

Quinn looked to Angie. "Tell him I am not lying."

Angie's face filled with the makings of a dark storm. "In the most thin lines of truth, yes. You are a master vampire."

I looked to Angie. "You knew this?"

"It's only a technicality. I knew you would over react. Plus, you know as well as I do, they are only using it as a loop hole to kill you within vampire and human laws."

I let out a disgusting yell. Vengeance took over as panic set in. I dug the Magnum in his temple. "You did this to me, you fucking dead maggot. If it weren't for you, none of this would be happening, would it? Would it!" My hands shook with rage. "Tell me why I shouldn't just waste you here and now?"

On his face I saw the overused smirk I had seen so many times. Even with a Magnum pressed against his temple, the master vampire failed to show emotion. As twisted as it sounded, I think he enjoyed standing right on the edge of true death, and seeing if he could walk away from it. I wanted to push him off that edge, but found my finger paralyzed with lack of guts and overabundance of fear. Not a combination to have when threatening a master roach.

"So that's why Sasha was hell bent on killing me tonight. He wants to beat this other vampire to my…throne?"

Quinn gave a chuckle and shook his head. "Ah, Avenger, you shall make a wonderful pure blood master vampire. Do not fight what you truly are."

"I am not and never will be a damn cockroach. So tell your little blood buddies to fly back out of town." I would put the Magnum to my own head before I acknowledged the monster in me.

I could feel his power rise. Either he would kill me, or I'd kill him. "And if you kill me, what of the young man you seek? What do you think will happen to him? I am the only vampire that can convince this new vampire not to kill the boy. Any wrong move on your behalf and he will surely die." He looked at the Magnum and laughed. "There is an old saying that every bad situation has a silver lining. Perhaps we could search for the one that pertains to this."

"I'm getting ready to blow your silver lining all over this nice restaurant, unless you produce Josh Price." Angie said as she dropped the vampire head and raised the 9mm in Quinn's direction. I kept the Magnum at his temple.

"There will be no need for violence, I assure you, wolf. I will do everything within my power to make sure that the man in question is released to the proper authorities. Please show me the dignity of not having your weapons at my head. You know as well as I do that there is far too much at risk to kill me, so if you do not mind, let us not play such foolish games." His stance grew confident. "Besides, Avenger, if you kill me, then you will be the master vampire of two species. I highly doubt that you would invite such added stress."

I started to pull the trigger anyway, when a caramel hand jolted me back to my senses. "As twisted as this dead piece of shit is, he's right. Don't give him the satisfaction."

"Listen to her Avenger, killing me will bring you only temporary satisfaction and long term complications." Quinn's voice grew darker with each word.

"Oh, Quinn, that's where you're so wrong," I answered. "Putting a bullet in your head is not complicated for me at all."

"Then have it your way. But if you refuse to negotiate on such trivial things, I assure you young Josh Price will die." His voice fell to a whisper. "When the body of the vampire you just killed is found, your life will suffer things worse than death. I would give me the benefit of doubt at this point. I know of the source behind those that seek you. There is much to be learned and told. I only hope you will become wise enough to listen. The more time you spend with a weapon to my head, the more your life is at risk."

"And the more bullshit you spew, the greater the danger," the werewolf responded. Unlike myself, Angie hoped Quinn wouldn't cooperate. She hadn't had her fill of killing things tonight and had far less to lose.

A new rush of power filled the room. Stronger than anything I had ever experienced before. Everything around me stopped breathing, moving…living. Death had entered and gain control in a stranglehold. "Perhaps it is too late for negotiations," Quinn mumbled.

"I can't believe my eyes!" a shout rose from the far end of the room. I looked up to see the silhouette of someone, but I couldn't make out the face. The form moved forward out of the shadows.

"Judas," I heard Quinn whispered. By the tone of his voice, I could tell Judas' appearance hadn't been welcomed or expected. By the undead electricity that dripped from the very walls of the Coffin Restaurant, it became clear I found myself between a rock and a hard place. I didn't bring enough bullets.

CHAPTER SIX

"This calls for a toast." His southern accent so thick it almost sounded fake. The dirt napper held a gold goblet in his right hand, turned to the tables of already terrified humans, and lifted it high in the air. "Ladies and gentlemen, may I have your attention please. It seems as though we have a celebrity among us. I wish to introduce Mr. Paul Isaac to you. Not only the greatest vampire slayer of our time, but also a master vampire who by all human laws, should be killed just like the vampires he hunts." He began to slowly walk towards us. "Tell us, Mr. Isaac, how you have left a trail of blood and death so vile that even after the bodies may have blown away, the stench upon your skin remains. And by the looks of the crowds on the streets, it has happened yet again. Only now it has happened to one of my own."

My hand instantly held the butt of the Magnum. I'd have already blown his head off his shoulders by now, but he and I both knew what remained at stake. No pun intended. A human life hung in the balance. Killing him before I got my answers didn't get me any closer to Josh. Still, I stood there, planning his death. But extracting information from him had to remain my top priority. Dark eyes returned to me. He drank from the goblet before he continued. "In all the years I have walked this earth, I have never heard of something like you. Mother a vampire, father a human. A mutated virus that no one ever thought could exist. Yet here you are before me. I can smell the blood in your veins, and understand why it is that all are attracted to you." After he finished the goblet of blood, the maggot mouth licked his lips. He had a slender frame, with a narrow face and handlebar mustache. His southern charm still showed through in his ageless face. "Raised by Father Garcia at the church to be a killer of your own kind, while he and the others hid your real identity from you. Lied to you about your mother and father. Tell me, master vampire, what angers you the most? Knowing your mother was one of us, the man you thought of as a father had been nothing more than a love struck fool, having a father that made his fortune off of the filth of vampire/human sex, or that everyone knew it and lied to you?"

"You don't know me." I did my best to hide my anger.

He watched my fingers twitch around the butt of the Magnum. A thin grin formed along his pale lips. "Apparently, I know you better than you know yourself. I know what you truly are and I find it vile and disgusting. And for that I will surely watch you die, but for now, let us simply talk about what hangs in the balance and what we are both willing to risk and sacrifice." Judas stopped and looked back to the diners. "And such a thing could ruin their appetites and be bad for business."

"Give me Josh and I'll forget you were here."

His answer grabbed my attention. "Perhaps I could trade him for Isabella since we are both in the market for humans?" I tightened as I heard that name from my not so distant past. Isabella had been a human servant for the cockroach artist Dubro, owner of a defunct vamp art gallery called Crimson Madness. Dubro and his lover Sylvester, had killed investors of his own gallery and faked his own death in order to slip away with the millions of investment dollars. Isabella had embezzled her share of the money and art in order to pay off the executioners looking for her newly turned brother. I had killed Dubro and Sylvester, but Isabella lurked out there somewhere, running from the vampires that didn't see her saving the life of a bat head as worthy of staying alive. Some would hunt her down for the artwork and money she now had, while others would simply hunt her down for the sport of it. Either way, she wasn't on my radar, not to mention, I had no idea where she had disappeared to. She had brought her own death on herself. As for her brother, the human laws are clear. If a human rises as a vampire after the laws went into effect, he or she is to be beheaded and never rise again. Sooner or later, Isabella will run out of money and time and she and her brother will find themselves on the biting end of a set of fangs.

Judas broke out in laughter. "I find it most intriguing that this human nearly kills you, yet you hesitate to deal with her life. But fear not, I have no interest in sweet Isabella. No more than I do young Josh Price. I am here for far larger prizes." He moved his hand around the room with exaggerated fanfare. Cold, dead shock danced across my skin. Pricks of pain caused me to whence.

I looked around the room, surprised by the lack of response. Hundreds of glass eyes stared back at me; an eerie silence as though death itself had entered the room. Every human in the restaurant looked back at us with doll eyes. Life no longer behind the faces. I realized what he had done. "You hypnotized them with your magic you twisted piece of shit."

"Would you prefer them to be huddled together, whimpering and crying, as my coven sucks the life out of their pathetic necks? With what I have to discuss with you, I will leave no witnesses to. So choose what you wish me to do. I do not care whether they suffer or not." Out of the shadows appeared two more figures. I think my heart stopped altogether as the light caught the shapes of Victor's and Sasha's faces.

Quinn remained seated with his hands folded on his chest. If he feared for his own life, it didn't show. Seeing a monster like Judas kill me would be pure joy to him. He would be rid of me and there would be nothing tied to him. He could simply walk away unscathed while his nemesis died before him.

While my eyes remained on the monster, I spoke as softly as I could to Quinn, who now stood as lifeless as a corpse. "I don't suppose you wish to tell me what this is really all about would you?"

"I fear the window of opportunity to talk may be breeched for the moment. Judas has blessed us with his presence as a representative of the pure blood vampires I told you about." Quinn's words were solemn and cold. "It would appear as though Josh Price's life depends upon the death of the current pure blooded vampire of the city."

"Care to elaborate?"

"It is really quite simple. If you want the boy to live, there must be sacrifice upon the part of the master vampire."

Quinn's eyes rolled to me. "You."

Judas picked the dead cockroach head up from the floor and lovingly kissed its cheek. "My dear vampire brother, we will have your revenge in its own sweet time." He sat it back down and looked back to me. I could now see the form of his face. "I have to admit it, Mr. Isaac, your reputation precedes you. I am impressed that you were able to kill this one. I had sent the very best." An evil smile rose. "It is such tragedies as this that will make your death sweet. To take your power and life will be nothing short of euphoric." Dark eyes looked to Angie. "Now it appears as though you have taught your wolf the ways of violence as well."

Angie took a step forward, "Just ridding the world of one piece of blood sucking slime at a time."

"Your wolf is full of spirit, master vampire. I understand your attraction to her. Both beauty and beast. Breaking her will shall be a challenge. I am already excited."

Angie started to speak, but it Quinn beat her to the punch. I thanked God he did, but wasn't sure why. "As I told you before, Judas, Mr. Isaac would seek me out for the human at stake even though no vampire of my coven had tried to harm him in any way. He is nothing short of a creature of habit. Now if you do not mind, I wish for a gesture of truce between our covens. I request that you kill Mr. Isaac somewhere else. Death in my restaurant would be seen as bad for business." Quinn moved away from me and stepped toward Judas' approach.

"So you allowed Judas' thugs to kill your vampire in order to save your own ass. How noble of you Quinn." Breathing became thin.

Quinn sipped from his glass as though nothing had happened; his conscience as cold as his skin. In fact, he looked bored of the whole event. "As I have told you before, vampire way of life is not like that of the human. There is only black and white. No gray to cloud the mind. The death of one, saves the lives of many. You will understand that all too well in a few moments."

"I came here only to kill you, Paul Isaac, master vampire, but now that you have brought about unneeded death to my coven. I am afraid that more deaths may be required to pay your debt. I ask for blood in return. Yours is non-negotiable. I will take it either way. If you refuse, I will take it at my own digression." I could feel the breath of his words hit me as he stood inches from me. Thick and impossible to wipe free. He wore a black button up silk shirt and pleated black slacks. A true southern gentleman to the untrained eye. A snarl formed on his upper lip and he huffed in gothic humor. His glare stuck on me. "You have created death and chaos for my species for the last time. Killing Asa has brought about tangibles that you will never be able to kill your way out of. Now you have not only placed your life in the cross-hairs, but possibly the lives of those you love." We were now so close, our noses touched.

"I won't allow you to take my blood or the blood from anyone else here. I owe you nothing short of a stake to the heart. As for Asa, he got what he deserved, so don't treat him like some kind of martyr. Let the bodies outside be a warning to you and all the maggot taxis with you that you've bitten off more than you can chew."

I could smell the metallic stench on his breath as he remained stoic. "Pity for them."

I stood my ground. I had to at least put up a façade of bravery. "Asa died because of his own selfish actions. Don't make the same mistake. Cross me and you and your coven will end up as fang flurries before it's all over. Give me back the human you have, I let you leave here with your head still on your shoulders." I could feel his incredible power roll across my skin. I fought the urge to react.

He began to laugh. "I give you this, Paul Isaac, you make my decision to kill you all the more pleasurable with each word that slips from your mouth." He looked at Angie, then back to me. "As for the human life, his fate is up to you. Do as I ask and everyone gets what they want out of this."

Judas walked around the tables as the countless patrons still stared into space. Time had suddenly stopped. He twirled, facing me. "I may not be up on all the human laws, but I do believe the government of the United States would concur the vampires you killed were protected beings." He looked back to Sasha and Victor, who so far behaved themselves. "But it is not human laws that I am interested in, nor do I follow. I will allow you to pick any two lives close to you as payment for the deaths of my vampires. If you agree, I will not kill the Detective's grandson. If you disagree to meet my demands it will be seen as an act of hostility and a broken code of ethics. I will kill everyone you love." As the words slid from his lips, he looked to Angie.

She walked toward Judas with her stripper stroll. "You want us to give you a human life for your vampires? You pathetic blood leech. That's what you wanted all along isn't it? They weren't your best hit men, you sent ones you knew we could kill. You set your own vampires up to die. You trapped Paul in vampire politics."

Judas gave a deep growling laugh. "Your wolf is smarter than you give her credit for, Avenger." His hand reached out to touch Angie's hair, but she stopped him before fingers could grasp her locks. My hand wrapped around his wrist. Power burn through me with a hellish wrath. He grinned a toothy smile as his focus remained on Angie. Without incident, he recoiled his grasp. "Well, I guess we know what is at risk if you refuse my demands. It would be so unpleasant to have to kill something so beautiful over the tedious task of vampire politics."

Sasha spoke. "You speak as if your coven will be allowed to come into our city and take over without resistance. I am the rightful heir to the throne of master vampire." He looked at me. "Unfinished business as it were. I will choose which of my coven will be given to you for the murders of your men, not Paul Isaac. He is not a pure blood vampire and by no means the master vampire of this city. Anything to do with vampire politics or law will go through me, not Paul. Otherwise, I will call upon the Vampire Council to intervene."

Judas turned to Sasha. "We all have something to gain and lose in this situation. To bring war against you, will weaken the overall covens. Making this land far less stable. But the glaring truth remains. Paul Isaac is the master vampire of Orlando, which means I cannot and will not discuss this matter with you. In fact, I find you highly out of line." He moved closer to Sasha. "Mr. Isaac's death will be our doing and no one else's. I have already sacrificed my vampires to flush out the great executioner. If I will kill my own, make no mistake that I will do far worse to you."

"You are a sadistic son of a bitch aren't you?" Angie started to move toward Judas. I stopped her with a touch of my hand, but I could not stop that mouth. "Sacrifice and death of humans or vampires means nothing to any of you as long as you get what you want. It's disgusting to think that you are able to hide behind laws meant to help you."

Judas gave a grimaced nod. "Call it what you will, wolf. It is simply the price of doing business. I knew Paul would not come here over the death of one of his vampires. He does not understand vampire politics and would not see it as a threat." He lifted his finger and smiled. "But put a human life in the balance, and I have negotiating power and leverage. Paul's one true weakness is his loyalty to the humans. I find it humorous that a master vampire would have such love for them. That love will be his downfall and we all know it." Judas smiled and gave a Gaelic shrug of his shoulders. "And now it would seem he has grown fond of the wolves of the city as well."

I stood in front of not one, but two master vampires as well as two others that had already attempted to kill me once tonight. And to make matters all the rosier, if I killed any one of them, I ran the risk of not getting Josh back. I really hated being me right now. "You heard me the first time. Consider this your last warning to crawl back into the hole you came from. Return Josh and I'll do my part to make sure you leave the city in one piece."

Judas threw his powerful glare toward Angie. "Perhaps losing the ones you love the most has not been weighed. I am not here to pick a fight, as you might say, but instead make things right among my kind. An opportunity to strengthen what we all have. It is you that is willing to risk the pawns in the game."

Angie held her ground against Judas. "If you're threatening my life, bat boy, you've under estimated my ability to give a damn. As I see it you have nothing to keep me from dusting your ass." Intimidation just wasn't her style, no matter how big and bad the monster tried to be. She looked to Sasha and Victor. "Don't go anywhere boys, because when I'm through removing his skin from under my fingernails, I'm going to rip your throats out. I know what fun things you were up to last night too."

Sasha opened his mouth to say something, but then grew a brain and remained silent. I knew he would wait in the weeds to make his kills. But then again, when Angie talks smack, it's best to hold your tongue. They, like me, knew, the girl could back it up.

The whole situation seemed so absurd to me. I had no issues with giving up my status as a master vampire. I didn't understand all the fuss about it. "I'm not agreeing to any of this. I don't negotiate under vampire terms," I said with as much defiance as I could muster.

"As you wish, master vampire." Judas grabbed a woman next to him. He exposed her neck in one swift move. Her eyes still glazed over with roach magic. "Then I start the killing now. Blood will be on your hands long after the life leaves her pathetic body. I, along with all the other vampires with me, will kill each human here one by one until you give your blood to me as well as the two vampires you choose to die for your mistakes."

When in Bat Town, do as the bats do, I guess. "Okay, I choose Sasha and Victor." God, the looks on their faces were priceless. I did my best not to smile, but failed miserably.

Judas gave in without a fight. He gave the boys a big smile. "Very well, Sasha and Victor it will be, but you must die first in order to save the others."

I pulled the Magnum out of my shoulder holster. I had to walk a thin line, but I wouldn't stand and watch as he drank the blood of everyone around me. I'd do everything I could not to kill him yet, but my idea of compromise continued to shrink at an alarming rate.

He laughed loud. "How does it feel, Avenger? Knowing there is a room full of witnesses and not a single one of them will ever hear your cries for help as I drain you dry. Perhaps you are not the great vampire killer that the stories speak about. I only hope you will be brave in death."

Angie pulled the 9mm on Judas. Until now, I had forgotten that she had it. Still, thankful all the same. "Walk away now, while you still can, or..."

My muscles tightened with anxiety. My mouth moved but nothing came out as a million questions filled my head, each fought to come out first. The blood lickers filled the room with eye blurring speed. Each one exposed a human throat. Fangs only a layer of skin away from jugular veins.

Judas' fingers played with the woman's neck. Nails threatened to break skin. "You make any sudden move against me and my coven shall take life from every one of them. Decision time, Avenger. Their lives or yours."

I weighed my options. Surely he didn't think he could get away with such carnage? But never under estimate a vein magnet. I gave a submitted nod to Angie. She brought the 9mm down to her side with hesitation and a frown.

"I am so glad to see that we could reach an agreement without more needless deaths." Glazed eyes returned to human form as each guest recovered from the cockroach magic. I shot the Magnum in the air, which ignited synchronized screaming and running throughout the room as silence broke. Each human face looked at me, faces showing the horror that drove them. They saw me as the mad man, not the savior.

An exodus of human lives rushed past me, headed for the exit; slamming me to the ground. Tables overturned, chairs and dishes crashed to the ground, candles flickered along the path. My eyes searched for any humans being attacked, but there seemed to be nothing more than pandemonium as they escaped the room. At this point, it didn't matter to me that they thought I had been the one taking life. I wanted them scared. It made them run faster! The roaches in the room watched the madness in curiosity as they blocked the exits. I waited for the inevitable attack.

Being on the ground put me at a distinct disadvantage. I jumped back to my feet. I waved the Magnum around me. The threat of a cockroach attack still loomed high. At any second fangs could be deep in my neck and the necks of those around me. I searched for Judas.

"Drop the weapon!" I didn't have to look up. Ezekiel Kansas. I hadn't seen him enter the room, but all too thankful for his presence. Doors around me opened and people spilled into the safety of the streets. I looked in the direction of his voice and started to say thank you, when he interrupted. "Now!" He had his own gun drawn on me.

Okay, now I was confused. Coffin freaks were about to dine on the patrons, yet Kansas' Glock looked back at me. I searched the room for Judas and the others. I knew they wouldn't let a little thing like the police stop them from getting to my veins. "Are you insane or just blind?" I knew losing my gun would leave me with no protection. "Besides, aren't you the one that wanted me to come down here and talk to Quinn so bad?"

"Drop the gun and put your hands behind your head!"

"Not until I get some answers," I started. "For the love of God, don't tell me they put you up to this."

"Isaac, don't make me do anything I'll regret in a few minutes. Now do as I say!" He began to move deeper inside the restaurant. His own weapon drawn and ready to fire.

In the thin light, I could still see the silhouettes of cockroaches in the room. I wouldn't be able to kill them all. I prayed to Baby Jesus that Kansas wasn't still in their pocket. If so, none of us would make it out alive. Note to self: Next time, don't help anyone.

CHAPTER SEVEN

I could already tell there would be no reasoning with Kansas. He had the look of a madman. Hopelessness cascaded over his features. His face looked tired. Bloodshot eyes descended on me with hollow expression. The hand with the gun shook with such force I knew any sudden move by yours truly would get me shot.

"Detective Kansas, thank you for leading the pure blood master vampire of Orlando to me with such haste," Judas said from the stage where the band had been playing. If he hadn't talked, I wouldn't have noticed him. He hung in the air like a shadow, weightless and timeless. My Magnum instantly went to him. I should have shot and asked questions later, but stopped short of pulling the trigger. "But I do not recall asking you to join us here tonight."

I kept my attention on Judas, but spoke to Kansas. "What does he mean by that?"

Kansas slunk into view in front and to the right of Judas. "Nothing personal, Paul. I'm doing what I had to do. I know you'll hate me, but I didn't have a choice in this."

I took it all in. "I see. So you are working for fang heads full time now." I did my best to remain calm. It wasn't the first time that Zeke Kansas did a little dirty work for Quinn and the other leeches in the city. Being betrayed and double crossed by the monsters in Bat Town didn't surprise me, but when it came to not only humanity, but someone who hid behind a badge sworn to protect that humanity, it stunk. Knowing that he had saved my life at my home simply to bring me here to be killed put him at the top of my shit list right now.

Angie now found herself in the custody of Victor. One

hand coiled around her throat. The other bound her arm behind her back. Our eyes met and I tried to assure her that I'd get us out of here one way or the other. I only hoped I could make good on that promise.

Her eyes led me to her hand and I followed. The trail ended with the 9mm still in her grasp. With all eyes on me, she had gone unnoticed. So had the Magnum in her hand. They had all come here to kill me and overlooked the fact that something else in the room might side with me. It didn't have ultra violet bullets, but it would still hold the plasma slugs off long enough that we could escape with all our fluids. The silver bullets in the gun would make a nasty wound that wouldn't heal overnight.

"I said drop your weapon," Kansas yelled. "Please Paul, don't make me do this. I *will* shoot you."

"Why shoot me when you have a room full of perfectly good coffin divers all around us. If you really wanted to kill me you already had your chance tonight. Why here? Why now?"

He gave a hopeless grin. "It's not that I want to kill you, Paul, I can't take the chance that you will kill him."

"Meaning Judas?"

A quick nod. "Please, you can't kill him. If you do, I'll never get her back."

"But it's okay if he kills me?" God, why does everyone see me as the bad guy these days?

"Just put down the gun and I'll explain. Please, don't make me shoot you."

I shook my head in defiance. "No chance, Kansas. I don't know what's in all this for you, but if it means me giving you my gun, you're out of luck." I shot a quick glance to him, then refocused on Judas. As fast as the bloodsuckers were, he could easily been gone by the time I looked back, but to my satisfaction, he remained in sight. In fact, he looked more distracted about Kansas than me.

Judas and I continued our staring game as he spoke to Kansas. "As I told you on the phone, Detective, I did not wish for your interference in this matter. You are jeopardizing any chances of gaining back what you love with foolish chances." Judas smiled wide and exposed his white fangs. His wide eyes rolled over to Kansas in defiance to the Magnum that pointed to his heart. We both knew killing him now left me with no chance of getting Josh Price back alive. Secretly, I began planning all their deaths to the smallest of details.

"What's that supposed to mean?" I asked to no one in particular. My eyes raced between Judas and Kansas.

Kansas continued with his rambled apology. "You don't understand, Paul. This is out of my control. Please, drop the Magnum and do what they say." Kansas wiped away the trickle of sweat from his brow. He moved within inches from me. Close enough I could reach out and grab him, but his gun still stared at my temple. I had to think before I acted. Call me silly, but having my brains splattered across the floor and on the walls didn't sound any more appealing to me than having fangs in my neck. "I'm doing what they told me I had to do. Please Judas, tell me where she is."

I could smell the alcohol on Kansas' breath as he eased closer. I knew all the pieces would fall into place in their own sweet time, but I began to panic from the inside out. In the past, Kansas had threatened my life more times than I could count, but we both knew it hadn't been anything more than empty threats. Not this time. He had been possessed by things only found in the darkest of nightmares.

I took another quick survey of all the major monsters that I had come to love to hate. Dead eyes stared at me. Quinn had disappeared somewhere and, *if he proved to be the coward I thought he was*, wouldn't be a problem tonight. Sasha stood in the corner of the large room. He sipped from a goblet and appeared bored with the evening's entertainment. Judas now eased his way across the vacant dance floor with the grace and ease of an alley cat.

"I'm asking this question to anyone here with enough guts to give me a straight answer. What the hell is this all about?"

"God, forgive me for this, Paul. I had no choice," Kansas whispered. His voice shook so badly, the words nearly broke apart. "Please put down the gun before they kill her."

"If I drop the gun, they will kill us all, if you shoot me, they will still kill you. Come to your senses and turn the gun on the real bad guys and we might make it out of here minus some very nasty bite marks." Truth be told, I remained more concerned with the fang heads than Kansas. My hands kept the Magnum moving. So much to shoot at, so little time. "Now, who's *her* and what makes her so damn important that we are all going to be killed?"

"They have my wife," he said matter-of-factly.

I nearly fell to the floor as I heard it. I froze mid-motion. She was pregnant, which complicated things on so many levels I couldn't fathom the thought. I prayed that I heard it wrong. "Stephanie? The baby?" If Judas had had a brain, he would have killed me then and there. With that bombshell, I couldn't have pulled the trigger if I had to. But under no circumstances could I allow Kansas or Judas to take the Magnum.

Before he could answer, Judas had made his way down the center of the room, toward us. "Enough of an answer for you, Mr. Isaac, or do you prefer to see how many more lives I can destroy tonight?" His power raked across my skin and stung the flesh on my arms. "Now if you do not mind, I would prefer you to lower your weapon and hand it to the detective. As I told you earlier, there were far too many lives at stake for you to play the role of hero."

Judas waited for my reaction. I played all the scenarios in my head and tried to find the one that had a happy ending, but none of them did. I couldn't give up the gun. I knew Judas had no intention of keeping his side of the bargain if I did. "You've already killed them haven't you?" I'm guilty of jumping to conclusions, but this time the dark side in me told me I had jumped in the right direction..

Kansas kept his gun on me, but turned to Judas. "Let me see her. Let me talk to her. Please." I found it pathetic and sick at the same time. I wanted to put a hole in Judas so bad, but everyone in the room knew I couldn't do it. I might as well have been holding a banana.

"Tell me you didn't help them set Price's grandson up, just so you could get me here. I have no doubt that by the time the sun rises, you'll be dead. I need to know that you didn't turn on Price too."

Kansas turned to me. "I had no choice. He sent a few of his men to my office looking for you the other night. Saying you were some sort of master vampire that had questions to answer. I blew them off, thinking they were nuts. Then I get a call about Price's grandson being in trouble tonight. I go to Bat Town only to find that the same vampires had already taken him. While I'm there, I get a call on my cell, Stephanie is gone. Just a voice saying they had her and cooperate if I wanted to see her alive again. Judas told me Sasha and Victor were planning on killing you over being a vampire or something and I had to go to your house and stop them from doing it. If I failed and Sasha and Victor killed you, they would kill Stephanie." He wiped away the trickle of sweat that ran down his cheek and looked deep into my eyes. "I was told to bring you hear to talk to Judas. Just talk."

"Vampires call on you to find me. I'm a vampire executioner and hated by every one of them without exception. And you thought they just wanted to talk to me?" I whispered. My arms grew tired of holding the Magnum on Judas, but I refused to lower my aim.

"My God, Paul, I wasn't thinking straight. They have my wife and unborn son. I'm afraid of what they'd do." He paced. "Hell, I'm afraid of what you might do."

I cursed under my breath. It really sucks when you can't even trust the humans. "Chances are good you're still going to get to find out."

Victor and Angie stood only feet away from Kansas. Those dark eyes on me. I had to shiver as I saw her hair matted in the wet wound on Victor's cheek. Sticky blood and infected liquids slid down her skin. I cringed with anger as I watched his pale hands trace her cheeks. Fingers raked across her breast as he sniffed her hair. Eyes always on me.

A laugh to escape his throat as he looked down at Angie. I tried not to look at the Magnum this time. I didn't want to give away our advantage. In my peripheral vision I could see she had it tucked close to her side away from deadly eyes. "If you really do care for the humans as you say, you will allow Sasha to bleed you and become the rightful heir to the pure bloods. Not everyone has to die tonight." He kissed along Angie's neck with uncaring demand. "Or perhaps it is not the humans that are the key to your heart, but instead something a little more animal."

My eyes locked on Angie. Anger and pain swirled in her eyes. Raw animalistic vibrations came from her direction. She showed signs of changing, but looked as though it had been against her will. Victor's undead surges pushed the animal inside her closer to reality. A deep groan escaped Angie's throat as she wrestled with the parasite force. I knew if Victor could force her to change, he would own a piece of her will. Victor forced my hand in all of this. I had to speed things up here a bit. If Angie lost the battle and went to animal form, the gun would fall from her grasp and end what little advantage we still had.

Judas spoke, "Only another fact that you can't protect the wolves at your feet, Avenger." Black hair danced in his face. "Love and loss of life are the things that bind all humans and I have always used this against them. In all the centuries of my life, I have taken out credible vampire killers and the authorities just like the two of you, all with the common threat of death. In the end, it is the one thing all humans fear the most." He moved closer to Kansas. "With you however, things were a little more complicated. You seem to love no one and no one seems to really love you."

That hurt, but then again the truth usually does.

Judas continued. "Mr. Isaac, you know as well as I do that in a few moments I will grow tired of this little cat and mouse game and kill Detective Kansas unless you put an end to all of this nonsense. I will slit his throat long before your finger can react to pulling the trigger. So let us not complicate matters and put away the gun." He watched the game between Victor and Angie with jaded boredom. "Now with two of my vampires dead, it is only fitting that I take the lives of two of your own. I know that killing two of your vampires will mean nothing to you and not draw a conclusion to this stalemate we find ourselves in. So, I must step outside common vampire law and take the lives of others." He stopped short of me and looked at Kansas. "I am talking of the lives of Ms. Kansas and Joshua Price."

"Please, no!" Kansas screamed as he fell to Judas' feet.

"Best advice I can give you, fang head is to let them all go. You sent those blood lappers to their death, not me. And just because you may be a vampire, doesn't mean that human law doesn't come into play here. Consider yourself lucky that you only have two dead vampires and slither back into the hole you came out of." I tried again to swallow both my pride and the anger that wrapped around it. If I allowed them to get out of control, I'd lose more than my life.

Judas shrugged. "Very well, Avenger." He picked up Angie's hand and kissed it softly. "Perhaps there are things close to you I have overlooked."

Victor laughed as he kept a strong hold on Angie. His fingers edging southward. He looked at me with evil eyes and waited for my reaction. Pale hands caressed caramel skin along her inner thighs. Her sultry eyes gazed at me as her body reacted to Victor's touches. Not of pleasure but of hate. The 9mm twisted in her hand, the barrel slowly turned toward her first kill.

Sasha slithered through the shadows. To the untrained eye, it appeared as though he had been lost to the chaos only feet away, but I knew better. He knew as well as Judas that killing me would make him more powerful and the master roach of the city. He moved into position for a quick kill. If things worked out right, I might get them to go after one another and slip away with minimal damage. I, no longer looked at this as a rescue mission. No matter what I did, I knew Stephanie and Josh would be dead.

Victor continued, "Do not worry, Avenger. I will take very good care of your wolf. She will be most popular in the dark alleyways on her knees." His dark eyes looked at Angie with crippling power. My own body picked up on the animalistic pulses in Angie's body. Clawing closer to freedom with each deep breath she took. "Killing her right away would take all the fun out of it."

"You harm a single hair on her head and I'll never sleep until your ashes are strung from ocean to ocean."

Judas turned his head and looked back at me. His face showed a genuine surprise. "So it is true that this one means something to you?" He laughed. "Fascinating that you will not submit to my bidding for the blood of a true human, but when a common wolf is thrown into the mix, you grow agitated." With pale long fingers he touched her cheek. I made an effort not to look at Angie or the weapon. "Lust is such a powerful factor for the living as well as the undead. And with this one, I see why you would be willing to die for her." He scanned her from head to toe. "In all my centuries I have never seen such perfection. But it is lust that clouds the mind of rational thinking. It is here that fatal mistakes are made."

"She means nothing to me. One monster's no different from another," I lied.

"Then you wouldn't mind if I rip her throat open and lap her blood here and now?" With a long fingernail Judas sliced enough skin that blood began to trickle down Angie's neck. She never reacted. As the animal in her fought to break free, she went deeper in some sort of trance.

He smiled as his fingers washed over the blood that trickled down Angie's skin. He licked those fingers with great care and closed his eyes and enjoyed the blood as it rolled down his throat. Then he refocused on me. "You do know under vampire law, your wolf has cast war on her own pack for what she has done tonight as well do you not?" I didn't answer. "She is responsible for killing my vampires same as you and being a wolf, she and her pack must be held accountable for those actions. But you can stop their demise by dropping the weapon and giving yourself to me. Do this without further complications and I will give not only this wolf, but all the pack sanctuary from my vampires."

Sasha acted first. He rushed toward me with paranormal speed, mouth wide open.

The 9mm in Angie's hand rose from the darkness and jammed in Victor's abdomen. I swung the gun in Sasha's direction as I heard the 9mm explode in synchronicity with my Magnum.

Victor spun free. Blood gushed from the wound as he drifted into the darkness, doubled in pain. Sasha threw a large round table in my direction as the second bullet from my gun missed its mark. Kansas shot at something, but I didn't care. I aimed for another attempt at Sasha as Judas, simply evaporated. It caused me to hesitate long enough that I lost any advantage I had.

Sasha nailed me with a boot kick to the skull. I swung at him, catching nothing but air. My balance betrayed me as I slammed into a wall. Large hands grabbed me by the neck and threw me to the floor. I landed face up. Dark eyes looked into mine.

Victor stood above us. His face still showed the pain from the silver bullet inside him. I looked away in the nick of time as drops of slimy blood leaked from the wound on his face and splattered on my cheek. My skin crawled with revulsions. With every ounce of strength I had, I brought the Magnum in Sasha's direction.

Gray nails raked across my face, cutting deep trenches of flesh. Before I could react, the weight on me lifted. Angie's nails had dug under his chin and pulled him up with one quick snap. The roach managed to wiggle free and elevate above us before he vanished in the dim light. Angie shot once hoping to get lucky.

I pushed Angie out of the way as Victor came from above in a swooping slash. His long fingers gripped me by the shoulder and spun me upward and across furniture that had already been overturned by tonight's adventures.

My cheek fell into a pool of blackened blood. I could feel it slither against my skin with a life of its own. I could smell its copper-like odor. It ran along the crease of my lips in a thick syrup. I licked it with repulsive afterthoughts. Sasha's power escaped the room.

Angie writhed in pain. The wolf in her tried desperately to get out. I could hear the growls of animalistic tones escape her throat. Claws and fingers fought for domination. Human sounds returned. A scream. Skin and fur twisted. Bones broke. Reformed. Something kept her from turning. "No!" she shouted. Her eyes were as wide as baseballs. White and rolling in the back of her head. The 9mm spun across the dance floor.

With every ounce of strength I had, I lifted myself to my feet. I had to get to Angie despite the power of daisy pushers in the room. "Victor!" I shouted as I started to run, only to hesitate.

Ahead of me, I saw a fresh trail of blood and followed it with my eyes to the source. Judas stood at the entrance of the room. He held a woman's body in his arms, his mouth covered her throat as he swallowed. She dangled lifeless in his arms. A crimson trail flowed down her limp left arm. Droplets of red pooled on the floor.

The vein weasel lifted his fangs from her neck and looked at me. Blood dripped from his chin. "That will be far enough, Avenger. Take another step and she will die."

My muscles tensed enough that my forward motion stopped. The woman's eyes rolled toward her capture as she choked on blood in her throat. Mesmerized by magic and bleeding badly, I could see the terror grow as life drained from her. A steady stream of blood exited the wound and soaked the upper part of her evening dress.

I looked for Kansas and any of the other creepy crawlies that might still be in the room. I found him on the floor with a gash in his forehead. Sasha remained in the shadows, but hadn't retreated as of yet. If the opportunity granted itself, he still wanted to be the one to take the first swing at my neck. I had little doubt he would stay close by.

From behind, the scent of vanilla gathered in my senses. Angie moved beside me. "I can get to him before he kills her." Her face still drained from the near change she went through. Hair drenched with sweat and leftovers from Victor's face. The caramel skin nearly as pale as mine. She looked tired as she fought the pain that ran through her. I knew, in her condition, she would never have a chance to get to Judas before he could react. She shook with fatigue. I changed my mind about Victor. He hadn't been the source behind her battle with the inner beast.

Judas looked at Sasha and then back to me. "Perhaps it is the chase for me that I thirst the most. Remember, Avenger, I am not the only one that sees your death as an opportunity to gain power. For you, the old saying is very true. You can run, but you cannot hide."

Angie shot Sasha as Judas started to bite into the woman's neck again. Power shot through the room as all the roaches began to move with lightning speed. Heat hit me with a force strong enough that it buckled my knees. The woman flew towards me and landed on one of the tables no more than ten feet from me.

Sasha screamed with pain as he and the other fang heads made their exodus from The Coffin. Power rippled through the air as the scent of blood grew strong. I started to move toward the woman with concern. Not for her, but us. When the dirt nappers realized Angie's 9mm didn't have ultra violet bullets, I had a bad feeling they would return in greater numbers.

I took a step back and noticed the scene before me. Kansas and Angie had their guns pointed at each other. "They're going to kill Stephanie now, you bitch!" Kansas screamed.

CHAPTER EIGHT

"If they do, it'll be because of your head being in the sand. With the little stunt you pulled, we'll all probably end up dead, so give me one good reason why I shouldn't shoot you right now." Unlike Kansas, I knew Angie wouldn't think twice about pulling the trigger. Add Victor's little molestation act a few minutes ago, and I knew killing something male would be physical as well as mental therapy for her.

"Angie, put down the gun," I said as non-threatening as I could. "He's not worth it."

Kansas moved his gun on me. Note to self: Trust and friendship are highly overrated. "If you had just gone with them like you were supposed to, this would all be over by now. Now they're going to kill my wife and baby."

"You really think they'd have turned Stephanie over to you? You're a police officer with the ability to have vampires executed. You should be thanking us your throat isn't spread all over Bat Town as we speak."

"Do you really think I'm so naïve that I don't know they will kill me eventually? I'm out of options, Paul. I don't have a choice in this. I either put the bullet in your head or mine. Sad thing is, I don't think it'll matter." He gave a snorted laugh. "Maybe if they see I killed you, they'll at least let Steph and the baby go." He wiped away tears from his eyes. "Stephanie had a sonogram last week. It's a boy. I was going to have a boy until you and your bitch shot everything to hell."

"You know as well as I do that roaches only care about power, lust and blood. By killing me, you decrease your options and chances of seeing your wife alive again. Besides, it would take a spine to shoot me, and I think someone shoved yours up your ass." I looked down at the woman Judas had attacked. Her eyes were wide with shock. She never blinked. Blood still dripped from the wound. I turned to Kansas. "Honestly, I don't care if you two shoot each other or not, but one of us has to hold it together enough to get this woman to a hospital before she bleeds to death."

Angie gave me an ever-so-slight nod and began to lower the 9mm. Better to save a life than take one for now. But in the back of my mind I knew, Kansas lived on borrowed time. I had defused half the situation, but when there's a gun still pointed your chest, you're never sure if you've really gained anything.

Kansas remained rigid. His face reflected the hollow man inside. Tears streamed down his cheeks. Kansas had started to see that no matter how politically correct he tried to be, no matter how many times he kissed blood sucking ass, they were nothing more than manipulating monsters. These dirt maggots would continue to erode his authority and trust until nothing remained but an empty shell.

Worse, I saw myself in him. A true reflection of the hatred and how it manipulated us to the point that simple thought and action no longer existed. As I stared at Kansas, I saw why so many hated me. I had become nothing more than ugly vengeance wrapped in skin.

"Put the gun down, Kansas. We're doing exactly what Judas and his coffin creeps want. Instead of driving wooden stakes through the hearts of the undead, we're at each other's throats."

"If we don't get this woman to the hospital, she'll bleed to death," Angie said to Kansas as she took a slow step toward our cockroach victim. She held her hands where Kansas could see them. Her restraint impressed me. "I'm just going to check on her. Don't do anything stupid. Oh yeah, you've already done that haven't you." So much for the restraint.

I watched as Angie bent down next to the woman. She gave Kansas quick glances from time to time. His Glock volleyed between the two of us, making up his mind which one to shoot. "I think she's going into shock, Paul. We have to move her out of here." She looked at the wound and seemed to search for a pulse. Then something bazaar happened. She jumped back to her feet. Angie looked at her hands, then looked around the room. "Besides, we don't know when they'll be back." Fear seemed to seep into her eyes as she looked at Kansas. "Get that gun off of me."

"Not a chance," Kansas replied.

Blurs of speed moved past me. Kansas lay on the floor, unarmed and unconscious. She met my gaze and smiled with her hypnotic eyes. "Tell him when he wakes up, he had his butt kicked by a girl." My jaw dropped. A combination of pure disbelief and humor. She had been faster than the human eye. Kansas resembled a crumpled piece of paper on the floor. Angie had flat out knocked him cold.

Angie's strength evaporated and her eyes rolled into the back of her head. She grabbed my shirt with hands far too weak to hold. I softened her decent to the floor as her knees gave way. It didn't take a rocket scientist to figure out something still controlled her, but my conclusions jumped to Judas and Victor. I knew they were able to possess a body without being in the room. I scanned along the tops of the tables for any signs of them.

I knelt next to Angie and cradled her head in my left hand. Lazy eyes smiled up at me like a lost puppy. I took it as a good sign. "What the hell's wrong with you?" My lack of bed side manners were blaringly obvious. I never took my eyes off of her as she slowly returned.

A smile formed as color returned to her face. Her skin glistened in the mixture of faint lighting in the room. The back of her hand traced my cheek lightly. "You're so beautiful." Chills ran along my spine. I had no way of knowing if the reaction was primal or paranormal. Or if it made a difference.

"I know." I took the hand that traced my cheek and placed it in mine and kissed it lightly. She smelled like a bouquet of freshly picked roses. "Are you going to be okay? What happened?"

Angie giggled. "Why Mr. Isaac, is that compassion showing up on your face?"

"No, it's my scared shitless look. We've got to get you to a doctor."

Her light heartedness disappeared. Eaten away by some secretive fear. "Absolutely not. I'm fine. Just a little tired." She fought to stand, but I continued to push her back down. That alone scared me. Angie had the strength to knock me to the other side of the room if she wanted to. But now she had a frailty that scared me.

I smiled at her attempt at anger. Latin blood boiled and I used it to my advantage. "Sure you're not pregnant?"

She gave me a playful slap to the face, followed by a kiss. "Only in your wet dreams, baby."

As bad as I tried to stop it, a smile broke through my façade. "I'll be back. Sit here and rest." I lifted her into a sitting position and waited to make sure she had the strength to stay there. Relief dripped over me as I stepped away. I found Angie more than a little enticing, but I didn't have enough room in my tiny heart to take on anyone else. The truth hurt. I considered myself nothing more than the Grinch with stakes. I brushed away the hair from her cheeks and fought the urge to kiss her. The timing would have to be better. A victim of a vicious vampire attack needed our attention. I swallowed my lust and refocused.

She lay on her side and held her neck with red fingers. Her eyes rolled open and close as she drifted in and out of consciousness. I did my best not to let my fear of what might happen to her show as I placed a cloth napkin over the wound. If we got the blood flow to stop, she might be okay, but then again, I was no damn doctor. Far as I knew, she might already be on her death bed.

I looked around the room for the Vampire Bite Kit, that all public buildings were required to have in case of something like this. Even those owned by the roaches had to have them in open view. Inside, I would find a coagulating serum that would act against the bat saliva.

The woman's eyes rose to meet mine, hollow and full of questions all at the same time. Purple lips gave their best attempt at a smile. I touched her hand. Ice cold flesh made me jump with panic. She didn't have much time. No kit in sight. I cursed Quinn.

I shook my head and looked back at Angie as she came back to her feet. "We've got to get her out of here as soon as we can." I didn't want to cause the woman any undue anxiety, but something that had me on edge. Somewhere in the darkness, I could still feel the power of a coffin freak. Looking over to

Angie, I could tell she felt it too. She burst to her feet and appeared to be sniffing the air. My eyes darted in the limited light. I hunted for anything that had a throat fetish.

"I felt it too." Angie drew close to me. I jumped as she placed her hand on the back of my neck. I didn't want to say it out loud, but I had a feeling that the power might have been channeled through the Angie somehow. I had seen it first hand when Maximilian forced the wolf in her to attack me.

I reached down to pick the young woman up. "Let's get her out of here."

Her hand reached out and grabbed my arm. Power shocked me with so much force, I dropped her to the floor again.

"Holy crap. The power is coming off of her!" My mind raced as I took a slow step back, keeping my focus on her. I reached for the Magnum and aimed for her heart. Better to be safe than sorry. "What the hell are you? You're dripping with power. Only daisy pushers do that." I pulled off one of my pure silver crucifixes and held it out to our new friend. To her dismay, the Magnum remained ready to do the dirty work. "Here, put this on. It will either burn you or keep you safe depending on what the hell you are. In the meantime, pray to God it doesn't glow."

Eyes formed a million questions as she volleyed her stare between the crucifix and me. "Safe from what? Vampires or you?"

"The immediate answer is me until you prove otherwise. If you're nothing more than a human victim, the decision should be an easy one. If you don't do what I say, at the very least, you'll bleed to death right here on the floor."

She started to smile, but it evaporated as quickly as it formed. Eyes stared at the crucifix necklace as though it would bite her. Now, I had her undivided attention. "Why are you doing this?"

"You're producing power. We're in a vampire district. Not the best of combinations. Now if you would be so kind, please put this around your neck." I allowed my lack of patience to bleed through my voice.

The young woman looked back to Angie. "Is he kidding?"

"He reads obituaries to cheer himself up. Kidding's not his forte," Angie said. "Who are you?"

"Apparently, I'm not whom you think."

"Wasting our time is only going to turn you to ash a little faster, so if there's anything you wish to say or prove, I recommend you use that hole in your face," Angie said as she approached the woman with her strut. I loved watching her move away from me, even though the distraction could leave me cloaked in a body bag. At least my last memory would be a lustful one.

The woman looked at me for help. I simply shrugged and continued to watch Angie.

"Give me the Magnum, baby," the lycan said, holding her hand palm up behind her, while the other still held the 9mm. "She either holds the crucifix or a bullet. Her choice, but I have no problem making it for her." I didn't want to give the Magnum to Angie yet. She remained in a bit of a bad mood to begin with, and with a vein weasel possibly pulling her strings, I sided on the side of caution.

"What is it?" I asked. I now focused on any movement our lady in distress might show. If she even breathed wrong, I knew Angie wouldn't hesitate in pulling the trigger.

"She's leaking power."

"You can't be serious. I told you, I'm not what you think." The woman began to appear agitated and nervous. It grew contagious in the room. She tried to crawl away from Angie, but thought better of it.

"Unlike Paul, I will shoot you and ask questions later. Whether you bleed or burn will simply be a matter of physics. Now why the hell is there power dripping off of you? I felt it when I touched you, so don't lie."

The woman's breathing increased. "You think I am a vampire?" Power continued to burn hot across my skin, as she reached out and grabbed the silver crucifix. A tormented smile gleamed as the chain snaked through her fingers. "See." The crucifix glowed for a moment but returned to normal in a matter of seconds, leading to even more questions. Power pulled me closer.

"So, you didn't start cooking right away. I'm not convinced yet. There is power on you, in you and around you. Better have a good reason why the crucifix glowed." With a quick pinch, I grabbed her by the lower jaw and pried her mouth open. I expected to see the razor sharp fangs, smell the blood on her breath. A gasp let go from her throat. Hands grabbed my wrists. But inside, I found nothing more menacing than incisors.

"That only leaves one possibility." Angie dug the 9mm into the woman's temple. "Do you want to tell him or do you want me to do it for you?"

"She's crazy," the woman responded as she tried to back away from the gun.

"Name," Angie commanded.

The woman thought for a minute, then did the smart thing. "Olivia."

"Good. I wasn't going to ask it again." Angie moved the 9mm from Olivia's temple to her heart. Angie looked at the wound on the woman's neck again. "Look here, Paul, it's stopped bleeding." Back to her victim, "Now, for the last time, are you going to tell him or do you want me to do it for you after I scatter your brains?"

Olivia looked up to me. "What's the difference? You're vampire executioners. You're going to kill me either way."

"What is she, Angie?" I asked.

"She's a living dead girl. Known in vampire terms as a blood host." A term I had heard before, but knew little about.

"You mean like a zombie?"

Angie shook her head. "No, a zombie is something that is raised from the dead. She has never been allowed to die." She looked at me and searched for the right words. "She's a lot like you. She has the virus, but isn't a vampire. The difference is that she has been bitten enough times by the same vampire that his power runs through her, keeping her alive."

"Then kill her," I said. I meant it. Negotiating with anything that had any ties with the vein sucker world didn't get my sympathy. Unfortunately for our new friend, all I saw was the monster inside her. I let her mouth go and grabbed a wooden stake. "And I'm no damned cockroach."

Olivia wiped her cheeks as though she could rid her skin of my intrusion. "I belong to Judas. I came here with him. I'm his mistress with benefits. As your wolf put it, his blood host." She wiped away a crocodile tear and had gained enough strength to come to a sitting position.

"Is she full of shit or is this for real?" I asked Angie.

Angie shook her head. "Vampires have the ability to animate and suspend death. With what we have here, her death has been suspended as long as Judas' power is close by. Take away the vampire and she will rot and die before your eyes."

Olivia shook. Her hands rubbed up and down her arms. With a nonchalant pitch, she threw the silver crucifix back to me. "So you see, in every way, I'm a slave. A slave to life, to death," she paused. "And to him." Her eyes watched Angie as she spoke again. "So killing me isn't as bad of a thing as you think." She looked at my Magnum, which still waited for its turn to interrogate. "It's either your bullet or his fangs. I don't have any other options."

"Why did he attack you?" I asked.

"All smoke and mirrors. It's a game we've played before. Those that witness the attack never think about me being part of the show." She ran her fingers through her hair and closed her eyes and tried to shut out the thoughts trapped in her head. "Until you, no one had noticed the power or knew of it. I'm nothing more than a distraction to allow Judas to get away. By the time I heal and move on, no one is the wiser and Judas is safe." She stood.

Olivia walked toward me. Judas' voice filled my head. *"We are kindred spirits, Avenger, whether you like it or not. Deny it all you want, but you know in your heart that it is true. Kill Olivia if you wish, but it will not stop your own fate."* I stood my ground, hand still played with the butt of the Magnum. If this roach host thought she could intimidate me, she had another thing coming.

She drew close enough that I could feel the breath from her words hit my cheek. The wound on her neck now nothing more than dried blood and scabs. In the candlelight, I noticed her for the first time as more than a victim of a blood bat attack. I wanted to pull the trigger as I listened to Judas' words, but his power rode across me and paralyzed my hands.

Olivia inched closer. I traced her face with my eyes and melted as her voice whispered in my head. She looked to be in her mid-twenties, long black hair, slender and an abundant supply of breast. Her pale skin glistened in the candlelight. Our bodies collided. My heart raced. Lust filled inside me and I wanted more. Warm and safe. I closed my eyes and tried to fight it. I knew roach power and it flowed through her. Perverted visions flashed in my mind, her skin and mine intertwined in erotic balance. My hands reached out to her.

"Back it up a bit," Angie replied as she moved Olivia further away from me. The green eyed monster rose in her stance. "Touch him again and your fang boy's going to be the least of your problems."

My body crawled with beads of sweat. Breathing became shallow. I found myself disoriented. I swallowed the nothingness in my mouth as I regained control of my thoughts and strengths.

Olivia never tried to resist Angie's retaliation. Her eyes stayed on me. *"I can feel the power rising off of you. Stop denying what you are. You are a master vampire and in the darkest depths of your mind, you know it is true. The taste of blood calls to you."* Judas called out again in my head. His laughter dominated. *"I will allow you to kill her while you mount her like a wild beast. Put a bullet in her brain as you succumb to her flesh."* The room grew cold and damp. Musty smells gathered at my nostrils. Invisible hands seemed to molest my skin as they passed. *"I shall bring upon this city a plague none have witnessed before. Blood shall run along the streets as a reminder of the wrath I have unleashed. I own you, master vampire. You just do not understand that yet."*

Olivia rose above us and fed off of the fear in the room. *"Your death shall be inevitable, master vampire. Question for you shall be, who I will kill before I chose you."* Olivia's eyes looked back to Angie. Unlike before, I now saw the dead skin and rotting flesh as the façade broke free. Maggots crawled through the meat on her face. Odor filled my nose. I fought the urge to vomit. Death gathered in the room.

Killing Olivia did nothing but pacify my anger. Keeping her alive might prove to be beneficial if it got me closer to Judas. I second guessed myself, but placed the Magnum in the holster and did the unthinkable.

I closed my eyes and grabbed her. Cold clammy flesh

slipped through my fingers and fell to the floor, as decomposing odors filled the darkness. My hands melted into her arm. Fingers sunk deep into loose flesh. Veins and arteries tangled in my fingers. Worms slithered from open wounds and tried to burrow into my skin.

Angie grabbed the other arm, and together we wrestled Olivia to the floor. I wrapped the crucifix around her throat and this time it didn't simply glow pink and go out. It caught fire and seared dead flesh into charred matter of indescribable grossness.

Olivia screamed with pain as the power forced Angie and me to let go. Demonic sounds filled my ears. Olivia writhed on the floor. Her hands reached for the crucifix, but unable to free it.

"It is her pain you are hearing and seeing, Avenger, not mine. Torture her all you wish. I will be waiting for you in the shadows all the same." But something told me my little act had more of an effect on the vein diver than he wanted me to know. If not, he would never have retreated in the thick of the fight. Not if my death was as valuable as he and Quinn said.

The power left the room and warmed to a temperature above freezing. I took a quick survey and made sure we were still alone. Olivia returned to the beautiful woman she had been earlier, but the word beautiful didn't quite fit. It was nothing more than cockroach power and trick of light. Chest muscles heaved with heavy breathing. Blisters and red skin wrapped around her neck. Puss oozed from open wounds. She looked wild and cornered as she screamed and rolled in pain as she fought against the crucifix. Pleads to release the chain bellowed from her throat, but I ignored them as I waited to see if Judas returned for his little accomplice.

I pulled the silver bladed knife from its sheath around my waist, drove the tip between two of her ribs and pulled her to her feet. The blade sang with the power that remained. Olivia's screams shot shards of pain into my brain. Black blood formed around the metal.

"Kill her now, Paul," Angie shouted.

I shook my head as I looked into Olivia's eyes. "I have a better idea with this one." I began to move her toward the opening of the restaurant. "I'm going to chum the city with her blood until he comes for her."

"Where are you taking her?"

"Where I can torture her at my convenience and Judas can't do anything about it." Inside, I knew I couldn't kill Judas this way, but he could still feel any pain I inflicted on his host. I planned on him having a very restless night.

With a free hand, I pulled out a Cuban cigar and lit it, feeling its flavor fill my lungs. It would be all the solace I'd get for a while and I needed it. I knew if I controlled Olivia, I could weaken Judas. I'd distract him enough he'd have to make the next move.

Angie grabbed my arm. "What about Kansas?"

He remained out cold on the floor. I turned to see his frame sprawled out and took in and blew out the taste of the cigar. "Leave him there. Something will find him. Cop or cockroach it doesn't matter. But to be honest, I'm kind of hoping cockroach." I drifted out of The Coffin, Olivia in tow. I had my bargaining chip.

CHAPTER NINE

Father Juan Pablo Garcia's eyes looked deep into my soul with the emotions of a dead man. I knew the stare all too well. He had raised me from age eight, so I knew his idiosyncrasies. And like in my childhood days, I knew better than to do anything other than remain quiet. But something else dwelled behind those black eyes. Fear. Not the tried and true fear that came with hunting these creatures down, but a new kind of fear.

I stood before him in the large cathedral, questioning my actions and knowing the answers would have grave consequences on a fragile ego. Words formed in the back of my throat, but I didn't have the nerve or ability to spit them from my lips.

Olivia hung above us, about a foot off of the ground, her hands bound to a rope that I had attached to one of the rafters. Her eyes dug holes into Father Garcia, while the rest of her remained practically lifeless. I felt hate dripping from her, not the fear I intended. I watched her chest for any signs of breathing and if she did, it remained too shallow to notice. And with breasts like hers, I'd have noticed.

I had brought her here to partner with the father on a good round of torture, and gather needed answers, but now I wished I could simply wave a wand and disappear. I hadn't come close to the welcome I had expected.

If I hadn't had doubts about my actions before, I made up for lost time now. The woulda, coulda, shoulda's collected with an avalanche of second thoughts. I had expected Olivia to be weakened by hanging in the House of God, but instead, she remained defiant and quiet. Not a true vein bat, but her placid demeanor took all the fun out of it for me. The power that rode on her seemed to grow more intense rather than recede. It pricked my skin like a thousand tiny knives. The torture intended for Olivia had turned on me.

I took a deep breath and started to speak. "Do not even open your mouth," the father snapped. He balled his hands into fists. His face turned a deeper shade of red. I knew he would never strike me, but I had had enough experience with him not to push it. Everyone, even men of God, had their limits. By the looks of him, I had gotten him out of a deep sleep. His thinning hair sprouted in several directions. Dressed in a worn brown t-shirt and jeans, it took a few minutes to remind myself of who he represented. But fashion had never been his strong point.

"How dare you bring such filth into the House of God." I looked back up to see his eyes had shifted from me to Olivia. Relief washed over me to find his stinging stare on someone other than me. It gave me a false state of solace, but I remained far too self-indulged to look at it any deeper than that.

In all our years as executioners, we had never brought one back to the sanctuary to question or kill. It had been an unwritten rule never to bring something so unholy into God's house. Why I thought this time should be different I rested on so many things. Other lives were at stake. Lives that I prayed were still in the balance and still alive. In the past, when we killed a monster like this, the lives in question were victims, as in already dead, so killing had been no more than restitution for their wicked ways.

But under it all slumbered something far more menacing that the possible deaths of fellow humans. I had come face to face with a fact that couldn't possibly be true. I hunted roaches. The thought of becoming one, never entered my mind. Though I had been categorized as a vein weasel in the most technical sense of the word, it didn't make my life any easier to understand. I was no more a master fang freak than anyone else, yet my life also hung in that balance for killing Asa. Like Olivia, I hadn't died at the mouth of one of the blood drinkers, but that didn't change the way they saw me. I had been painted into a corner, and I had become very bitter about it.

The sanctuary grew as bitter cold as The Coffin had been. I could see my breath as I exhaled. As I looked at Father Garcia,

I tried to justify my means. "There's a new fang head that's kidnapped Kansas' wife and Price's grandson. His name's Judas." Father Garcia's face never changed. "Ever heard of him?" Nothing. "I brought her here to try and save their lives." Nothing. "He wants to kill me." Nothing. "Damn it to hell, Father..." He grabbed me by my shirt and squeezed.

"Don't you ever say anything like that again in the House of God." Fingers unwound. I didn't move. His stare remained on my new friend. "Get her out of here, now." His voice not much more than a whisper, yet the words held more emotion than anything I had ever heard him say before.

I touched his shoulder and stopped him. "She's not a roach," I repeated.

"I don't care, you do not disgrace this sanctuary with such methods of any kind, no matter what she is." He looked back to Olivia again. He took a deep breath. "If she's not a vampire, what is she?"

"According to Angie, she's a blood host. She belongs to a tick named Judas, who thinks I'm the new master of Orlando and wants to kill me. He's been a busy boy the last couple of nights. And I don't even want to get into what Victor and Sasha have been up to."

"A blood host. How fitting." Father Garcia continued to stare at Olivia. "We shall be lucky if there is a single living soul here in the morning." His eyes moved to me. "This was a grave mistake, Paul. We know how to kill vampires, but this...this is something very different. She has abilities that the vampire does not have. I'm afraid you have opened a lot of lethal possibilities." I could tell by his voice, he wanted to say more, but not with Olivia present. "As a blood host, she can walk in the sunlight, wear a crucifix and be the eyes and ears of the vampire that owns her. I guarantee you, she's more powerful than you are giving her credit for." He gave me a strange look. "She's not that different than you."

Okay, that's the second time tonight I had been compared in that way and I had grown sick of it. In denial, I chose to ignore it. I needed to justify bringing this fang banger here and honestly, *I* didn't buying my excuses anymore. For me, killing Judas would make the other problem go away.

Temporarily anyway. I knew there would probably be others, but I would deal with that when the time came. One pitfall at a time. "She tells us what we want to know, then we kill her. I don't understand the problem. She has no power here." I started to move forward, but stopped.

"She doesn't need it. She's shielding under your power. A blood host is an extension of the vampire in control. You kill this thing and you still have a vampire to deal with. It kills you…well you know the rest." I watched as Olivia and Father Garcia played chicken with their eyes. Good and evil staring into the other's soul. A twisted blend of poetic and pathetic. "If you didn't have the virus running through you, this would be simple. But that is not the case."

I started to open my mouth when cold power brush by me. That sadistic laughter rolled through the air. *"Are you ready to meet the God you serve, Father?"* Judas said through a sugar-coated taunt. I waited for any sign of emotion to flow back into Olivia's face, but nothing changed. No more interaction than that of a plastic doll. Her eyes were rolled back in her head, allowing only the whites to show. She vibrated with power as she swung only feet off of the ground.

My eyes darted throughout the room for signs of Judas. Chills ran down my spine. Pushing the panic deep inside me, I stepped deeper into the room, Magnum ready to go. But shooting and killing something that wasn't there would prove to be a bit tricky. I had underestimated Judas and had done it at a very inconvenient time.

"Get this thing out of here, now!" Father Garcia's face started to show the cracks of humanity. I marked it up as nothing more than the cantankerous behavior of an old man set in his ways. But as I listened and watched the father, more questions surfaced and I didn't want to hear the answers.

Olivia's stoic stance lifted as she smiled and licked her lips. Dark, sinister white eyes bore down on me. *"Do not think that all my power is restricted from killing you now. You have severely underestimated me. You have done exactly as I had hoped you would do. Now, not only will I be able to kill you, but the priest as well."*

I had lost interest in torturing the truth out of Olivia. In the few minutes of watching Father Garcia's actions, and hearing his cryptic version of what a blood host entailed and could do, my intentions changed. I brought the Magnum up on her.

Father Garcia stopped me. "No, Paul. If you kill Judas' blood host, he will be able to ride off of your power, making him stronger and you weaker. Right now, all he can really do is threaten us, but if you kill her, it will release the power in her and it will attack your virus. You will not be powerful enough to defend against it."

"What do you mean, my power?" God, why did I ask that question?

Father Garcia never answered my question directly. "A powerful vampire can parasite off of its host and gain control of another vampire. Judas knew this. As with Asa, if you kill Olivia while Judas is here, that power has to go somewhere. He's hoping that he can possess you when you take her life. That's why you must get her out of here and as far away from her as possible. If he gains enough control of your virus, he can kill you from where he is."

Olivia's eyes followed me. Dead eyes, absent of all emotion. The human inside her had already died years ago. What I stared at now had become nothing more than evil in sheep's clothing and I had been too ignorant to see it.

Father Garcia's hand wrapped around my elbow. I moved before I knew it. "I will not ask you to leave again. You're covered in vampire power. Right now, any vampire can walk in here if they can ride on it." He let go of me and looked me from head to toe. I saw a terror in his eyes I had never seen before.

"I don't…"

"Now!" His voice echoed through the sanctuary and vibrated through the emptiness. I started to speak, but held my tongue. The man before me no longer saw me as a son or even a fellow cockroach slayer. He saw me as dangerous as Olivia and about as human.

It took everything I had not to dump every profane word I knew on him. When Quinn and Judas called me a master coffin head, it didn't matter to me. I had considered the source. But when Father Garcia saw it in me, I grew hollow. I struggled to stand. Stupidity and betrayal left me numb with denial. "Grow a spine and say it, Father. You don't see me as a man anymore do you? You see nothing but the virus. Well damn you all to hell along with your hollow little world, hiding behind crosses and Bible verses while Kansas' wife and Price's grandson die at the hands of blood suckers." I said it with as much malicious intent as I could. I wanted the words to be covered in barbed wire.

Olivia watched with curiosity. *"You can feel it can't you, Avenger? The power wrapping around you like a warm blanket. Winds of change is coming. Even the father cannot save your soul now. He has betrayed you just like your parents. Kill him for his lies and deception."* She licked her lips in permissive strokes. She turned her wrath on Father Garcia. *"Tell him of his mother and her kind. The truth shall set both of you free in your days before death."*

I pushed the Magnum against her throat. A hollow threat at best, but I had nothing else. "Listen up and listen up good. I'm not a cockroach, much less a master cockroach. As for my mother and father, keep them out of this. You know nothing about them. Nothing more than lies made up by cockroaches and the humans that kiss their asses." Truth be told, I tried to shut the truth out. I refused to allow Judas to convince me of lies. If there were any more dirty little secrets about my mother and father, I no longer cared to hear about them. Inside, I begged her to stop.

"If you truly believe that you are not a master vampire, then kill Olivia. If you are in fact nothing more than a pathetic human, I will have no power over you. Do it. Kill Olivia, Avenger. Prove your worth to the Father and yourself."

I looked back to Father Garcia and saw the truth in his face. Anger consumed me. Denial raced through my mind. "You *do* think I'm a cockroach."

He had grown cold and distant much like I had seen him be with other stake magnets back in the day. Pitiless eyes looked back at me.

"Why don't you kill me? If I *am* a roach, that's the law." I pulled a wooden stake from my jacket pocket and handed it to him. "If you really believe it, do it. Do it now!"

He shook his head and looked back into my eyes. Tears streamed down his cheeks. He yelled at me in a controlled whisper. "I know better in my heart. But you carry the virus and you have killed a master vampire. In vampire culture, these articles of facts condemn you to what Judas says you are. I don't agree with those conclusions, but it doesn't change how they see you or what can happen. They can ride on your power do things they shouldn't be able to do. I cannot take the chance of having you here ever again." Father Garcia yanked the stake from my hand and pointed it at my chest. I closed my eyes in anticipation of the sharp pain still to come. I heard the crash of wood hit somewhere in the distant pews. I opened my eyes to see the Father still standing there, minus the stake. "Do not ask such things of me. Just know that you cannot come here again. Not that I do not love you, but because of the danger you put us all in. I have tried to deny it for far too long and kept secrets far too close. I will never be able to kill you, Paul. I have neither the strength nor the heart."

He blessed me.

I shoved him away. "You don't bless blood suckers, Father. Hate me, fear me, and disown me if you want, but for God's sake don't be condescending." I wiped my eyes free of tears. "If you were half the man I thought you were, you would have killed me."

"God may forgive me for killing you, but I never would." He looked up at Olivia with worry, then simply walked away.

CHAPTER TEN

Candles flickered in the distance as I stared up at Olivia and licked my mental wounds. I pulled the silver bladed knife from its sheath and cut the rope above the knot that bound her hands. She had been nothing short of a beacon to all the other blood lovers in the city as to my whereabouts, and it would only be a matter of time before they learned they could use Olivia to enter the church. I had to get her out of here as fast as I possibly could.

Olivia seemed to be content in staying still as I cut her free, but I dug the tip of the blade under her skin for good measure. She knew our being here made those she served stronger, not weaker. Even the silver seemed to struggle with the power. I had a real bad feeling I controlled her only because she allowed it.

The evil magic in the cathedral grew into an invisible fog. It engulfed everything that breathed. My chest grow heavy. An invisible force pushed against it. Muscles protested movement as though rigor mortis had set in. Power rode through me and from me at the same time. Some of it mine. Some of it from sources still unknown to me.

I pushed Olivia toward the large doors that seemed to still be a mile away. Her demeanor made me very nervous. She remained calm. The hand with the knife begged to go deeper but I resisted.

The church grew so cold that I could see my breath. Clouds of desperation reminded me of my no win situation. Chills ran down my arms. Lights flickered against the walls. The large crucifixion of Christ at the front of the church bled from its palms and feet around the nails. Fire ignited against the skin, turning it black. I picked up my pace.

As I reached the large cherry wood doors at the entrance of the cathedral, Olivia broke free and turned on me. My knife twirled in the lights and landed out of reach. Nails dug deep into my chest as I flew over several pews. My spine landed against a backrest, resulting in breath-taking pain. My legs tingled with pain. My head lay against frozen darkness along the once plush carpet. Blood escaped from torn skin. Warm liquid oozed from wounds on my elbows. In her eyes, I could see Judas' reflection. He looked back into my own fear and laughed. He hadn't come here to rescue Olivia, but to imprison me.

I lay there for a few seconds and tried to ease the throbbing in my muscles and bones. I regained my breath in small gasps. Bites of pain would not allow me to take in a full amount. Above me, I could hear the rafters creak with pressure as the evil filled the room. The rope where Olivia hung, swung softly in the under current.

I lifted myself upright and began to crawl across the overturned pew. I reacted to both the jolts of pain and the coldness. Part of me wanted to run. Part of me knew I couldn't. All of me wished I hadn't come here.

My eyes searched in all directions for the blood sucking power source that dwelled here as Olivia bore down on me. Eyes rolled back in her head. A stroke of darkness outlined her shape. I tried to flank the monster. I lost ground in the move. While I hurdled over broken pieces of pews, she simply floated across the sanctuary with ease. My fingers were so cold they threatened to break off from my hands. I could feel the evil, see it, touch it. All too real. Far too real. And knowing that I couldn't kill her to save myself, made things seem impossible. According to Father Garcia, it would be suicide.

With all the human strength and speed I could muster, I moved in on her, ripped and tore at her dead skin. Muscle peeled away in my hands and slid through my fingers. Things slithered along my arms. Warm liquids bathed my cold flesh. I closed my eyes and released my grip. With every ounce of human thought I still had, I pushed those memories to the back of my mind. Locked them away and threw away the key.

Olivia pounced on me. I swear I saw fangs jut from

those extended jaws. I clutched the side of her cheek and pulled. Flesh broke off in my hand and turned to powder. Bone and dead muscle peeked through as maggots rained down on me.

There was no blood. Instead, rotten meat fell to the floor, followed by thousands of real cockroaches and earthworms. Deadness filled my nostrils. I shook with fear, but blamed it on the Arctic tundra of the evil in the church. Temperatures so low that icicles formed in my goatee. Stench suffocated me. I grew light headed and disoriented, a lump of vomit grew in the back of my throat.

She jumped free of my swings. Dust filled my eyes. More specifically, dead ashes gathered against my flesh. I spat and blinked in synchronicity. I jumped to my feet, knowing she wouldn't be far nor would she run away. My ability to come back to my feet would determine if I lived or if I died.

Olivia laughed I turned to find her. I knew things were about to get worse as I saw Father Garcia in her grasp, his neck stretched tight. His airway evaporated fast, mouth opened and closed as life escaped his lungs.

I could feel a force hit me and roll me along the floor. I had suddenly become nothing more than tumbleweed. The momentum impossible to slow, much less stop. I grew dizzy as invisible nails scratched deep trenches into my flesh. Ghost-like images swirled around me, glowing in a hellish image of Judas.

I came to rest at the feet of the life-sized crucifixion of Christ that hung on the wall. It still dripped blood. Only now it dripped on me. Real blood. Not some trick of vein sucking magic and illusions. Real. Warm. Blood. I spat as it ran into my mouth and wiped it from my eyes. I coughed it from my lungs. I savored the metallic taste. I licked my lips in non-voluntary laps. Tasting it as sweet nectar and horrified at what I had done. Repulsed by my actions, I couldn't stop it. The virus in me wouldn't allow it.

Along the walls of the sanctuary, I could see hundreds of faces of lost souls form. Each screamed in tormented agony. Flesh pulled free from bone in eternal decay. Maggots writhed across the floor giving them a life of their own. Faces I knew. Eyes gazed back to me with the same screaming pain I saw in their eyes when I staked them. Each reached out to me. Not for help, but to gather me in.

Stained glass from the over-sized windows shattered and rained shards on me in a rainbow of death. I threw my hand up to shield my eyes, as small pieces found their way between my shirt and skin. Small cuts widened as I moved.

I looked up to see the cringed face of Father Garcia, still in the hands of Olivia. She hovered silently in the air, watching me, daring me. My Magnum firmly in hand, but reality told me that I could fill Olivia with bullets and it wouldn't help anything. Judas had me at his mercy and I cursed under my breath. My guilt crushed me.

My lungs burned with the cold air as I stood. Maggots and other creepy crawlies fell from my skin as I attempted to move forward. *"Give me what is mine, or the priest will die. Slowly,"* Judas' voice slithered out of Olivia. *"Give to me your freewill and bloodline, and all shall be forgiven. For it is you that is the envy of all night stalkers. The one that can walk in sunlight, into a sanctuary, out of a grave. I covet your bloodline and all that is promised to it."*

"Do you really believe your own bullshit, Judas?" I said to thin air. In some twisted way, he had become my new demonic imaginary friend. Note to self: Imaginary friends suck dead ass.

Like Quinn, Asa and Maximilian before him, Judas believed in all the hype that spewed from his mouth. Fang heads lived in their own little world of fantasy and narcissism. Perhaps the better word here would be delusion. For now, I'd let it go. My mind filled with infinite possibilities. I couldn't handle anymore at this time.

I looked back at Father Garcia again. I had to get to him. "Run," he gasped as I started toward him. But I couldn't.

Leaving would have proven once and for all that I had been no better than the leech that held him even if it saved his life. I didn't know if I could admit who or what I had become, but to leave the father in the hands of vein heads and do nothing would have been unforgivable. If I left, it might pull all of the power out of the church. Olivia and Judas would no longer be able to stay inside. I knew it would prove to be a gutsy move, but all I had.

"Come to me, master vampire and surrender all that is

yours. For now you see that even your God cannot save you."

I heard the bones crack. Olivia began to twist Father Garcia's spine. Her hand pierced his chest and pulled out a still beating heart. Sharp screams filled my ears. She took a bite of the heart ripping away muscle with animalistic power. Blood squirt in all directions, dotting her face with small crimson spots. I shot the Magnum until every bullet emptied, and still the screams remained.

Horror hit me I smelled the sulfur. Ash floated through the air and flurried to the floor. A coldness still lingered around me. My eyes landed on the large crucifix which moments ago had been a bleeding Christ. Large nails pierced Father Garcia's hands and feet. A crown of thorns wrapped around his head. Bathed in blood, Father Garcia's body hung in tattered chunks.

I shook and shivered. Fear washed over me. Not of vein maggots, not of death, but of what I knew hid under this skin. Denying it any longer would only lead to more death and destruction to those I loved and vowed to protect. I had become everything I hated.

I pulled the cell phone from its leather holder on my belt to call Price. I noticed the dripping blood from my hands. Thick. Slimy. Dark. Warm. Fresh. I denied my first thoughts. No God, no. It couldn't be that.

I brought a hand to my tongue and tasted it. Fresh blood that still moved with life. I could smell Father Garcia's scent. With methodical care I turned my hands palm up and stared at the blood that dripped in between my fingers. They left no doubt as to what had happened and who did it. I had killed, not for the blood but because I could no longer control the urges. I couldn't deny the truth any longer. I had become a predator. A fucking cockroach.

I shouted for Father Garcia as I moved through the large sanctuary. I needed some indication that everything I saw had been nothing more than vampire trickery. My heart pounded in my ears. Shivers returned, but this time from a different source. Call it a gut feeling. A gut feeling that would remain unthinkable.

"What have you done, Avenger?" Judas' cold voice returned. Humor laced around the words. He laughed. Deep and loud. *"Do not blame this on me. For it was you that has left the*

priest in peril. I do not have to tell you that it is the priest's blood that drips from your hands."

I stopped and looked at my hands yet again. Shook my head with disbelief. Olivia had vanished. With Father Garcia's dead body hanging from the cross, I had nothing to protect here anymore. I ran from the church. Not out of revenge, but out of denial.

My knees buckled in the front lawn. I grabbed fistfuls of grass as I wept. Mixed the blood with the fallen dew. I cursed God and myself. Anger filled me. Aches of coldness threatened to explode me from inside out.

I reached for the phone and called Price. "Price, it's me. I killed Father Garcia." Cockroach or not, I had a conscience. That sucked more than anything.

I put the Magnum up to my temple. I would take the easy way out. Far better than allowing Judas to kill me or having a stake driven through my heart. I would end it on my own terms. Better yet, I was too big a coward to face my reality.

CHAPTER ELEVEN

I don't remember how long it took for Price to get there. His shadow engulfed me. With any luck, I could hide in the man-made darkness and simply disappear, but something told me it wouldn't last. How long I had been sitting on the ground, I had no idea, but long enough that the dew had soaked through my jeans. I shivered with cold, even though the air around me had been warm and thick.

I tried to stand, but Price simply motioned for me to remain sitting. A gentle smile broke through on his tired face. He meant it to be genuine, but I could see through to the pain that lay under the surface. In an agonizing free fall with loss of his own, Price tried to comfort me. I appreciated the attempt, but nothing could be done about the heinous thing I knew I had done. Now that I had time to think about it, I wished I hadn't called him. He had enough twisted things going on right now to be dealing with mine. I returned his badly sold genuine smile.

My stare hit the wet ground. I couldn't face him. Whether by Judas' power or my subconscious evil, the result stayed the same. Father Garcia had been killed and his blood stained my hands. Instead of doing what Father Garcia had asked, I stood there and argued my side of the story. And why? To be right? To justify my actions. I looked back on it all and saw how trivial and self-serving I had been.

"Paul," Price started. His voice soft and timid. "I got here as fast as I could." He had left the rest up to me to fill in. I couldn't blame him for avoiding the real questions. Even more afraid to know the answers.

"He's in there."

"What happened?"

I stood, in spite of the second protest of the detective and brushed away the grass and dirt from the back of my jeans. It looked like I had pissed my pants. And with what I had experienced, I wouldn't have been surprised if hadn't. "I don't know."

Price turned his head like a dog that had heard a strange noise, not sure how to respond.

"I could tell you Frank, but you wouldn't believe me."

"Try me."

I took a deep breath and swallowed. With every ounce of strength I had, I turned and faced Price. "I'm a fucking cockroach, Frank. I ripped out Father Garcia's throat and lapped up his blood. I'm sure of it. Best thing for you to do is stake me here and now. If I can kill him, I can kill anybody."

Price let out a nervous laugh, pushed his glasses back up his nose with his index finger and shook his head. "What are you talking about? You ain't no more a vampire than I am." He had slowly taken a step backwards which proved to me that actions were louder than words. I couldn't blame him. Not exactly the response you heard every day. And after what I had reported, trust had found itself in the crosshairs of our friendship.

"The vampire poison in my veins is growing, Frank. Judas used it tonight to enter the church. One minute I was trying to free Father Garcia from Judas' blood host, the next he was dead and blood covered my hands."

"Judas? Blood host?" He gave me a half grin. "Let's start at the beginning."

I did and it didn't make any more sense the second time around. To him or to me. I knew to be sensitive enough to leave out the part about Judas having his grandson and the possibility that his grandson could be dead. Telling him would only make things worse.

Price waved me off and shook his head in denial. "I don't believe it, Paul. You know as well as I do that you'd never do anything to hurt the priest, even if you were a full blown cockroach." His eyes grew with horror. "Christ, Paul, I'm sorry, I didn't mean to imply…"

I stopped him with a raise of my hand. "No offense taken. I yam what I yam," I said in my best Popeye impression.

Again, he shook his head. "I don't believe it. Even if it is true, Paul…" His words trailed to nothing. He began to pace and made a conscious effort to not look at me. "Even if he's dead, this Judas thing did it, not you. To hell with blaming it on a damned virus. You wouldn't have done something like that on your own." He took a deep breath. "I don't believe it." I don't think either of us bought it.

I pointed to the church. "Neither did I until tonight, but Judas found a way to get inside the church through Olivia's tie to him. My power conducted the energy somehow. Now Father Garcia is dead because of that ignorance. Even if my hands didn't do it, my power and stupidity allowed it to happen."

"It doesn't make sense to me, Paul." He placed his hands on his hips and turned in circles, deep in thought. He pointed his finger, eyes well focused. "You're a good man. Without you, I know there would be no way of getting Josh back alive. I would never have come to you for help if I didn't believe that." He pinched his fingers against the sides of his nose in an attempt to keep from crying. He shook it off with a bad attempt at a laugh. "Show me the body."

Now I let out a nervous laugh. "It won't be hard to find. It's hanging on the cross just like Christ. Apparently I crucified him afterwards."

I could see the wheels turn in his mind. He grimaced. "You crucified him?"

In frustration, I pulled out my Magnum and handed it to him. "I don't know anything more than what I've already told you. Take this and pull the trigger right here. I would have done it myself, but I didn't have the guts. Apparently, I can destroy every life but my own."

Price waved the Magnum off as he moved past me and toward the church. "Let's not get the cart before the horse yet. You've said yourself that vampire magic is pretty convincing. That you will see things the way they want you to see them."

I had said that. Wanted to believe it. But damned if I could. I looked at the dried blood on my hands and showed them to the detective. "Does this look like magic to you? This is blood, Frank. Father Garcia's blood." But as the words dripped from my lips, I noticed my hands were nothing more than skin and bone.

No blood to be found. I tried to speak, but it grew impossible.

Price looked at my hands as we walked and shook his head. "See, I ain't gonna have to shoot you, Paul." He gave another nervous laugh and patted me hard on the back. "You've put your life on the line for me and mine far too many times for that."

I looked at my hands again. "Impossible," I thought aloud. But in the back of my mind, hope grew. "Maybe it was all an illusion." They had a certain way with magic. To the living, their dead and decaying bodies looked beautiful and sexy because of it, get trapped in their gaze and you become hypnotized by it, so there's a million to one shot that I had been duped by Judas' magic. I looked back to the church. Better to get it over with sooner rather than later.

It seemed to be a mile to the front door of the church, but in all the steps, I never took my eyes from it. Unlike the detective, I knew the nightmare that possibly waited on the other side. Price severely under estimated the death that waited for him. I shook with apprehension of what we would find.

I could feel my knees start to rattle again. It made each step more and more lethargic. A bad dream coming true. You know the one I'm talking about. The one where you try to run but you can't. Even as the sunlight started to shatter the darkness, I could still feel Judas' presence.

Price stopped at the closed door and took in a deep breath. He turned to me with a wily smile. He waited for me to talk him out of pushing the giant door open. Another few seconds and I would have.

For the second time I handed him the Magnum. "Frank take this. You may need it."

He looked up at the starry sky, wheels turned in that mind as he put all the pieces together as only a well-trained detective would. "You ain't no vampire. I've seen your pasty white skin in the sunlight." He smiled at me. "You're a pain in the ass recluse, but that doesn't make you no vampire. If you were, you'd only have about fifteen minutes before you start smoking."

"I've been able to walk in the sunlight before, Frank, but things are starting to make me doubt who or what I am. My reality started to unravel. Vampires aren't supposed to be able to go inside a church, but one had entered here tonight." I shook the thoughts from my head as I pushed the door open with all the strength I had.

Frank's attention followed the door as it swung open. He stared inside for a few seconds, then turned to me as the door slowly returned in our direction. I could tell by his body language he hadn't seen the same things I had.

I pushed him aside and looked inside the sanctuary. For now, I had no intentions of stepping foot in there again. Not because of what I had done, but because it could drag more creepie crawlies out of their hiding places again. I could see the length of the church and questioned my sanity. "This is impossible." Thoughts volleyed back and forth as to whether I should be jubilant or shitting my pants.

The church appeared as pristine as it had been when I grew up here. Not a single thing had been molested. All the pews were perfectly aligned, all the stained glass windows were in place along the walls. No signs of a struggle. No smell of fire. No blood. No body.

I looked toward the front of the church and nearly passed out. The large life-size Christ that filled the wall hung unmolested. Father Garcia's body had vanished.

"Impossible," I continued to repeat to myself as I moved inside the church for a better look at things. Not in my best judgment, but better judgment didn't seem to be my strong point anymore.

Price followed me. "What? What is it, Paul?"

Out of the corner of my eyes, I could see him look at me, but my stare remained on the crucifix. "He was hanging right there." I pointed to Christ, turned and looked throughout the sanctuary again. "This whole place was torn to shreds. I don't understand it."

Price gave out a small chuckle. "That's what I've been saying to you, Paul. It was all a dream or something. You've been burning the candle at both ends lately and part of that is because of me. That woman you brought in here probably put some sort of vampire spell on you. You couldn't see past her boobs to make a clear decision." He slapped me on the back and pinched my shoulder. "Looks like I won't have to kill you after all."

Unlike Frank Price, I hadn't been totally convinced. It seemed so real. I could still taste the blood. Feel the bruises. I touched the stained glass window closest to me and refused to believe what my fingers were feeling. Smooth glass, unbroken. My hands ran along the pew in front of me. I remember my back coming down on it. The vampire magic that had overpowered me, no longer existed. The nothingness had become my sanctuary. "I can't believe it was magic."

"Come on, let's get out of here. If Father Garcia catches us in here, it'll be us that's hung on that cross." He pushed his glasses up his nose again and let out a large huff of air. "Any word on Josh, Paul?"

I bit my tongue and refused to answer. "Something's not right, Frank." I shook my head. Doubt cluttered my mind as I watched the detective move away from me toward the large door. He didn't want to find evidence that I might be right. I let him go. I inherited this nightmare. He had his own to deal with. I felt silly even calling him. "Go on home, Frank. Sorry I brought you down here. As for Josh, I will do whatever it takes to bring him home to you."

"You sure you're gonna be alright? Maybe I should drive you home." Price did his best to avoid the conversation. I think we were both afraid to ask the real questions, much less answer them.

I shook my head and tried to smile. "I'll be fine. Like you said, I just need some sleep and get my head straight."

He started to walk out the door, then turned. "Paul?"

"Yeah?"

"Thanks for helping me with Josh. It's going to be alright. God won't let anything happen to him."

I watched as he left the church. At least someone still had faith in me. The dark doubt in me, though, never gave in to what I saw. I needed another pass on things to convince myself of what really happened. In retrospect, I wanted him gone. Judas had ridden my power once tonight, and nothing guaranteed he couldn't return. Even if Father Garcia was right, and Judas could do nothing more than threaten us, I didn't want to take the chance with Price in the room. No need to keep taking chances with lives I couldn't protect.

If it all had been a roach magic show I knew what I had to do. Nothing else would give me peace of mind. I had to see Father Garcia face to face. His old scowl would be the most welcomed sight in the world right now.

I picked up my pace as I moved through the church toward the front door. He lived in a small apartment to the left of the sanctuary. I prayed to God, Father Garcia would open that door and prove to me once and for all, I had lost touch with reality.

But when I opened the front door to the church, my inertia came to a stop by something with the consistency of a brick wall. I hit about chest high, long dark hair meeting me in the face. I bounced back and nearly fell on my back end. My heart rattled against my chest. I convinced myself that Judas had returned to finish what he had started. But instead, another object of my continuing macabre soap opera stood before me. "Kasey, what the hell are you doing here?"

Kasey's face remained stone-like. "I need to talk to you."

"I'm a little busy right now. Whatever it is, it will have to wait."

"It won't wait. Now."

He remained in front of me and something told me not to try to push him or my luck. He was built like a rock, wide as a bus and not known as someone that had a lot of patience. To be honest, he came off as more than a bit nerdy. If he had been five foot eight and a hundred and fifty pounds, he would have had his lunch money taken from him every day. But that hadn't been the case. Cartoon big described him the best.

At first glance, he reminded me of one of those male models on the cover of a romantic novel. Chiseled chest, muscles upon muscles, tan skin. Most women melted at his feet. All but the one he wanted most, that is.

We had a history. He was the alpha male of the local werewolves and to this day, I still doubted he wouldn't break me in half at any moment. His crush on Angie made us rivals in his mind. Telling him that I didn't want her as my little woman didn't change the dynamics of our friendship, so I didn't bother with any conviction.

I looked past him and guessed he had come here alone. Dressed in a white t-shirt and faded jean, he had on far more clothes than the first time we had met. Thank you, God.

I pulled out my silver bladed knife. "Move or I'll carve little wolf cookies out of you."

"It's about Angie." Kasey said about as matter-of-fact as it could. "We'll take your car so we talk."

Regardless of what I might say out loud or even admit to myself, hearing her name send tingles and chill throughout me. Instead of being pounded to the ground, I simply gripped the knife a little tighter. "What is it?"

"What it is, Avenger, is a matter of life or death."

CHAPTER TWELVE

I looked at myself in the rear view mirror as I sped along Highway 50, trying to make as much distance between the nightmares of the church, Father Garcia and myself as I could. Eyes stared back as death and vengeance piled on top of me. The reflection showed the same, but what it represented had taken on a whole new meaning that I neither believed nor could ever come to terms with.

My hands gripped the steering wheel tight. I feared it would break off in my hands. No matter how hard I tried to suppress the images of the events in the last twenty four hours, they seemed to return. They dominated my thoughts stronger with each visit. I didn't have time for this, and my mood grew darker by the minute.

"Want to tell me what this is all about, Kasey?" I kept my eyes on the road ahead. I needed a distraction of any kind. The fur ball next to me would have to suffice. The moon gave everything around it a mysterious glow as it reflected in the trees along the road.

"I want you to stop leading Angie on." He looked straight ahead. The werewolf beside me wasn't only as big as a brick wall, he had the emotions of one as well.

I had to let out the quick surprise of a laugh. "Leading her on? What the hell are you talking about?"

"She thinks she has a chance of winning your heart and it's killing her."

Okay, now I looked at him. He still refused to meet my stare and remained stoic. "I don't know what she's told you, but we aren't an item in any way. Tell her to keep her sweet ass out of my life. I don't care. I don't date monsters."

With robotic motion, he turned. "That's the problem."

"So you want me to date her?"

His frustration made me crack a smile. I tried to pick a fight. Unfortunately for Kasey, the night had been a little too eventful for me to play twenty questions. Finding Judas and Olivia left me more than a little distracted. I still couldn't get those images of Father Garcia crucified to the cross out of my mind. Helping Kasey or Angie, for that matter, wasted valuable time that I couldn't afford.

I slammed on the brakes and stopped in the middle of the road. A trio of horns, tires and headlights filled the air in an opera of sights and sounds as the cars behind us swerved. "Tell me what you're talking about. I'm a little bit wired right now and you're bugging the living shit out of me. Grow balls and get it off of your chest, Kasey. This is about you, not Angie." Some loser drove around me in a white BMW, showed me the middle finger. Goodie for him.

Kasey gave a slight nod, then looked forward again. "The pack is concerned with your involvement with Angie. More importantly, I am concerned with your involvement. Your presence is going to drive her to things that we would find unacceptable. If she doesn't change on her own, it will make things far more complicated than either of us can imagine. You must make it clear to her that you have no intentions to accept her heart. While you see all this as nothing more than a game, to Angie, it is very real."

"My presence? I've made it clear to her that being boyfriend/girlfriend isn't in the cards. I have bigger things going on right now than grabbing Angie's ass. Now if you don't mind, I'm going to turn around and get to things that are a bit more in the world of reality."

He motioned for me to drive on. I did. "Have you noticed anything different about her lately?"

"Her tits do seem a little bigger."

You know the old saying, "If looks could kill", well that's the look I got. I thought about it as I shifted. I knew if I wanted this to end anytime soon I would have to play by his rules. I thought about throwing him out, but knew the act would only get the hell beat out of me. "She passed out the last time I saw her. Are you telling me it has something to do with me?"

He nodded. "It's killing her." His glowing eyes looked through me. "If a werewolf does not make the change at least once a month, we can lose strength, go mad and eventually, we die. That is, if we're lucky. What you saw with Angie was the effects of not changing. It will get worse. Most fall victim to vampires who can gain power over us, much like the blood host you saw tonight."

"So you know about Olivia?"

He shook his head. "Angie told me about Olivia and Judas as well as your situation. That's how I knew where to find you. Vampire stench isn't all that hard to track." He gave me a quick look. "You being dead might be the silver lining we're all looking for."

He baited an argument. I chose to avoid it. His opinion didn't matter to me one way or the other. "What does this have to do with me?"

"Like I said, Angie thinks she can win your love and admiration if she can suppress the change. I think it is preposterous, if not right down pathetic. I have told her that you are incapable of loving anything." He shrugged. "Her will is stronger than her intelligence." He looked out the side window for a second or two, then returned the animal-like stare. "She is weak and time is running out. I'm afraid that if Judas finds out that she's this weak, he will kill her. You have to tell her this morning that you don't love her and convince her of it." He remained as emotional as a corpse. All fur and no play had made Kasey a very dull boy.

"How am I supposed to save her life by telling her things I've told her for the entire time I've known her? Subtle hints and being blunt seem to have the same effect on her. It's not easy being this sexy."

"You must break her heart quickly instead of giving her hope. Even if that hope is just in her head." He cleared his throat. "She is at the Silver Priapus. Turn your back on her now, and I'll give the loyalty of the pack to Judas. With you dead, Angie will change and grow strong and I can help her to see what real love is all about. In the scheme of things, you are less of a threat to this city than Judas, but I will still do what is best for Angie. She may not mean anything to you, but I'm willing to risk everything on her life."

"Have wet dreams about her, do you, Kasey?"

His large hand gripped my throat so tight and so quick, I nearly lost control of the car. We swerved into the path of oncoming cars as I tried to slow the 'Cuda to a stop for the second time. "Don't tread lightly on this. I know what you are and believe me, there are those in the pack that see you as more than a vampire killer. You carry the virus of the lycan, making you a threat to the pack. Virgil had refused pack demands, and you know very well how that turned out."

I *had* seen what he had done to Virgil. I tried to nod the best I could, while his vise-like grip remained tight around my throat. I had learned tonight that if I wanted to stay alive long enough to save the lives that were in cockroach hands, I'd need all the allies I could get. I needed enemies with benefits. Cooperation went a lot farther than resistance.

"You will turn her or we will eat you alive in front of her. Either way, Angie loses you tonight. Forever." He took in a deep breath as he released me. Kasey tried to suppress his anger by looking out the window again. He gathered his thoughts before speaking again. To my advantage, he wore his emotions on his sleeve. "Then there is the other threat that seems to be growing with rumors. One that I know to be irrational, but there are others that don't feel as I do." Now came an uncomfortable glare. "Things that threaten my position in the pack and that's the fact that you also have our virus in you. As with the vampires, you could be an alpha to our pack. There are those among us that want you dead in order to make sure that doesn't happen. They've seen what has happened in the vampire community because of you and we don't want it to happen to us. For now, I am able to keep it as nothing more than talk, but those loyal to me and my status might allow those rumors to grow into more than a war of words. That's why we have to address this thing with Angie with kid gloves."

I had to laugh. "You think I want to be the leader of your pack?" I saw it as a joke, but I could already see on Kasey's face, he didn't. The pack hadn't come up with the irrational thoughts. Kasey had. "You think I want your job to get Angie don't you?

God, the boredom of humanity never sounded so good."

"Joke all you want, Paul. I'm telling you what you are up against. Even if you do, this favor with Angie, there will be those that see it as an aggression against the pack. Like with the vampires, you are in a no win situation with the wolves as well." He looked at me again. "That is why I wanted to talk to you alone. The pack thinks your association with Angie could bring about changes they will not accept."

"Meaning the pack thinks I will try to get to the alpha spot through Angie's crotch."

He nodded. "More than that. You see, you represent something that none of us knows how to deal with. You are part vampire and part wolf. That makes you hated by my pack in two ways, not one." He gave me a wide smile. I wanted to knock that smug grin off of his face so bad.

"So what happens if my telling Angie doesn't do the trick? Then what?"

"Turn her."

I gasped for air. "How the hell do you want me to do that?"

"We don't have time for your petty denial, master vampire. You know exactly what I am asking you to do. I can feel the power on you. Even if it is against her will, the turn will save her life. The virus in you is strong enough to make her change." He leaned close to my ear. "That's why I'm telling you that by doing what might be necessary could still get you killed if I can't convince the pack that you are not trying to change her for the wrong reasons. Like I said, my wolves see you as both vampire and wolf. If you don't change her, they see you as a threat to her and the alpha male position of the pack. If you do change her, they will see it as vampire aggression. Either way, there will be those around me that will call for your death."

"Damn monster politics!" I searched for things to say that would convince not only Kasey, but myself, that I hadn't become a daisy pusher, but every excuse seemed to make me guiltier. So I did the thing all unintelligent people do. I used profanity. "I'm not a fucking vein weasel, you furry prick!"

Kasey simply stared back, unimpressed. "Angie's place is by my side. I will not allow you to turn your back on her simply because you don't have the intelligence to come to terms with it. You do not mean enough to me to beg you for your cooperation. I'm not asking for a favor. I'm demanding it. Turn her and I will keep the pack away from your throat."

I smiled at him as I digested his words. "Well, it's about time you showed some sort of balls. But as for Angie, I will never allow you to turn her into your trophy bitch. She's better off dead than that."

"We will have to come to terms on that issue in the future. Most believe you will be dead soon anyway. I happen to be one of them, which is why we have to do it now. " With that, the giant wolf man smiled.

CHAPTER THIRTEEN

The Silver Priapus sat on the far side of Orlando in the middle of nowhere. Unlike the blood drinkers, the fur balls enjoyed their privacy, more or less. But their love for lust put this place at the pinnacle of sexual imagination mixed with reality.

The club had a reputation of being one of the best strip joints in any of the monster districts, filled with some of the most beautiful women in the world, but also some of the roughest customers. It had become one of the hubs for wolf activity and the management didn't take lightly to those customers that had fangs or were of the common humanity type. Trust didn't come easily here. If you didn't grow furry, you might have to fight your way out at the end of the night. And something told me that tonight might not be all that different.

The Priapus shined in chrome and pink neon, but with the house lights up, they lost their charm and welcoming spirit. It now looked industrial and cold. Heavy smoke hung overhead in spite of the tobacco laws. A mammoth bar with countless bottles of booze squatted in the corner, decorated with thousands of lights and an etched mirror of a naked woman and werewolf being more than a little intimate. A bartender filled drinks for the 'managers' sitting at the bar. Waterfalls of wine trickled into shallow pools and large marble statues of Greek Gods sat on pedestals throughout the club. But if you looked closely, you could see that the statues were in fact nude live female models. Beautiful. Dangerous.

Every eye seemed to watch me as I walked further inside. I counted fourteen male and six female. All the females were still nude and watched by the males. Wolf property. My guess, the men hanging around were probably the boyfriend/managers. It didn't really matter. I didn't have enough bullets and blades to kill them all.

I smiled back at a black haired baby doll in a schoolgirl uniform as she sucked on a red lollipop. She gave me a teasing wave as she continued to stare at me from between her legs. Her ass stuck up in the air, exposing the lack of undergarments. Again, I reminded myself I had been brought here on business, not pleasure. And if I have said it once, I have said it a million times, just because it's beautiful and nude, didn't mean it wouldn't chew your throat out.

As we entered the main room, pounding bass bounced against my chest. All eyes watched a stripper on the stage leave nothing to the imagination. She had a large snake of some kind wrapped around her as she spun on a pole. Years ago all of this would have been shocking, but not anymore.

"Over there," Kasey pointed to a table where several other male shifters were seated. He motioned to a woman server and pointed to the table. She nodded and a drink magically appeared at the table practically before we did.

"This is all a little too familiar," I said to myself, remembering the time I had met Kasey and Angie at the Lunatic Moon. I recalled how that night went down, and it hadn't been pleasant for yours truly.

I took a seat next to a pack member that appeared to be in his late twenties. He had a tattoo up the right arm of a green parrot. Several piercings in his face gave him the look of a magnet gone awry. He looked me up and down, hunger in his eyes. At any moment, I expected him to be at my throat. "Well, look what the cat dragged in," he finally said as he took a gulp of the beer in front of him. "Question is, Avenger, do we kill you for being a vampire or for being a shifter." He swallowed more of the beer. "Guess it don't matter as long as you're dead." I heard laughter echo from around the room. Not a good sign.

I smiled as I lit and puffed on a cigar, still staring at all the piercings. "I'm curious, when the full moon comes out, do you turn into a werewolf or a pin cushion?"

He started to lunge toward me.

"Sit down," Kasey commanded Pin Cushion. "I have told you my reasoning for bringing him here and that has not changed." Now, he turned to me. "And you keep your trap shut."

Pin Cushion spoke anyway. "And I told you my reasons for *not* bringing him here. He's a threat to us all, having vampire and shifter virus in him. You see what's happening with him and the vampires already. We don't need that here too."

Kasey leaned across the table to the man. "He'd have to kill me first, and I'm not going to let that happen. As we discussed, this is pack business and my decision. If he doesn't change Angie, we are all a threat to Judas and his vampires."

"Then he changes her, then we kill him." As Pin Cushion smiled I saw the crooked yellow teeth behind those lips. "But under no circumstances does he get out alive." I had no doubt. I would have to fight my way out. "Just because he does us a favor, doesn't mean he's not a threat to us." He stared deeper into Kasey's eyes, "Especially you." His eyes turned back to me.

We sized each other up with long piercing stares, but something far more dangerous caught my attention. Angie appeared from the mist of pink neon and dry ice that hung in the air. By the look on her face, my being there had been a surprise.

She entered dressed in a slinky white see through dress, complete with white gloves and stiletto heels. Under the material of the dress, I could see all the prizes she had to offer. Her hair flowed along her shoulder in neon green, her face painted in tasteful makeup. Long eye lashes batted at me. Her face glowed with excitement. She sold her eroticism with grace and class.

I stood in the nick of time. Her arms wrapped around me in a tight hug that allowed all those things under the dress to press against me with sensory overload. Skin softer than a new born touched me with electric shock. I held on a few extra seconds as I smelled the lust that radiated off of her. Plus, I knew it would piss Kasey off.

Angie pulled away enough that I could see her wide smile. She gave me a wet, heavy tongued kiss on the lips as her hands explored my behind. "Hey baby, what are you doing here?"

I looked to Kasey, but didn't say anything yet.

She followed my glance, then came back to me. "Did you kill, Olivia?"

"Not yet."

"Do you know where Josh and Stephanie are?" She sat

next to me. Close.

"Not yet."

Now a puzzled look hit her face. She watched as Pin Cushion left the table, leaving only Kasey and the two of us. "You didn't come here on your own did you?"

I could feel her power raise the hair on my arms. My eyes surveyed the room around me, taking in all the exit routes, placement of all the wolves still close by and anything else that I might, in a pinch, be able to use as a weapon. I had the 9mm and the silver bladed knife, but that wouldn't be enough to defend against all of them. "What happened to you at The Coffin?" I'd try to play this off as easy as I could.

Angie stood. "I told you. I was tired. There was too much vampire power in the room." I saw the concern in her eyes as she looked to Kasey. Gone were the lustful eyes and pouty lips. She grabbed my arm. "Come on, let's go kill something."

"Want to tell me the truth?" Unlike Kasey's approach of black and white, I wanted to save as much of her as I could. The thought of us being bitter enemies remained a little too raw yet.

Again, she looked to Kasey as she released my arm. "You brought him here didn't you?"

"You need to change, Angie. You are putting the entire pack at risk." He looked at me, but still spoke to the beautiful wolf. "And at what cost? The love of a half vampire that wants nothing to do with you. It's pathetic. Your place is here with us. With me."

I took a deep breath. Things were suddenly going my way. Her wrath descended on Kasey. Wolf power vibrated through me with a musky scent and raw energy. "He turns me, you kill him, is that the plan?"

Kasey played it smart. He remained silent.

She walked to him. I slid my chair as far in the other direction as I could, trying not to be noticed. I watched the other wolves in the distance, re-surveying their numbers and locations. One of them could put me six feet under.

"This isn't about me, this is about you. You think with Paul dead, I'll crawl to your bed don't you?"

Kasey stood, stopping her momentum. "I am the alpha male here and I will do whatever it takes to keep you alive and safe. If you don't turn, you will either die or much worse, become Judas' slave. I won't allow you to become his new playmate. Your place is at my side, and I will not lose you to a power hungry vampire or a man that doesn't even see you for the beauty and prize you are."

"Prize? That's the problem with you, Kasey. I'm not a prize. You want to control me like the vampires do and you hide behind pack concern to do it. At least the vampires are up front about it." She looked back to me. "So why are you really here?"

Oh God, the attention slammed on me again. "Kasey's right, Angie. You have to change. You've seen what these vampires are up to. They'll stop at nothing to eliminate all of us. Not to mention the reason you haven't changed is really stupid."

Bullets couldn't have hit me harder. I choked on the words that escaped from my mouth. Now I hoped that one of the wolves were at my throat. It would have been far more pleasant than what Angie had in store for me now. "Stupid? Please Paul, elaborate. Me, being such an ignorant woman might find it hard to understand, so please in all due respect, use little words." She crept my way with more than just a little swing in her hips.

Angie towered over me, her hands on her hips. I took in her body from toe to head and all the magical play lands that were under the see-through dress. Words suddenly escaped me. Even a blind man would have been distracted by what I saw. "Angie, there is no us, never has been, never will be. I don't love you or any other monster down here. If you don't change, Judas will do things far worse than kill you. Don't let him enslave you over me."

She looked across the table to Kasey. "I'm having a hard time deciding which of you are more pathetic. I have one that wants to control my every move and another that thinks I love him and will throw everything that I am away to get him." A lunatic laugh escaped. "Let me see if I have this right, Paul, you come here and tell me that you don't love me, I get my heart broke and change into wolf form again, rip your fucking heart out, Kasey wins my heart and we all live happily ever after. Did I miss anything?"

"Angie it's not…"

"I live my life for me. I don't need either of you." She

looked at Kasey, "You will never have me after this little funfest." Back to me, "And my changing has nothing to do with you. I don't want the picket fenced house and the bed of roses. I make my own rules and neither of you or any vampire in this city will change that. I control me." She bent close to my ear. "We both know it's you that wants me, lover, not the other way around. I know I can stop at lust, but you're afraid you can't. I'm comfortable with my wants and needs and who I am, can you say the same?"

"Change or I will do it for you," I bluffed.

The statement seemed to catch her off guard. "What did you say?"

"You heard me."

She shook her head. "Yeah, I heard you. Not sure if you did. And how do you think you can do that?"

"I have the virus in my blood, same as the wolf virus from when you bit me. I don't like what I am, but I'll change you, like it or not." I didn't even believe it. My voice broke up several times trying to say it. It sounded silly.

I don't think I ever heard her laugh as hard as she did. "You actually believe what Judas told you?" My cheeks burned with an overflow of blood as the embarrassment set in. "So Kasey and the boys have convinced you that you're a vampire and painted you into a corner, haven't they?" She walked to the edge of the stage and leaned against it.

"What do you mean?"

"Kasey gets you to change me in order to save my life, proving to the pack that you are a vampire hell bent on possessing me. Having vampire virus in you, makes the act seen as vampire aggression. Having shifter virus in you makes it aggression against the alpha male. Either way, Kasey kills you and eliminates what he sees as his biggest rival. Looks to me like I'm not the stupid one here. All Kasey had to do was shit. He knew you'd step in it." Her glare hit Kasey, "Congratulations." She rose from the edge of the stage and came back to me. "So change me, master vampire. Let's see what you've got." Her body seemed to be clawing its way out of the skin tight dress as she swayed back to me. My eyes took in the lust overload and I didn't have a single weapon on me to stop it. I wanted to reply, but Angie's eyes focused on me. I could feel the blood race through my veins. Sweat began to bead on my head. A stiffness formed between my legs. Hot breath danced on my skin as her hands touched me. "I've always had a thing for master vampires, baby."

She gave out a seductive lick of her lips, followed by a faint smile. Above me, I watched her move with angelic grace. She floated on thin air as she peeled away the left silk glove with methodical care. As she pulled it from her fingers, she laid it on the table beside me and gave a long wink.

The second glove came off with the same production as whistling began around us. Angie acted as though she never heard them. Her focus remained squarely on yours truly. Angie had challenged me as a man and as a roach and I lost at both.

I squirmed in my seat. My eyes traced every inch of her body from the Key Lime colored hair to the platform white stilettos. As if my eyelids were sown to my forehead, I couldn't look away.

Angie reached behind her and with great care and unzipped the silk dress. It began to give way to more of the hidden caramel skin, revealing her ample breasts.

I swallowed hard as the dress drifted to the floor with no effort at all, exposing Angie in a white fishnet bodysuit. Material around the butt cheeks conveniently missing. I could hear the catcalls and whistles escalate in the corners of the room.

Behind the fishnet, I, along with everyone else, could see her well-sculpted body glitter with a light coat of sweat. My eyes engulfed the large nipples, each decorated with diamond rings, as they caught rays of light from the mirrored ball and sent them back out over the crowd in spikes of beaming prisms.

As my eyes sank further south along her body, I followed the flat stomach and belly button, also decorated with a diamond stud. She continued to be perfection even further down.

I shook with desire and heat as I imagined touching her caramel skin. My fingers had at one time run along it and I remembered and relived it every day. I could smell the lust from her body as strong and recognizable as a freshly grilled steak. My mouth watered and grew dry at the same time.

Jealousy began to build in me, as I heard several

insulting comments about her from behind me. I wanted all this for my own personal show, but knew all too well that my own hang-ups had kept it from becoming a reality. I could tell Kasey enjoyed the show. That made matters worse.

She licked her lips again as she pulled on the top of the bodysuit and allowed her breasts to bounce free. I swallowed hard with desire. I wanted them in my hands, in my mouth. I groaned with excitement. My breath grew quick. The room spun.

More calls came from behind me. Even though the same fantasies ran through my head, I turned it personally. I refocused on the degrading act Angie performed. My hands clutched tight. I grit my teeth.

I had had enough. I grabbed Angie by the wrist and pulled her to me, as several bouncers moved in. I pulled my silver bladed knife from its sheath and pointed it toward them with my right hand. The left hand still held on to Angie's wrist. "Show's over, fur balls." Around me, I could hear sarcastic boos as I continued to try and keep the bouncers at bay.

Angie's face showed restrained anger mix with fear as she pulled back on her wrist. Confusion and questions grew in her face. She smiled and started to say something, but I cut her off. "Look at you. You're a mess. Not to mention acting like a whore." I knew it had been the wrong thing to say the minute it left my mouth, but that seemed to be a re-occurring theme tonight.

Angie slapped me hard across the face. If her strength had been compromised, it hadn't been in her ability to connect with my head. I let go of her wrist. The ringing sounds in my ear let me know she wasn't the helpless babe in the woods that Kasey made her out to be. "So you like parading up here like some freak slut?" I stood and shook her. "If you thought this would make me love you, you are dead wrong. What you did proves to me that you're nothing but monster trash."

Angie fired a glare at Kasey, then back to me. "Let me tell you something you male chauvinistic pigs. I don't need an erect prick to make me feel powerful. What I do, I am confident in and I answer to no one." She moved closer to me. "And baby, that includes you." Her breathing became hard as she tried to keep her emotions in check. "You may be wound a little too tight when it comes to sex and nudity, but that doesn't mean I have to subscribe to it. You don't own me. Just because I'm beautiful and a woman doesn't mean I'm helpless or stupid." The last word slid out with great annunciation. I started to speak but smart enough to close my mouth. "It's me that sees you as the monster now."

Angie laughed again. "That's right, Paul. You're one of us now. A monster. The very thing you love to hate. So either throw me over your shoulder and take me home, or get the fuck out of my way and never beat your hairy ass in here again, because your jealousy and judgment is really getting old."

"Quinn and Judas and the other cockroaches in this city can suck you dry all they want. I'm sure you will return the favor. You are nothing more than another piece of coffin bait in this town. You're a dime a dozen." Before I knew it, I had the knife pointed at her. I never intended on letting her get to me, but in the back of my mind, I knew it would end up this way. We were both trying to deny what we were, but in the long run it played into my favor. It made her hate me and me hate her enough to do my best to change her. Even if it proved I had crossed the line of humanity.

"Is that why I could feel your body heat, taste your lust, see your bulge." She began to move toward me. Splitting through the empty tables with aggressive speed. I had suddenly become the hunted. Angie looked down at my hand. "You plan on using that blade on me or do you want to keep it in your hands like your penis." Sucks to be me. A smarter man than me, would have turned and ran, but I stood there.

I gave her room as she descended. Out of fear, not courtesy. Unfortunately, it still didn't stop my mouth. "Just because you think I want to fuck you, doesn't mean that I love you, respect you or need you. I can find sex anywhere. It doesn't take as much talent to get a man hard as you'd like to think. So don't read so much into it." I wanted her to be angry with me. I wanted her to hate me worse than any son of a bitch she had ever come across before. I would much rather deal with her wrath than with her tears.

Angie looked over to Kasey. "You put him up to this didn't you?"

Kasey simply shrugged as he sipped on his drink. "One quick rip is better than a thousand small tears."

Her eyes turned to Kasey. Now a deep laugh. "How pathetic, Kasey. If I wanted a boring fuck," she turned to meet Kasey, "I'd have been in your bed already."

Kasey's mouth dropped open. I fought a giggle.

She moved between Kasey and me with a light shove. Flipped over the table in front of her and made her exit. Glass shattered across the floor as the other fur balls at the table stood, trying to avoid the mess. I could see her reflection in the mirror behind the bar. This conversation would be brought up again at a later date.

She stopped and turned, facing me. With a quick step she leaned against my ear. "So you think you can live without me? Not think about me? Deny your hidden desires of love for me?"

I couldn't give in now. I had to make her believe everything I had said. "Yes."

She sniffed me. "I smell it."

"Smell what?" I asked as I tried to put a little distance between her teeth and my throat.

"Bullshit."

CHAPTER FOURTEEN

I watched her walk away, hypnotized by the sway of her perfect ass. Dirty thoughts raged through me. I grew embarrassed as I caught myself licking my lips with animalistic heat. I wanted to turn her into my personal wet fantasy, not a slobbering, wild animal.

Around me, I saw the gathering of faces. All looked at me to see what I would do. Some hoped I would do the bidding of the Alpha male, others blamed me for ending Angie's little show prematurely, all wanted me dead.

"You better do it now," Pin Cushion commanded. The words were hot as they crawled down my neck. His southern accent stretched the words out far longer than they needed to be. I hadn't forgotten his threat to kill me. I kept him in sight.

Kasey waited for me to make the next move. A circle of fur balls closed in. I replaced the knife with the 9mm, armed with silver plated bullets. I'd be able to bring a few to their knees, but there were far too many of them to make it out alive. I knew it. They knew it. Question was, who would be loyal enough to the pack to die for it.

"She already hates you, might as well do it," Kasey smirked.

I wanted to turn around and at least give him some sort of comeback, but I knew that in the long run it would only cost me more bruises and broken bones. I got those enough without letting my mouth get involved. Why poke a stick at such things?

"Kasey, I've already told you I don't know how to turn her into anything other than a miserable person like myself." Inside, I searched for anything that might get me out of this situation. And it *was* a no win situation. Either I didn't turn her and get eaten alive by werewolves or I turned Angie and proved once and for all that I had become more vein weasel than human.

Pin Cushion chuckled and sniffed the air around him. "Funny, I smell blood sucker." Yellow eyes hit on me. He raised his palms and turned in small, slow circles. "And I feel the power." I took a step backwards, only to fall into the chest of another fur ball.

I watched as Angie moved further away from me, increasing the pressure to do something. Death had already rolled dice on my bloody bones. And to think after what I had said to Angie, I would be the only one coming to my rescue. Especially considering what I had come to do.

"Concentrate!" Kasey shouted. "I don't have to tell you what will happen if she leaves here."

From deep inside, something began to crawl out of me. Clawing and twisting with the pain of barbed wire. Almost overpowering. It shook me as it reached out from me. Screams filled my mind, similar to those I heard at the church. Grotesque fingers stretched towards Angie. I wanted to call them back but didn't know how. My body ached as the source of the power ate at me from the inside. Muscles trembled, vision blurred. I couldn't stop it now if I wanted to. I could no longer control it.

Cold air rushed through me. I swallowed hard as I looked around. The scent of blood lingered thick in the air. Unbelieving eyes shifted to me. The wolves winced as the entity inside me gathered in the room. Somewhere in the back of my mind I knew the power didn't belong to me. The power washed over me with ancient vengeance causing me to scream with the dead voices inside me.

My eyes opened wide. I had nothing to go by, but the power seemed to wrap around me. My God, Judas and Father Garcia were right. Panic washed over me. I tried to pull it back but couldn't.

Angie must have felt it too. She stopped in her tracks and turned to face me. She sprinted back. "You son of a bitch!"

As Angie moved toward me, two things happened. One, she gained speed, and two, she changed form. Her nude body streamlined before my eyes. Caramel skin changed into something far more beastly and a lot less attractive.

She grew less and less human with each step. My feet wanted to move, but she crashed on top of me before I could do anything about it. The 9mm slammed against her chest, but I refused to pull the trigger, which sucked. I had been attacked by her in this form once before. She would make it painful. I had little doubt she would make me bleed. A lot.

Her claws hit me in the shoulders. Weight pinned me to the floor. Claws sliced with precise action. Warm blood spilled from my wounds. I moved my right arm over me to cover my face. Clear, thick fluids from her change soaked my shirt.

Kasey and others howled with excitement. I knew it would only be a matter of seconds before the entire room turned into a pack of werewolves, moving in on a kill. Kasey wanted me to change Angie, but eliminating me from her heart had been the bonus prize in this twisted box of Cracker Jacks.

Deadly claws stabbed me. Flesh ripped. Excitement grew. Cheers filled the air. Growls took their place. Angie pulled me to my feet and flung me across one of the tables. Luckily my back broke the fall. Table, glass and human flesh all splintered to the floor in synchronized pandemonium.

I became nothing more than a human kite to the female wolf. I finally landed face down on the stage of the Silver Priapus. I choked in my own blood as it filled my nose and mouth. I spat, only to have more take its place.

One growl became many as I tried to make it back to my feet again. A musky odor replaced the stale cigarette and beer cloud of moments ago. I gripped the 9mm tighter. Kasey and the others were no longer in human form either.

I looked up with the one eye that still worked. All the wolves stood at attention. White teeth glared in the dark room. Hair on the nape of the neck stood on end. My urgency declined ever so slightly as I tried to meet their stare.

Things started to turn for yours truly. None of the wolves looked in my direction, but instead toward the entrance of the club. I followed the glares to a single figure at the doorway. Judas' silhouette overpowered the room. I saw Father Garcia hanging in the church. Revenge outweighed my rational thought.

CHAPTER FIFTEEN

He walked into the room with cocky movement as he clapped his hands in sarcastic pleasure. He held a southern gentleman's swagger that almost appeared arrogant. I started to right myself. "There will be no need to get up."

"To hell there isn't," I thought. I stood.

Shadows gave way to light. I saw the evil that had filled the walls around me. Judas strolled forward, dressed in attire better suited for a Dickens novel than a master neck biter. His dark gray shirt and white pants were overshadowed by the full length maroon coat. A gravely laugh filled the otherwise silent room.

All this led me to give Kasey a deep stare. Judas had been here the whole time. Kasey had invited Judas to do his dirty work. He had hoped I would piss Angie off, she would leave, there would be no witnesses, Judas would kill me, and he would get the girl. The Reader's Digest version of things, but in the end it all meant the same. Me leaving alive hadn't been part of the plan.

I thought about the events of the night and had to laugh at myself. Everyone from the humans to the fur balls to the coffin nappers wanted me dead for different reasons. Some good, some not so good, but when everyone you know thinks their life is better off with you dead, it's time to re-evaluate your priorities.

I started to reach for the Magnum when he stopped me.

"Ah, Avenger, that is not a way to welcome kindred." He moved close enough that I could see him in the grotesque light. His black eyes swallowed me whole as he played with the ends of his handlebar mustache. Judas took a survey of the room and seemed content with what he saw. His gaze stopped at Kasey only for a moment, "Or should I call you, Alpha?"

"Nice little trick you pulled at the church last night." I pushed harder through his power and tried for the Magnum again. Given the chance I had to shoot him and not hesitate.

He bowed. "I aim to please, my friend. You know, things did not have to end the way they did. Knowing your limits is what keeps things like us alive. It is what separates us from the humans. "

I wanted to ask him about Father Garcia, but I knew I wouldn't get a straight answer. God, Father Garcia had to be alive. I pushed harder through the thick power. My hand grasped the butt of the gun. I turned to look up to Kasey. "You'll fry for this."

Call it lack of blood, too late of a night, whatever you want, but before I could get the strength pull the Magnum free. Judas' power had me by the throat and began to squeeze. If I thought I was up shit's creek before with Angie and the fur balls, this had to be an all-new level of having no paddle. "You underestimate the time it will take to kill you, Avenger. If you think my coven will allow you to become a master vampire in this city, you are sadly mistaken." He looked down at the hand that tried to reach the Magnum. "You do not have the strength to reach it and even if you were able to get to it, you have not the speed to pull the trigger before I crushed you."

His power unwrapped from me and I dropped to the floor. He didn't want me dead yet. I hadn't suffered enough. He wanted me to reach for the Magnum. A way of highlighting his strength over me. Master blood head to master…well you know.

I knew better than to try and reason or deal with him. "Unlike Quinn, I have not come here for sex or money. I am a pure blooded vampire. I live in the ways of the old world. Power and blood are the only things that matter. I don't make deals or compromise. Other than your life, you do not have anything I want. There would be no truce. You are nothing more than a weak master that had not truly earned the position. Taking your life will give me great pleasure. Blood will be spilt."

Angie shook on the floor, caught midway between wolf and woman. She bellowed and twisted between quick pants. Judas bent low and took her by the arm. He lifted her to a chair at a nearby table. It sounded like bones breaking, reforming and then breaking again as she struggled to take one form or another.

"Leave her alone," a voice behind me resonated. Kasey stood at attention, blocking the main exit. Sweat and grime shimmered across his naked body. He moved next to me without making a sound. "You were to kill him and leave. Kill Paul and we all get what we want out of this."

Judas turned to him and gave another laugh. "I am the one that turned her, not this pathetic master vampire. That makes her my personal blood host if I wish it so. My Olivia has worn out her welcome, so to speak." He smelled Angie's hair. "And in all my time, I have never seen or smelled such beauty. I am sure her taste will match the other senses as well."

I glanced over to Angie. She had taken on human form again. Her head lay in a pool of sweat and other unknown fluids on the table. I couldn't tell if she was conscious or not. Nothing had proven to me that she had turned enough to gain any of her strength back. I didn't know how it worked, or how quickly it took. Other than what Kasey had told me, I had nothing to go on. I had doubts that even that held any truth.

Judas gazed back to me. "You didn't really think you had turned her did you, Avenger?" He started to laugh. The blood bat followed my eyes to Angie. "At least you have come to terms with what you truly are." His hand reached over to touch along the wolf's back. I saw her flinch. "So now you know the game, Avenger. What will your choice be? You have a man's grandson, another's wife and unborn and the princess of your heart all out of reach and in the hands of a vampire." He licked his lips as he stepped on my back. "A very dangerous vampire. One that wants what you have. In fact, one that covets it." He tried to catch my stare. I closed my eyes. I couldn't afford being caught in his gaze. I wouldn't get out alive.

"A great dilemma awaits you now. Before you die, I will allow you to fulfill a legacy of sorts. You may attempt to save the life of one of them. But the others will surely die. Killing you will be the easy part. Watching you struggle to save this one's pretty head while turning your back on your own kind will be most delightful."

I struggled against his grip, but found it impossible to

break free.

"I have tasted the blood of the young man you call Josh. Sweet and innocent. Think you could decapitate the grandson of such a close friend?" He smirked. "And then there is the beautiful wife of Detective Kansas. Ripe with child."

The words seemed to take on a life of their own. I fought against the grip, only to fail at gaining anything. He continued to laugh. It had become apparent to me that I had fallen into his trap.

He looked down at the fallen wolf and held out his hand. She rose without question, but not without pain or reluctance. "I will show you soon enough what a true master vampire can do."

If I could have breathed and spoke, I'd probably have thanked him. It at least gave me some sort of solace in believing I might be more human than monster. But deep inside, I knew that we were all at the mercy of this vein licker tonight. One wrong move and he would kill Angie. And to top it all off, Kasey had delivered her to him. He might eliminate me, but it would cost him the real prize in all of this.

"My first thought coming here was to kill you and simply take over the territory, but after meeting you, I have found you to be a most interesting foe. We shall play a game and see where your loyalties lie. I will place the Price boy, Kansas' wife, and this lovely wolf in different places in the city. You will only be able to fight for the life of one."

"Killing him is one thing," Kasey reluctantly added, "but I will not allow you to leave here with Angie." Behind the night crawler, I saw fur balls move in front of the exits. "We have given you what you came for. Take Paul Isaac and do with him whatever you wish, but we will fight you to the death for the wolf. Release her now, or we will consider it an act of war."

Judas licked Angie's cheek. "So you are willing to see the deaths of all your pack, wolf? I will start with her, but do not think I will spare any of those that try to stop me. Unlike the master vampires in this city now, I show no mercy." Angie hit the floor in agonizing pain. Pure power swept over all of us. "Your actions shall leave you with blood on your hands, wolf. I do not bluff. Thoughtless acts such as this shall only bring about pain and bloodshed for them all. Your wolf's fate lies in the vampire hunter's decision. He controls who lives and dies tonight." He smiled at me. "Actions of a true vampire master."

Power injected in me so hard, I couldn't speak. Crushing venom spread through every bone and muscle. My mind went blank. My knees buckled and I crashed back to the ground. Flashes of light moved through the room. Angie screamed in the distance. Howls from wolves echoed in the darkness. Blood filled my nostrils. Animal excitement left the room with a thick wet dog smell.

Judas attempted to keep the entire room from turning into wolves. He pulled the animal our of each human frame. Energy pushed against us all, threatening to crush every bone. The walls of the Silver Priapus exploded with plasmatic parasites. Vampires rushed into the room, attacking with blurred velocity.

Speed and movement filled the club as the shifters struggled between states. I grabbed the Magnum from the floor and the 9mm from the holster. With each touch of the trigger I plowed my way through the monsters. For now, I considered everything an enemy. Judas and Angie blended deeper and deeper into the sea of fighting and closer and closer to the exit.

Kasey moved past me caught between wolf and man. He sliced through the air in lethargic moves. His huge claws caught one of the cockroaches in the throat and human canines finished the gruesome act. I could hear the muscle tear. The bones crush.

I jumped across several overturned tables when I heard a second set of shots go off. Instincts told me to move low. Whatever pulled the trigger couldn't possibly be on my side. Not to mention odd. The monsters never were big on carrying weapons.

As the second shot rang out, I recognized the sound. I glanced up as a cockroach landed on my right shoulder. Fangs exposed. I fired a bullet in his gullet and sent him to the floor in charred demise. I kicked the corpse for good measure.

"Kansas!" I called out. "Keep Judas from getting out!"

My feet tripped over a dead wolf as I moved toward Kansas and the doorway. Before I reached the floor, an over-sized hand grabbed me. I pulled the Magnum around. My finger released the bullet. It nicked Kasey's shoulder.

Kasey put his hand across the wound and pulled back a palm of fresh blood. Amazement filled his eyes. "You shot me?"

I shrugged. "Oops." Unlike the daisy pushers, shooting a wolf with ultra violet bullets wouldn't be a death sentence. I moved toward the door, dodging both cockroaches and fur balls as I went. Judas disappeared from sight. I knew finding him would be the only chance I had of getting Angie back alive.

Kasey held his wound. He read the answer in my face. "We have to get her back. He'll kill her simply because she loves you."

"If it wasn't for you, she wouldn't be in the hands of roaches." I didn't wait for him to respond or try anything. In quick hops, I danced over the dead daisy pushers and fur balls around me. I spun again to find all the roaches escaping in retreat.

Except for one.

Kansas had his Glock pointed at the hissing vein freak and about to get himself killed. When it came to daisy pushers, you never hesitate pulling the trigger. It only magnifies the chances your throat will be slashed. "Where is she?" Kansas asked.

I started to pull my Magnum up and took aim at the blood drinking bitch, her back still to me.

"Don't do it, Paul," Kansas called out. His focus never left the monster.

"She'll kill you…"

He shot the first bullet into her thigh. She dropped to the ground. I could tell the way the bullet hit, he had the wrong kind of bullet for the job. Thus, adding to his demise. Then I shook with grief. He acted like me. Kansas didn't want this one dead. He wanted his answers first.

"I've killed three of the sons of bitches tonight, Paul. I'll kill them all until they start talking." And I believed him. As I grew closer to the detective I could see a mixture of blood, sweat and dirt on his clothing and hands. I could smell the alcohol on his breath. He had been on a mission of destruction. He didn't have the guts to commit suicide on his own, so being killed by a maggot taxi became his answer to his problems.

Kansas didn't have the mundane, lonely life I had. He still had a legitimate shot at the happily ever after shit. But I knew I had to choose my words very carefully. If Kansas knew I could only save one of the hostages and I chose a werewolf, the ramifications would be severe. And for that, I couldn't really blame him. I had always said I would save a human life before considering the life of a monster, and now I thought of nothing but getting Angie back safe and sound.

"Get out of here, Kansas. I'll kill her. God knows no one will question me doing all this." I continued to watch the coffin crispy on the floor as she bled and tried to gain her strength back. The roach didn't appear to be all that powerful, but then again, that's like saying, "It's not a very dangerous shark." They're all dangerous if they're still twitching. I pulled up the Magnum and again took aim.

Kansas spoke, "No, I said this one's mine. She'll tell me where Steph is or she'll burn in the sun."

We all needed answers from this coffin bait, but it wouldn't be easy. Kansas and I were on two different missions. We both had something to lose. I didn't have the patience or ability to think past having Angie safe again. I realized what I would do to keep her safe from all of this. And that included sacrificing a grandson and wife and unborn baby. I shivered inside.

From my right a large man approached in his patented naked stance. "Kasey, the only thing worse than you losing Angie in this, is that Judas didn't kill you."

Kasey growled at me. Anger bubbled through his skin. With one hard punch, he hit me square on the nose. Little yellow birds circled my head. Darkness filled my sight as my eyes rolled to the back of my head.

CHAPTER SIXTEEN

I woke disoriented but in no time at all, knew that things weren't all warm and fuzzy. My eyes started to focus on the ceiling of the Silver Priapus and the erotic art. I had a feeling the average customer that came here never even knew such art existed above their heads.

Flashbacks reminded me how I had come to be staring at the ceiling. I grimaced with the throbs of pain. With great care, I pinched the sides of my nose testing for broken bones. By the bites of pain that ran through my face, my guess had been, yes. For the first time, the lycanthrope virus had been an advantage. In a few days, I knew the nose would be as ugly as it had always been, but the pain and swelling would be nothing more than a memory.

As I pulled my fingers away from my nose, I determined I hadn't been out for all that long. The trace of blood on my face hadn't dried yet.

"Now you can tell me what I want to know, or I can make this last for hours," I heard Kasey methodically speak. "None of you will get away with this."

I sat up, only to find the roach bitch hog-tied and staring wide-eyed. Demonic jaws snapped at the wolf. Kansas stood to the side and paced, or better put, waited his turn to torture said daisy pusher.

"What the hell are you two doing?" I asked.

Kasey turned to Kansas. "I told you I didn't hit him hard enough."

I stood, only to feel the blood rush from my head. Darkness filled my vision. I grabbed a chair to keep from falling. As I closed my eyes, I smelled the death in the room. As predominate as any smell I had ever experienced. Every muscle in my body tensed. I fought the urge to upchuck all over the Silver Priapus' floor. "Angie," I said to myself. I wiped another slide of blood that oozed from my nose and headed for the door.

"I'll go with you," Kansas volunteered.

I shook my head. "I don't think so, Kansas. Trusting you will only get me killed quicker. Besides, I'm going after Angie, not your wife." One, I didn't trust Kansas, two, we wouldn't be on the same page as to who to rescue and kill, and three, and most important, if I got to Judas, I didn't planning on staying within the limits of the law to bring all this to an end.

Before I could take another step, Kasey had his hand in my chest. "No one will do anything dealing with Angie, unless I say so. And that especially means you. This is pack business." I looked around and didn't see any other wolves. My odds of making it through the night had vastly improved.

"Unless I've missed something, it involves the cockroach that also wants me dead. And that makes this my business." Taking a second glance to be sure, I finished, "For all we know, they're all dead anyway."

"If you had turned her when I told you to, we wouldn't be having this conversation. She would be strong enough to defend herself. Stop thinking you can always play the human card in this. If Angie dies, you die."

Kansas moved back into the room and stopped next to the wolf. "Do you really think she'll tell us anything, Kasey?"

He shook his head. "I think so. The sun is up. The only thing keeping her from smoking is the fact that there is no sunlight in the room." He went over to a window blind. I heard the coffin muncher breath hard. We both knew what he planned to do. "Last chance," he sang as he pulled on the chord to the blind.

Deafening screams filled my ears. Smells of sulfur added to the ambience. The leech twisted against her binds as the sunlight ate at her skin. Smoke poured around her so thick, I lost sight of her body. She screamed with madness, but never talked.

"Where's my wife?" Kansas asked as he moved close enough to the maggot biter that I grew nervous. He should have been smart enough to know that if that mouth could talk, it could also suck on a vein.

I walked within an inch of Kasey, who still faced the vein biter. "Guess you didn't think this little game of yours all the way through did you fur ball. She ain't going to tell you anything. They may be disgusting, but they know better than to tell on their masters. That death is a lot worse than anything you can dream up."

"Please Paul, help me find where Stephanie is," Kansas pleaded as he looked back to me. Tears filled his eyes. I still couldn't forgive him for what he had done. He had tried to get me killed and now wanted my help to save his wife? I didn't think so. I watched as he grew dangerously close to our hostage again. I tensed. "Make her tell me where Stephanie is."

"She not going to tell you anything, Kansas. She's nothing more than an expendable piece of meat. Like Olivia, she's nothing more than a diversion." I grew very nervous. If Judas could come through Olivia, nothing said he couldn't do the same with this little blood leech. As for all the people I needed to rescue, I remained at a loss as of where to start. There were a lot of nooks and crannies to hide people. Having Kansas along as a loose cannon would only complicate things more.

The detective ran to me and shook me out of desperation. "Please, Paul. I will do anything to get my family back."

I moved closer to his face. "You've proven that haven't you."

He jumped back, realizing what I meant. His mouth moved, but nothing came out. "Just try. Please," he finally spouted. "If anyone can get her to tell us where Stephanie and Angie are you can." I didn't know how to take that. "All off record if you want." I looked at Kansas and saw something more soulless than the neck biters. I didn't trust him, but I didn't have any other options either.

I shook my head. "Alright. We're about to find out what she knows, but I'm telling the two of you right now, this isn't going to be pretty. In fact, it's going to be real messy." As focused as I had ever been, I moved to my victim. "Get her up," I commanded to no one in particular.

"What are you going to do?" Kansas asked softly. He already knew he had pushed me too far. I wanted to make sure that what I did would haunt him for the rest of his days. But it's true, desperate men do desperate things.

I pulled out a long wooden stake with my free hand and tapped the point against the silver blade of the knife. "You wanted to get answers out of her didn't you? Perhaps I was wrong. Maybe she does know where Angie, Stephanie and Josh are."

"What are you going to do?" Kasey repeated. Fear grew in his voice as well.

"I said get her up. Now!"

Both men snapped to attention and did as I commanded. Each grabbed the bitch under the arms. Then in synchronized motion, turned to me for further direction.

"Take her to that wall." I pointed to a solid wall to my left with my chin.

The vein maggot looked at me and hissed. She fought against my two accomplices, but still her fate rested in my hands. The more she fought, the more justified I felt about it. It only proved to me that I had to be doing the right thing.

Again, I got synchronized stares from the two men. I could tell by their faces they already knew what I had in mind. And they would be right. In the back of my mind, I knew that there wasn't a snowball's chance in hell of getting any information out of this one, but it allowed me two things. One, blow off a little steam, and two, send a message to Judas that he had messed with an insane master roach. If he wanted to play twisted little mind games, I had one or two up my sleeve as well.

My little subject stared back at me with eyes wide with the unknown. Sure, she knew I planned to torture her to death, but not knowing how had her at my full attention.

I walked toward her. "We can make this very easy and quick, or we can do it my way," I explained. The point of the knife slide under her skin enough that the silver would sting and stink. Silver had become my favorite element. It killed fur balls and tortured fang heads. What in life could be better than that?

She remained silent. And to my surprise, she stopped resisting her captures. Either she had given up hope of making it out alive, or planned something that I hadn't thought of yet. Her eyes closed and she began to sweat, but still no sounds or confessions.

I came eye to eye with my victim. Like humans, she breathed, could give birth, and if things went well, feel pain. Thinking back to Olivia, I also hoped by torturing this little vampire would flush Judas out of hiding.

A stream of warm blood rolled from the wound. I imagined the pain. Fought back a smile. "Where can I find Judas?"

She shook her head in quick nods. Her breathing increased to shallow sniffs. Sweat began to form on her forehead.

Without warning I drove the first stake through her collarbone and into the wall behind it. Demonic screams filled the Silver Priapus. Music to my ears. She struggled against the piece of wood, but my anchor held her firmly in place. Her lips moved. She tried to speak, but the pain sucked it back into her mouth.

"I think I'm going to puke," Kansas said in a nervous tone. He only a few minutes, he had proven to be such a wuss when it came to interrogation tactics. I often wondered how he made it through as many crime scenes as he had. Then again, we had different ways of getting what we needed out of these things.

I kept my attention on Little Miss Fang Face. "Get him out of here," I said to Kasey. According to the laws of the land, I had already slid into deep shit. I had harmed a historical artifact but defacing it had been the least of my worries "Feel like talking now, bitch?" I asked as I moved within biting distance of those fangs. My own safety had fallen far down on the list of priorities.

I pulled another stake from my belt loop. I made sure to do it with as much methodical care as I could. Sometimes the presentation got me the best results. "You know, your bastard of a master has been a real pain in the ass. Now I would love to be doing all of this to him, but as you can see, he's abandoned you." I moved the stake by her wide eyes and creased her other shoulder with it. The point now perpendicular with the flesh. She looked away and held back a scream.

I drove the second stake into the coffin bait's other collarbone. Hurtful screams echoed throughout. She cried with pain, but again didn't fighting back. I started to get disappointed. I had convinced myself that this type or interrogation would bring our master roach front and center.

I drove the silver knife inside her rib cage a little deeper. I could smell the burning flesh. I twisted the knife slightly to get a better tone out of her.

Screams filled the room as she twisted against the silver blade. Flesh started to melt away. Skin rolled back and rotted on the floor. For now, the stakes held, but I knew better than to think that any of us were safe. With any power at all, she'd be able to pull the stakes from the sheetrock and the rope that held her hands would be no challenge.

The wolf pushed me back. "Let her go. We can't do this anymore."

I turned my head to the side. "Why the sudden change of heart? Don't tell me you're getting…feelings for this one."

"We need answers on where to find Angie, not this needless torture. We're wasting time!"

"Funny. I find that needless torture gets me the best needed answers. And unlike you, I'm willing to do whatever it takes to get those answers." And I meant every word.

He entered my personal space. "There's more to this than you know." His words came out laced with panic. A light coat of sweat formed on his forehead.

"Do tell."

"If you would use your senses for something other than being bullheaded you'd see that she's pregnant." Kasey made sure to slow down at the last word. He allowed the word to drip from his mouth. "We've already signed our death warrant."

I looked back at the vein biter. "How do you know?"

"I can smell it." He looked at her. "Tell him."

The roach worked her glare back to me. Tears fell from her eyes. A long nod.

She couldn't have been more than a month or two along and definitely not showing. My mouth opened, but Kansas that beat me to it. "Who's child?"

She looked away from me. Her breathing became even faster. Roaches don't spit out babies every day. Pregnancy in the blood sucker world is rare and very sacred. Most females will go a hundred years between births. And if this turned out to be Judas' little bun in the oven, I knew we might not have a whereabouts, but we had something far better than senseless torture.

My attention volleyed between Kasey and the mother-to-be. "Do you want to live to see this birth?"

She refused to look at me or answer me.

Kasey moved in on her. "Tell me where I can find my wolf." My mind tried to figure out if he had had a change of heart or simply tried to get his answers. I watched and listened for a few seconds. I hoped this would go easier than I had imagined it. "We both know this is Judas' baby. Tell us what we want to know and you walk out of here unharmed."

"Judas' baby," Kansas muttered. He grew zombie-like and nearly fell to his knees. Instincts took over. I grabbed him by the elbow to keep him from falling all the way to the ground.

"What's your name?" Kasey asked.

"Allana," the mother-roach-to-be responded. Her glare washed over me. Revenge alone kept her alive. "I tell you nothing until he leaves."

Kasey turned to me. "Go."

"I don't think so."

Kansas' hands reached for Allana. "I want my wife and baby back!" I struggled to pull his hands from her. Not because I disagreed with his actions but because we were still dealing with a very dangerous monster. Yes, she had been staked to a wall, but shit happens, and no one knows that better than yours truly.

"Where did he take Angie?" Kasey interrogated. His voice grew intense. "He was supposed to kill Paul and leave us at peace. We had a deal."

I stopped. Blood turned to ice. I pivoted to face Kasey. I saw the look on his face. "What did you say?" I pulled him back around. My hands shook with rage. Betrayal started to be the norm in my life. I knew he had sold me out to Judas, but to hear it come from his own lips made me hate him a little more. "What deal?"

Kasey allowed the air to escape his lungs as he looked back into my eyes. "Judas was supposed to kill you and leave. Nothing else was to be harmed or killed. I brought him to you on a silver platter. Angie would see you killed, forget about you. Return to being who she truly is. My pack would gain power from the new master."

"Instead, Kasey, you allowed him to take what he came here for with little more than a few dead fang heads." I looked at the two men before me. Both had betrayed me. Both had set me up to die, yet here I stood. "Sucks when the only one in this room that hasn't betrayed me has fangs."

I pulled the blade free from Allana and stuck it under his chin. It took all the restraint I had not to slice his jugular. "Your life depends on you telling me everything, Kasey. I swear to God, I'll leave you bleeding on the floor if you don't."

Kasey stood stiff. His eyes bulged as he felt the sliver blade prick his skin.

"You'll kill him," Kansas screamed as he tried to knock my hand away from Kasey's throat. "You can't do this."

"Oh, I can, Kansas. Both of you deserve to have me looking down at you as you fade to black." I kept the blade under Kasey's skin. "You tried to have me killed at The Coffin, so don't try to tell me what I can and can't do. The two of you allowed Judas to get power from you without a fight."

Kansas pulled his Glock from its holster and pointed it at me. "I won't tell you again to take the knife off of him, Paul."

With a quick pull I retracted the blade and allowed Kasey to fall to the floor. He held his wound and rolled in pain. Droplets of blood dotted the floor at my feet. I pushed him away from me with my foot towards Allana. "I hope she sucks you both dry."

As I turned away from Kansas, I could still see the gun pointed at me. I knew he might still shoot me, but I had had enough. In the end, he would probably be doing us both a favor. No more looking over my shoulder. No more alliances with anyone. Human or non-human.

I could feel the power in the room as it grew. I turned as I saw Allana pull free from the wall. I started to speak, but my words would never make it out. Everything moved in slow motion and fast forward, all at the same time.

I saw Allana descend on Kansas. She pushed him to the ground in a violent freefall. I pulled the Magnum free and started to aim, as I heard the shot. Blood shot through the back of the roach, bringing with it, flesh and bone. Some splattered along the wall opposite of where we were. Most found its way on me.

Allana started to stand and looked back at me. She no longer had the deadly eyes of a demon, but instead the eyes of a mother. Her mouth gapped open as she tried to pull in a deep breath. Both wooden stakes still attached at her collar bones.

Her fingers were held tight against the wound in her stomach. Once pale fingers now crimson with shiny thick liquid. Droplets of blood already started to stain the floor around her as she attempted to take a step forward.

Below her, Kansas scrambled free. His Glock still pointed at the monster above him, but now nothing more than an afterthought. With his left hand, he wiped away bits of flesh and blood from his own face, as his mind started to put together the events that had taken place.

He looked back at me, now nearly as pale as the roach. From what I could tell, Allana's fangs never met their mark. "God, Paul, what did I do?"

Allana fell to her knees as she continued to hold the wound with her hands. Hollow eyes now looked into nothingness. Tears rolled down her face. She grew hollow from the inside out.

Kansas gave Allana a wide girth as he came to a stop in front of me. Although I don't think he realized it, his gun had been pointed at me. The look of horror on his face led me to believe he might pass out. "What did I do?" he repeated.

"For a change, the right thing," I answered as I pushed his gun away from me. My eyes remained on the coffin bait. She crawled toward the sunlight.

"Olivia, help me," Allana gasped as she tried to crawl along the floor on her knees and one hand. The other remained tight around the wound in her stomach. The exit wound visible in her back along with another small pool of blood and guts. Her breathing became shallow with pain as she talked in some gothic language to invisible faces. "My baby," she cried out in English.

"I didn't mean to shoot her, Paul. We've got to get her to a hospital or something." Kansas started to move past me to Allana. I grabbed him.

"It's too late, Kansas." My mind couldn't land on all the unimaginable things Judas would do to Stephanie and his baby now. I didn't know whether to tell him to run or face the music.

All I knew, in the end, Kansas would die for this.

"But the baby?"

I shrugged. "Consider it community service, Kansas." I pulled out a cigar and lit it. I looked over to Kasey, who sat on the floor, holding his throat. Kasey stood a reasonable chance of dying if enough of the silver made it into his bloodstream. If I still had a sliver of humanity in me, I would have cared, but not tonight. I had no remorse for any of them. They all were getting what they deserved. As I began to walk out of the Silver Priapus, I looked back to Kansas again. "Better get him to a doctor before he bleeds to death."

Kansas looked to Kasey and Allana, then began to catch up to my stride as I hit the lobby. "You can't leave them here like this?"

I blew out the first puff of cigar smoke and surveyed the damage. I walked over to the damaged roach and lifted her head with my hand firmly under the chin. "Now a minute ago, you were calling out to Olivia. Where can I find her?"

Allana grinned through the pain. "In time, you will find her at your throat."

I blew the next lung full of cigar smoke in her face and returned the smile. "I will find her, find Judas and all your little friends. I'll ride off of your power to find Judas. You're tied to him and that power will lead me right to his coffin."

I saw a different look in Allana's eyes. I had only meant it to be a bluff, but somewhere in all the lies, either I had hit on something, or she believed it to be true. Either way, she remained trapped here and nobody could do a damned thing about it. I now had something to bring to the bargaining table.

CHAPTER SEVENTEEN

I could see the wheels turning in Allana's head. She tried to figure it all out, knowing this would be her prison until sunset. And like Allana, the sun held Judas in place. As long as the sun burned in the sky, I gained time. I planned to use it to my advantage.

The night played through my head again and again. Nothing seemed to make sense or have any direction about it. Judas still held all the cards as far as any of us were concerned. He had Frank Price's grandson, Kansas' expecting wife, and now the wolf that both Kasey and I lusted for.

I stared at Allana. If the vein weasels could channel their power through me because of the virus, maybe I could do the same to them. I knew hunting down a transient roach like Judas could take months to find, and I doubted I had that luxury.

In the distance, Kasey moved from the floor and fell across one of the tables short of the stage. Blood stained his naked skin. His hands still held the wound. I didn't care if he lived or died. And why shouldn't I be? He had brought me here, not to save Angie, but instead to deliver me to the creatures that would one day try and destroy him and his pack. If he died, he got what he deserved.

Kansas stood about ten feet from me. His gun ready to shoot God knows what, and that made me nervous. He had already gotten a bit trigger happy tonight. He shot a daisy pusher, yes, but in the end, he had made things far more complicated than any of us needed right now. His one bullet might very well have killed more than a baby roach. "Kansas, put that thing away. You're too far up the Council's ass to use it and she ain't going anywhere soon."

Allana watched me as I moved around the room. Her pain showed on her face. I could see it on her face, no matter how hard she tried to hide it. From time to time, she would recite some garbage in an unknown language. The wooden stakes I had used to drive her into the wall, still jutted out of her collar bone. The large hole in her back still oozed slime and blood, while her lungs whistled with labored breath. She continued to try to crawl toward the ultra violet rays of the sun. I kept an eye on her. I didn't want her to die just yet. Even if she survived her injuries, she had lost the baby. See, things were looking up already.

"What are you going to do, Paul? We can't leave them here to die," Kansas added as he put his gun away with trembling hands.

I looked back to Kasey who, I must admit, didn't look all that good. Something told me I might have left the silver blade in him a bit too long. He might die on me. If it ever got back to Angie that I had killed Kasey, no matter how justified it had been, she would come after me. Pack loyalty would trump love.

Kasey looked back at me with eyes of vengeance. Sweat had matted the locks of black hair to his face. His skin so white, he resembled a fang biter. Muscles twitched with pain.

I opened and closed my mouth several times trying to find the right words of apology, but nothing seemed to come to mind. I had no remorse for what I had done. Apologizing for something you don't regret never comes across as genuine.

"He will kill them all now," Kasey said, as he lay across one of the small tables near the bar. The fur ball's naked body reflected in the mirror behind the countless bottles of booze. A bare ass stared back at us as a reminder of how twisted this night had gotten. His head rested on his left arm. Only his eyes showed signs of life.

"What are you talking about?" Kansas asked before I could get the words out of my mouth.

Kasey propped himself up with a grunt. "It's quite simple, Detective, when Judas finds out that you killed his unborn child, what do you think he will do to Stephanie and your baby?" His eyes rolled to me. "Chances are we will all be burying something we loved in the next few days."

"Shit happens when you play with the neck biters, Kasey. Now shut up and die." I lifted Allana's head up and took in her features. She looked to be nothing more than a child. I second guessed her part in all of this, but I knew she had been left behind for a reason. I had learned that the hard way with Olivia. Still, if my theory played out, she would lead me to Judas. I thought back to the words Father Garcia said in the church. I acted without thinking things through.

"What are you going to do?"

Allana's face showed both fear and determination. I had to get inside her thoughts. "Probably committing suicide." I couldn't even come to terms with the plan I had. I didn't trust anything in the room with me, which made things even more insane. "If you ever want to see Stephanie alive again, you better come to your senses."

He shook his head slightly. "I'm with you. What do you want me to do?"

"Earlier tonight when I brought Olivia to the church, Judas channeled his power through her because she carried the virus. I think if I look into Allana's eyes, I can get to Judas. Find out where he is and where he's keeping all our little friends."

Kasey stood, still holding his wounded throat. He leaned against the tables and chairs as he tried to make his way to me. "You're an idiot if you think it will work."

I pulled the 9mm from my hip holster, loaded with silver nitrate. "I wouldn't take another step, fur ball or I'll finish what I started with you. And as far as Angie goes, Judas has her because of your own insecurities and lack of a backbone. I doubt you would put your life on the line to save her. That's the difference between you and me."

"I'm not going to have to kill you, Isaac. Looking into her eyes will be suicide. Go ahead and do it. If you do live to tell about it, I'll still be here to finish what Judas should have done."

"Paul, what do you want me to do?" Kansas asked as he moved between me and the two monsters.

"First of all, I want you to get out of biting range."

He looked back at Allana and Kasey, realized how close he had gotten to the blood roach and jumped.

"Second, I want you to help me. I'm going to try and ride on her power and see if I can communicate or locate your wife. I don't know if it will work and I need you to have my back if things go bad. I've been able to do it with a few less powerful vein suckers, but not one like this." Again, I didn't plan on telling him I would save Angie first. Not something to be proud of, but if I put my life on the line, I decided in which order I worked.

His eyes showed the uncertainty. "What do you mean if things go bad? What could go bad?"

"She overpowers him, attacks him, drains his blood and becomes a master vampire herself," Kasey added as he walked within inches of my face. "Then she turns on me and you and kills us."

My eyes locked on his stare as I shook my head. "Yeah, something like that." I took a deep breath. "If they go bad, kill her. Don't hesitate. And that includes fur ball."

Kasey looked over to me. I got ready for the attack certain to come. His eyes glared at me. I could feel the wolf rise in him. I brought his attention to the 9mm still pointed at him. It stopped his progress toward me for the moment.

I let out a deep breath as he sat back down at a table to my left. My muscles relaxed. I knew our little thing wasn't over, just over for now. I knew how dangerous Kasey could be. Just because I saw skin and not fur didn't mean he couldn't slice me three ways to Sunday. He had proven to be every bit as much of a killer as Quinn, Judas and the fang gang. Even injured, I didn't want to push my luck. I swallowed my fear, only to have it regurgitate in the back of my throat.

I looked down at Allana. "This is your last chance to do this the easy way. When I'm through with you, that bullet hole in your belly will seem like a paper cut. Now where the fuck are they?"

The fang bitch looked up at me and began to breathe hard. I followed her eyes to the door and smiled. She had nowhere to go. *"Come and get me, Avenger."* Judas' voice slithered from Allana's mouth, as it had with Olivia.

I grabbed Allana by the two stakes in her collar bone and positioned her against the far wall. I forced my stare into her eyes. Invisible hands wrapped around me Pain filled me. My body imploded. My will started to slip away. In ways I still can't explain, our bodies became one living and dying thing. Invisible hands reached out and grabbed me. Crushed me. Pain rode my nerves. I grit my teeth, tried not to scream.

I could see Judas' eyes stare back at me. Feel his breath. Taste his power. Smell the blood. Darkness wrapped around me. My hands stretched out, trying to find anything to hold on to.

My body grew wet, but not with sweat. Blood. Hip deep. Fingers touched me with the illusion of thousands of twitching worms. They tried to pull me down under the current of human liquid. I began to pant as my breath became shallow. Air evaporated from my lungs.

I focused on my own power and tried to push through. I was onto something and Judas knew it. I could feel his presence around me, lurking somewhere out of reach. Cold power vibrated on the blood.

"Can you taste your fear, Paul Isaac?" Judas' voice slithered over me. It echoed in my ears again and again and again.

Glimmers of light flashed around me as I caught the sight of skin. Flesh that had been peeled away from human bones. Large hooks held it upright. Stained with old blood and other fluids. Dirty and decayed. The smell. What oxygen had been in the room had been consumed by the odor. Rotting meat. Flies crawled along my skin. Maggots. So many the ground moved.

The room grew cold. Death stood close by. Stone walls dripped with crimson blood. I could smell the sweet scent of it. I swallowed the mouthful of saliva and tried to move forward through the hanging skins. Flickering candles gave me grotesque images of exaggerated things I wished I had never seen.

The last skin began to move its head toward me. Hollow eyes looked in my direction. It had been cut from the throat to the groin. The muscles and bones plucked out from its skin. Lips moved in animated methodical motion.

I stopped and reached for the Magnum, only to discover my nakedness. Judas' voice laughed in the distance. *"All things die, Paul Isaac. Some by the hands of God, but most by those like me."*

"Help me, Paul," the skin cried out.

"This isn't real," I said out loud to myself. I tried to convince myself that there were no such things as spooks. Somehow, I didn't come close to believing my own words.

"Help me," one of the other skins called out from behind me. Followed by another, then another, until the room filled with cries of agony and pain.

I covered my ears and dropped to my knees. Blood began to rise to my chest. Warm. Thick. Delicious.

The skins ripped free of the hooks and surround me. Paper thin fingers reached in my direction. Rubber faces looked through me. Distorted and hollow.

I swatted away the skins and rose. Without thought, I began to run through the hip deep blood. My strength faded as I fought against the current. It splashed on my face. I fought the urge to lick it. Fought the urge to throw up. Fought the urge to scream away the madness.

Ahead, I saw two shadows. I stopped and tried to focus in the dim light. One male. The other female. I couldn't tell much more about them than that. From behind I could still hear the skins calling out my name. I could hear them wade through the blood in slow pursuit. For all I knew, death had already found me and had sent me to eternal hell.

"Paul, you have to help them," another voice added.

"Olivia?"

Olivia materialized before me. I could see her silky skin. The light and shadows melted along her curves. Even in this hell, she looked beautiful, untouched by the filth around us. "Here," she said as she held her hand out to me. A wooden stake rested at her fingertips. "You have to kill them now. Allow them to escape the pain or Judas will continue to torture them until the end of days."

Light began to illuminate the male's face. I grabbed the stake. I expected to come face to face with Judas, but instead, I saw the muscles and bones of Josh. White eyes bulged out against the redness of the flesh. Teeth peeked through the network of meat. "Do it, Paul. Please do it now," the flesh called out.

"Josh?" I took a step back again.

"You've done this to us, Paul. You should have given Judas his payment for the vampires you killed. Chosen us over Angie. Now we all suffer for your decisions. Do the right thing and end our suffering. *Kill yourself. Kill yourself.*"

"Don't let Zeke find us like this, Paul. Please," the female voice said as it, walked into the candlelight.

"Oh God, Stephanie."

In her arms, I saw a small baby, absent of skin, simply muscle and blood. It cried out in pain.

"This can't be real," I said to myself. "Zeke, get me out of here!"

"He can't hear you, Paul. No one can," Olivia said as she touched my hand.

I moved it away as quickly as she had touched me. I shook my head in denial. "This isn't real. It can't be."

From behind the army of skins covered me. I tried to scream. They filled my mouth and swallowed the sounds. I couldn't breathe.

I couldn't hold back anymore. I vomited until my ribs cracked. "Zeke! Somebody help me!" I swung the stake around me, hitting at the nothingness. The skins got tangled in the strikes, wrapped around my arm. My fingers pulled away the skins from my face. I grabbed Olivia by the wrists and shook her. "Tell me this isn't real. Tell me!"

"Paul, I wish I could. I cannot do anything to help you. I am powerless against what you see. You have to end it for them."

"Where's Angie?"

Olivia's face drained of all emotions. "Enduring things much worse."

I looked back to the bloody bodies of Josh, Stephanie and the baby. "It's not real. None of this is real."

"Then you should have no trouble doing it." I looked her in the face again. That sorrowful look had returned. "Do not let them end up this way. An endless road to torture, suffering and bitterness. Do it for them and their families. They need the closure."

"Please, Paul."

"Please."

"Please."

Their cries echoed through the darkness again and again. Never stopping. Louder. Intense. Begging. Pleading.

With all the rage I could muster, I drove the stake into the beating heart of Josh. Without the luxury of skin, the blood pumped through it and exploded on me. Thousands of droplets of blood showered me. I spat it from my mouth. Wiped it away from my eyes. Screamed with madness.

"There! Are you happy now?!"

Olivia still stood there in front of me. A thin smile of gratitude formed on her lips. Eyes remained infested with sorrow. "They must all be given the same mercy." She looked over to Stephanie and the baby.

I pulled the stake out of Josh and shook my head. "No, I can't do this." I threw the piece of wood back at Olivia.

"Then they will meet a fate much worse than that of death." She picked up the stake and handed it back to me, blunt end first.

I screamed as I held my head in my hands. I closed my eyes, but the visions wouldn't go away. The baby continued to cry in pain. It ripped through my ears. I placed my hands on my ears in an attempt to make it stop. "Shut that baby up!"

"Do it now, Paul."

"Please, Paul. Don't make him suffer," the body of Stephanie pleaded.

More cries. I rocked back and forth with non-human emotions. I looked at the stake, still in Olivia's hand. Still outstretched to me. "I can't do this, Olivia. I can't."

"Then they will be mine forever, Paul Isaac," Judas' voice called out.

I grabbed the stake and drove it through Stephanie's heart first, then through the new born heart. The candles flickered madly before going out. The skins behind me fell into the pool of blood at my feet. The power left the room. Darkness. Cold. Alone.

I screamed until my throat bled.

CHAPTER EIGHTEEN

I woke on the floor of the Silver Priapus for a second time, gasping for air. A forest of tables and chairs surrounded me as I tried to orientate myself and determine reality from illusion. Something I didn't know if I could do or not. I tried to convince myself of what I knew to be nothing more than vampire magic, but it still seemed so real.

Zeke Kansas' pale face hovered over me. "Saving you from the grasps of vampires is starting to get old, Paul."

"Go to hell, Kansas." I sat up as fast as I could and looked around for Allana. She had curled up under a table resembling a frightened child, but had the deadly look of a viper. One of the stakes had been either pulled free or had simply fallen out. Her fangs showed through as she started to smile. Sweat dripped from her forehead. The gunshot wound in her stomach still bled, but her strength grew at an alarming rate. Even though I would never admit it, I knew she had fed from my power as well. I gave her as much strength as she gave me. Again, I hadn't learned my lesson on blood sucker power. "Did you find what you thought you would?" Allana asked.

"Where are they?" Kansas interrupted. "Where's Stephanie?"

I tried to speak as I looked at him, but couldn't. I refused to tell him what I had seen and done. It wouldn't do either of us any good. In my mind, I had to keep telling myself none of the things I did or saw could be true.

"Tell him, Avenger. Tell them what you saw."

"You miserable freak," I started as I ran to her, pushing Kasey clear of my wrath. I flipped her table over and grabbed her by the remaining wooden stake and lifted her to her feet. I could hear her collar bone pop as I pushed the stake upward. She gave a quick gasp that almost could be disguised as pleasure. "You know as well as I do that you will have to go to him when the sun goes down. You'll have to feed and you will take us right to Judas. Like it or not."

Jaws snapped at me. Hatred filled her face. "You will never be able to save them, Avenger. You will never be able to stop the onslaught of vampires that will come here to taste your blood and take your power. Tell the detective how you killed them."

"Paul?" Kansas' face drained in front of me.

"She's lying, Kansas. I didn't kill anybody. These are the things that have been doing all the killing. Unlike you and wolf boy over there, I'm still standing on the side of humanity no matter what."

"So what did you find?" Kasey asked. His wound already showed signs of healing. By nightfall it wouldn't be anything more than a nasty little scar. I noticed the wooden stake in his hand. I had little doubt of what he planned to do with it. Wolf boy wouldn't just let our little disagreement end here. Whether Allana or I pushed up daisies at the end of the day didn't make a difference to him. On second thought, he'd choose me for the pointed end of the stake if it came down to it. I represented a threat to his unattainable piece of meat.

As I thought about it, I grabbed the stake from his hand. No reason to give him a knowing edge. "Nothing."

"Nothing?"

"You heard me."

"Skinned alive," the fang head taunted.

"Shut up!"

Kasey continued to look at me. I continued to ignore his stare. "Who was skinned alive?"

I began to push Allana through the tables and chairs. She tripped over the dead bodies that had been wolves and roaches during the fight, but my grip on the stakes wouldn't allow her to fall. "It wasn't real and you know it," I said to the blood maggot.

"What makes you think that?"

"Who was skinned alive?" This time from Kansas. Allana gripped my hands. She tried to stop our forward progress, but my adrenalin and focus were too much for her. I had to keep her from telling Kansas about the things in the illusion. Truth or lie, real or magic, I didn't need those thoughts planted in Kansas' head. Knowing I had seen his wife and son skinned and then staked them would no doubt be the last straw. "Nothing, Kansas. She's just running at the mouth."

I pushed Allana closer to the lobby area and its ample supply of large glass windows and bays of sunshine. Her jaws continued to snap at me. She fought against my strength, but with the combination of me moving forward, her moving backwards, and my ability to push with the wooden stakes and keep her feet off balance, I could force her wherever I wanted.

Kasey's big hand grabbed my shoulder, slowing my momentum. "What did you see?"

"Tell them how you saw Josh Price and Detective Kansas' wife and child skinned alive," Allana sang.

"What?"

"She's lying, Kansas. I didn't see anything."

"Then he drove a stake through each of their hearts. Killed them in cold blood." Allana turned her stare to Kansas. "I saw the whole thing happen. Pity. If you had allowed me the time, I could have saved them. My death will not change anything for you, Avenger."

I tried to push forward, only to remember Kasey's big mitt remained still against my shoulder. "Where's Angie?"

"Tell me she's lying, Paul," Kansas said as he desperately tried to gain my attention.

The room spun with unanswerable questions. Visions I couldn't erase from my mind. Anger that couldn't be restrained. I did the only thing I knew to do. I ignored them all and planned on taking it out on my victim. Killing her would stop the lies and doubts, not to mention allow me to release pinned up frustration.

I pushed Kasey's big paw away from me. A throaty roar bellowed in his throat. A musky scent danced on the air. From everything I knew about shifters, he wouldn't be able to go furry full on. Werewolves didn't need a full moon to change, but they did need lunar activity, meaning a change in the daytime was nearly impossible. Still, I knew the man-wolf could still slice me into ribbons if I took too big a chance. He lived as comfortable in the sunlight as I did.

"Tell them of the screams you heard," Allana taunted. She looked Kansas in the eyes and smiled. She baited him with far more doubt than I would be able to remove.

Allana remained only a few yards from the weakest beams of sunlight. I grew so hollow on the inside that Kasey's and Kansas' voices seemed miles away. Dream-like and unreal. I had fallen into every trap that Judas had sprung. He knew I would kill his daisy pushers. My actions had now led to the possible deaths of Josh Price, Stephanie Kansas and her unborn child. My faults had led them to meeting a horrible ending. I could have simply given Judas two humans inside The Coffin and myself, and he and his blood suckers would have went on their merry way. But something inside told me different. The monsters didn't want me to be simply dead. And I could have given him every vein in the restaurant and he would have still made this a twisted nightmare. Judas and his coven wanted to see me desperate and alone. Killing me had somehow become nothing more than a twisted game of cat and mouse.

"Where did they take Angie?" I heard Kasey ask from behind.

I looked back into the eyes of Allana. "I'm about to find out."

"Are you insane?" Kansas shouted.

"Tell me where he is," I growled as I wrestled with her strength. My feet continued to push her toward the sunlight. She would answer my questions or bake in resistance. I needed her to talk, but my personal vendetta against her and her kind overwhelmed me to the point I didn't know if I could stop once I got started. The thought of killing her consumed every action I had.

She tried to shield against my invasion, but I crawled into her thoughts. I exposed everything I could. I didn't know Josh Price well enough to have a huge emotional attachment. Stephanie might be the wife of a twisted friend in a far more twisted friendship, but now Angie had been thrown into play. My personal feelings leaked through my reality and rational thought. Throw in the fact that Kasey wanted her for his own eye candy, made me far more defensive and jealous. I still hadn't come to terms that I had feelings for Angie, but that didn't mean I wanted anyone else to have her. In my own little shreds of reality, she had become me property and I would kill and torture anyone I had to in order to get her back alive and safe. I couldn't allow or trust Kasey. He had made it perfectly clear. He had no problem selling me out to the vein weasels if it kept me away from her.

Flashes of light fell across my eyes. I could hear Judas' voice. Smell the metallic odor of blood. Vanilla and sweet perfume. Angie.

"Run!" I heard her say.

"Angie!" I screamed.

Judas mouth dripped with fresh blood. His roach power crawled through the hairs on my arm and melted with Angie's as he tasted her. His pink tongue lapped at the droplets as they fell from his chin. He would kill her simply to flush me out of hiding.

Burned skin wafted into the air. Infection. Sickness. Victor stood next to Judas, smiling and licking his lips. "I'm next to taste her, Avenger."

I pushed against Allana's power, the nausea moved the vomit from my stomach to my throat. My hands hit the floor as my strength abandoned me. I gasped against the tightness in my chest. The power rising inside me had changed. Animalistic. Strong. Growing. Close.

I looked up to see not only Kasey, but several other fur balls. Carnivorous eyes glowed with blood thirsty appetite. "You've been a part of this all along haven't you?"

Kasey kicked me in the face, sending me spinning in the air. My back snapped against one of the railings along the stage. The pain took my breath. "You should have simply died when you had the chance." Although still in human form, his eyes and hands showed the signs of the canine that clawed under the skin. "This is for my kind and a favor to the wolves that see nothing in you but the threat of pack alpha. Don't take it so personally."

I swung at his approaching bite, but his fangs dug deep, causing my muscles to revolt and twist. Other wolves joined in the fray. I could hear Kansas screaming in the distance. Shots fired. Pandemonium. I could hear Allana as she ran toward the sunlight. The smell of death filled the room as she crashed through the window. Burned flesh took my breath. Deadly sounds moved around me as I tried to lift my head. Something tried to eat me alive.

CHAPTER NINETEEN

I came to, face down in sand and rotten oranges. Fire ants had feasted on my legs and hands and turned them into infernos of agony. Now, among all my other injuries, my body had another reason to swell. I spat grit from my mouth and swatted away the biting insects as I sat up tried to orientate myself.

The darkness told me I had been here for a while. My eyes searches in all directions for anything familiar. As I sat up, an orange tree thorn impaled me in the back. I cursed under my breath as I looked through the countless rows of orange trees for any clues that might be waiting for me.

My neck ached. Puncture marks littered my body. I had been left here for dead.

As I looked at my hands in the glowing full moon, I noticed the thick coat of blood that covered them. It glittered with silt and sand and the remaining ants. Only thin lines of skin under the redness gave me any hope that I hadn't become one of the skin creatures I had experienced in Allana's eyes. I had reason to believe this blood belonged to yours truly and not some sort of fang head magic.

Thousands of crickets sang in the distance. A large barn owl sat silently on a branch in an orange tree not far from me. We made eye contact for a second before he flew from his perch and grabbed a field mouse.

I pushed against the ground in a valiant attempt to stand. My muscles were sluggish and resisted any movement what-so-ever. Being the stubborn cuss that I knew to be true, I ignored the pain and got to my feet. Sure, I might be alive, but that didn't mean much. The night allowed things to hide among shadows, and I had grown really tired of being someone's chew toy.

Between the darkness and the disorientation, I hadn't decided which way to walk. Every alleyway between the orange trees seemed to be a dead end. I pulled a large branch of thorns from my jeans and moved along the path to my right. Eventually, it had to come out somewhere.

I checked my holsters for the Magnum, 9mm, stakes, knives, and holy water. It all seemed to be there. I continually checked them again as I walked knowing that by some mysterious force, they could disappear without constant supervision. Having all my weapons only led me to believe that whatever had placed me here, didn't think I'd ever wake up. Kasey and his fur balls didn't think it would matter if I had weapons with me, because they didn't expect me to rise from the shallow grave. This had been planned to look like a roach attack.

Habit had me reach for a cigar. I thought better of the act. My stomach threatened to revolt if I continued the act. I returned it to my shirt pocket. Fresh, warm blood tricked down my body from wounds I'd find later. It didn't make sense to worry about them now. I couldn't stop the flow of blood or dress the gashes at the moment if I had to.

My steps picked up pace as my muscles loosened. A full on run still didn't seem possible. It didn't matter how much cockroach and fur ball virus I had in me. When things bite you, it hurts and hurts a lot. I looked up at the glowing moon and knew the monsters that had her still roamed the streets at full power and at any moment I could be face to face with Judas yet again.

I thought about Angie. She had to be alive. Nothing in this city had ever proven to be more bad ass. But in the hands of these new coffin nappers, I knew even Angie had been out powered. Even if she had turned for a few minutes, I knew her strength wouldn't come back enough to protect herself.

I shuffled through the dead leaves and stepped on rotting oranges as I made my way through the grove. An overwhelming smell of life and death fought for supremacy. A light wind blew through the branches, setting off a chorus of dancing leaves that sounded more like a bucket of rattlesnakes than anything else. In the distance, I swore I heard footsteps matching my pace. I stopped and listened. Funny how the darkness played with the mind.

Behind me, I caught the glimpse of a shadow moving with speed. I grabbed the Magnum and hunched behind an orange tree. My muscles grew tight. Pain filled me. A rabbit scurried along the path, catching moonlight as he ran.

I exhaled as I laughed at myself. Relieved that the bunny of death had left me in one piece. I stood again, brushed away the sand from my knees and continued my walk.

Ahead, about five hundred yards, I could hear the sounds of cars moving by from time to time. I smiled. I had picked the right direction. Now, I frowned. No one in their right mind would give a six and a half foot man dressed in leather, covered in blood, with tats up his arms and a Magnum on his hip, a ride. My best chance of making it out alive relied on finding out where me feet were planted, call Price and have him pick me up. Once I got to the road, I would be able to know my whereabouts. All roads have a name.

To my right, a branch snapped. I did my best not to react. I continued to walk, pretending I didn't hear it. I pivoted my head with as little movement as I could. I could feel it now. Roach power trickled across my skin in countless droplets. My muscles twitched with electricity.

In the moonlight, I could make out a shadow. It tried to remain camouflaged in the trees, but the night glow gave it away. I gripped the Magnum again, but kept my pace the same. Whatever planned to suck me would have to do it on the run.

I sighted a clearing twenty yards ahead. I remained on the defensive. My stalked would have to come within inches of me to kill. I only had to get off one clean shot. I couldn't help the smile that rose on my lips.

The blood that covered most of my body had been nothing more than a calling card of every hungry vein licker in the area. I had risen as nothing more than a quick meal on the run. But tonight wouldn't be his night. If this vein licker wanted to stay alive, he would look elsewhere for a warm meal.

As I reached the clearing, I slowed my pace. To kill the enemy, you have to flush him out into the open. And to do that you have to appear vulnerable and delicious. I hoped in the end, I'd be neither.

The first attack came on my blindside. I refused to fall to

the ground as his fingers dug into my fresh wounds. His weight fell on top of me. I turned and slammed him against one of the orange trees, hearing the branch snap as it pierced him. Hands loosened almost immediately.

I spun to meet my attacker when the second coffin muncher appeared. His bite would come seconds too late. I brought the Magnum up and pointed it in his face. I puckered my lips and blew him a kiss as I pulled the trigger.

He tensed for the blow. Eyes grew as big as baseballs as the bullet lodged in his chest. Dead matter exploded through his back. Orange light flowed through the wound, ending in glowing ash.

Before I had time to dwell on my success, I turned to the other blood leech and gave him the same medicine. His hand reached out to me, begging for mercy. In my own way, I gave it to him. He would never have to roam the earth again as a blood bat. He owed me one.

In my peripheral vision, I could see him already as he stood along the path, outlined in moonlight. His power triggered the hair on my arm. A third vein weasel approached. I pulled the Magnum up on him.

As he drew closer I could see the smile on his face. They weren't here to feed. They were here to try and beat Judas and Sasha to killing me. Now my mind raced with thoughts of how many more might be lurking out of sight. Power attracted them every bit as much as blood.

I kept the Magnum on him. He raced through the trees, never giving me a clear shot. The shadows danced around him as he moved in and out of the moonlight. My eyes watched in all directions. There could easily be more. Something told me to simply run.

I pulled the trigger. It grazed the side of his head, but for all intent purposes, I missed my target. This blood sucker proved to be both, ugly and fast. I hoped and prayed the sound of the Magnum would cause any others to turn and run.

He slammed into me. Fingernails dug into my face. Hands turned into fists that pounded me again and again. My Magnum fought for another shot. His body forced the shooting hand to the ground. Nails dug deep. Muscles protested against the pain. Fingers released the weapon. I cursed under my breath. His face grew close to mine mixed with sweat and crud. "I've tasted her." A free hand grabbed a wooden stake from around my waist.

My body grew stiff. Fear raced through me. The removal of the stake a mere distraction. "What?" I had hoped I hadn't heard right.

The evil laughter terrorized me. "Her blood is as intoxicating as her beauty. Perhaps after I dispose of you, I shall feel her pleasure against me another time before draining her."

Then, I did the unthinkable. I pulled my head forward toward the slime ball and bit into his neck. I ripped and shook with every ounce of strength I had. Warm blood filled my mouth. I wanted to wretch and swallow at the same time. Skin stuck to my teeth. The roach howled in pain as he pulled away.

He stood over me and held the wound as blood leaked through his pale fingers. Disgust filled his stare, but then turned to joy. "That's more like it, vampire. Taste her blood. Allow it to linger on your tongue and trickle down your throat. You have come so far. It will be such a shame to kill you and leave you for the rats and dogs." He drove the wooden stake between my sternum and collarbone.

The pain took my breath away. Nausea nearly took me to my knees. Sweat sprouted across my forehead. Vision grew black. I found myself paralyzed, but able to think clearly. A very scary combination. My hands grabbed the stake. My body convulsed and I fought for breath. I could see his shadow move above me. His power added to my discomfort. Unable to stop him in any way.

I could feel his breath against my ear. "How does it feel, Avenger? Knowing I will be the one that not only kills you, but will suck the life out of your wolf as well." He pushed on the stake as he rose again. "My only regret is that you will not live long enough to know she is dead and being eaten by the zombies of the underworld."

His deadly power released me as he perched in the top of one of the nearby trees. I spat blood from my mouth. His, I hoped. There were some serious doubts in that, though. My hands remained wrapped around the stake. Not much larger than a tent stake in size, but the pain spread through me and grew from the inside and worked through my chest.

My fingers reached for the Magnum, still to my left. I refused to give into the relentless pain. I gasped for air as I drowned on my own blood. The metal of the gun made the pain subside. In the moonlight, I pulled the trigger, but fell back to the ground, unable to see if I hit my mark.

I knew the roach wouldn't live long enough to get back to Angie, even if he succeeded in taking my life. The roach energy coming from him had been rather weak. My death would be his demise. It would mark his own death. By taking my life, would make him the new master of the city and we both knew that Judas didn't care which of us died. The albatross would be around his neck if he became the new fang head. Knowing this little detail still gave me the advantage. For now.

My hands grabbed a nearby branch. With one knee on the ground, I caught what little breath I could. My muscles tightened, but instead of the weak feeling I expected, I actually felt good. That is, for someone that had a piece of wood stuck through their chest.

The blood of the roach had been my life saver. I couldn't deny it. When I bit the roach and drank the blood of Angie, mixed with his own, it gave me the strength that I needed to come back to my feet. For someone with a piece of wood sticking through their chest, I felt pretty good.

The monster came back down on me, but this time I had prepared for the attack. I pulled the trigger as he reached me. The heat of the bullet warmed me. A storm of ash spiraled across my face and danced to the ground.

I didn't have time to admire my handy work. I had to get out of here fast. I still had no guarantee that there weren't more waiting on me. And even if there weren't. They would be here soon.

The ground seemed to roll as I tried to walk. Visions were blurred, sounds muffled. I balanced myself by holding on to the stake. Somehow it seemed to help keep me from falling. Breath came in labored pain. If I had anything in my stomach, it tried to come out.

As I reached the black ribbon of the two lane road ahead

of me, I saw the approaching headlights and heard the growl of a semi. I stood in the middle of the road and waved my arms the best I could. The stake limited my movement.

With both hands I pulled hard on it, feeling it give a little. Pain forced me to let go. Warm blood moved down my chest. I gathered my strength and courage and yanked again. The stake came free. My knees buckled under me and I had to reach down with my hand to keep from falling on my face.

The lights of the semi grew brighter and closer. A quick blow of the horn let me know he saw me. Getting him to stop would be another job. But I held my ground and stood in the middle of the yellow lines, waving with everything I had, the best I could. He would either stop or run over me. I couldn't honestly say it mattered which.

I heard the Jake brake engage and my heart fluttered with excitement. With all the energy I had left, I ran toward the stopping semi.

The driver opened the door, grabbing his red baseball hat. He looked like a ball with legs, brown flannel shirt, jeans and boots. At best five and a half feet tall. I could tell I looked like hell by his reaction. "Jesus, buddy, what happened to you?"

"I need your truck." I grabbed the chrome railing and stepped on the fuel tank.

"What?" Confusion mixed with fear. I could see the wheels turning in his head. I didn't feel like fighting. Inside, I begged him to just play along.

"I'll get it back to you. This is an emergency." It took all my breath to talk.

"You ain't takin' my truck." He started to shut the door. I pushed it back open with my body.

I pulled out the 9mm from its holster. I didn't plan on shooting him, but he didn't know that. "Get out or move over. I'm not going to argue with you."

All blood left his face. Passing out suddenly came into play. He shook his head and slowly slid to the other side of the truck. I moved in and bent over the wheel. Vampire virus or not, the pain caused me to wince and grunt as I moved.

"What are you goin' to do?"

My anger rose as I looked ahead, along the shoulder of

the road. Victor's car sat there, only the park lights glowed. He had sent the roaches to find me. The scar faced son of a bitch had been waiting for me and if it hadn't been for the semi, he might have succeeded in killing me. I pushed myself back in the seat and swallowed. Thirst burned my throat. I closed the door, pushed in the clutch, and shifted gears. "I'm going to kill a vampire."

CHAPTER TWENTY

The massive diesel engine on the Kenworth growled along the narrow roads, Victor's automobile just out of reach. I shifted again, grinding gears as I pumped the clutch. Amber lights glowed in the darkness. Each shift reminded me of the wound in my chest, causing me to bend with pain. I fought the urge to pass out. I refused to think about how bad my injuries might be. Killing Victor gained me all the motivation I needed to stay alive.

Maps and adult magazines decorated the cab. A mix of stale cigarettes and old coffee filled my nose. The CB squawked with static as a dim light glowed from the front. A set of blue fuzzy dice hung from the visor on the passenger's side of the truck. The man beside me caught me staring at the novelty. "A little old for stuffed animals aren't you?"

"It's my handle. They call me the Gambler."

I felt bad when I remembered I still had my 9mm on him. Without fanfare, I put it away and hoped it wouldn't come back to haunt me. Chances were good that the Gambler had a piece in the truck and it would soon be pointed back at me. Better to die by trigger than fang, I will always say.

I never answered as I drove my attention back to the road and tried desperately to pick up speed. The big rig purred with power, but when you're used to a 426 hemi of Detroit horsepower, the massive monster I controlled now, could never feel anything other than sluggish. On the other hand it would get me back to Bat Town. I doubted that I would get there fast enough to suit me.

In the distance, I could see the taillights of Victor's black Chrysler 300. Revenge pushed me forward. I still had every intention of going on a killing spree once I got into Bat Town, but now I had the chance to get one of them on the way. Not your everyday bat head. The one responsible for most of my damages over the last forty eight hours.

The Gambler remained silent as we hit the interstate at nearly a hundred miles an hour. If he had a weapon, so far he hadn't reached for it. The weight of the truck shifted violently. The mike to the CB slide from its perch and slapped me in the face. My shoulder slammed against the door with the inertia. My chest bit with pain. I swallowed a scream. The Gambler's eyes never left me, mouth moving in silence. I couldn't blame him. I had appeared out of an orange grove covered in blood and sand and a hole in my chest, not to mention, I had pulled a gun on him and stole his truck. I somehow doubted we were going to be best buddies sharing stories over a hot cup of coffee anytime soon.

"You're him, aren't you?" he finally said in a nervous soft voice.

"Who?"

"That guy that got into all that trouble a few years back for killing the wrong vampire. The one with the priest."

"Yeah, that was me." I shot a glare to him. It still remained a touchy subject after all these years. After all the years of hearing it from vein weasels, I thought I had become used to it, but now my fellow man looked at me as some sort of monster. Nobody ever mentioned it and said thank you for ridding the word of one more vein mole. Instead, they looked at me as if I would do the same to them. I didn't get the reactions. I shook my head as I shoved my way through the traffic, keeping pace with Victor's car.

As we moved down the interstate, headlights blinded me. A sea of red lights moved in and out of my way as I desperately tried to catch Victor's car. I put a hand to my chest. Partly to try an ease the throbbing pain, but more to see if the bleeding had at least slowed. My hand came back warm and wet. Painted in dark red.

I looked down at my chest and along my arms. My concoction of viruses were keeping me from dying where I stood. The wound in my chest looked small, but deep. I hoped it didn't puncture a lung. Each time I tried to take a deep breath, the pain shot through my body, causing me to double over and scream.

Two cars separated Victor's Chrysler from the semi, each in a different lane and blocked my forward progress. My headlights illuminated the inside of the car in front of me as though someone had suddenly turned on a switch. I flashed the lights and pulled on the air horn. At first it didn't seem to cause my desired result, but as I added a little bumper, I gained all the necessary real estate.

Horns blared. Tires squalled. In my mirrors, I could see the car slide to the shoulder of the road. No more damage done than a few scratches and dirty underwear. All in all, in comparison to what I had gone through, they were lucky. "Sorry," I said under my breath.

"You're going to get us killed!" the Gambler shouted as his right hand shot up and hit the roof for stability. Honestly, he had been far less animated than I would have been in his situation. I kept the weapon I had in his view, hoping he wouldn't try something really stupid. That little fact alone made this chase easier to deal with.

I looked over to him, but again, never said much more than a grunt. My foot kicked something hard from under my feet. I mashed the accelerator again. Black smoke poured from the stacks. The smell of diesel filled my nostrils. Flashes of white paint zipped by as I pushed the petal as far as it would go.

"So, what did he do?"

I couldn't believe what I heard. "I'm covered in blood, a freaking hole in my chest and you're asking what he did?" I cursed under my breath. Then realized I had been a bit of an ass. "He's tried to kill me twice in as many nights. Not to mention I have reason to believe he has kidnapped a woman and possibly killed another and her child. Killing him will be too easy." I looked over to him again. "You do have insurance don't you?"

He shook his head and looked forward again. I had no doubt he wouldn't forget me as long as he lived. Our tale would be told in every truck stop across America.

In no time at all, we were approaching the exit to Church Street. I saw Victor hit the brakes slightly to make the turn. I would have to do much more. I planned on using the roach's car as my skid mark. The problem with the plan blared in my eyes.

There were a lot of innocent people that were within harm's way. My vengeance blinded my thoughts, but I couldn't simply slam into cars and take the chance of killing people. It didn't make me any better than the monsters. Then again, being a monster had put me in this scenario.

The light turned green. Brake lights went to dull red. Adrenalin pushed me forward. If I slammed into vehicles, at least they wouldn't be at a standstill. Not that it made it right, but justification for my future actions were based on my growing insanity.

I hit the Chrysler with all the force I could. It spun to my right. I could hear the glass in the back window shatter. Tires barked in protest. Metal crunched and ripped. The semi jumped in the air and came down with a violent bounce. My injuries forced me to bend forward. I let go of the steering wheel, shooting the rig inches short of jackknifing.

"You're going to get us killed!" the Gambler repeated. "Are you insane?"

"I tried to get you to jump out of the truck." I looked in the oversized side mirror, trying to see what damage I had done to Victor's car and hopefully its driver. Glass glittered in the headlights. My foot stomped on the brakes. I could smell the burning rubber as the lethargic beast tried to succumb to my command.

The Chrysler appeared to be crippled. Most of the trunk had become wadded metal, yet the fang head scrambled inside in jerky motion. Being far less fragile than humans, the daisy pusher would leave the scene of the crash with nothing more than an insurance claim.

The Chrysler now sat in the road perpendicular from my semi. Again, I pushed in the clutch and shifted gears. Drivers and passengers from nearby cars jumped and scrambled out of the way.

"Please, you can't do this," the Gambler called out. "Vampire or not, this is my truck. I'm calling the police." With that, he pulled out his cell phone.

"With everything that just happened, do you really think you need to call the police? I'm sure they have had at least a thousand calls about a maniac in a semi off of Church Street trying to kill someone. Save your minutes and hold on."

As we approached the car, I saw a figure move from the far side. Victor. His pale face shinned in the single remaining headlight on the Kenworth. For someone about to be road kill, he seemed to be moving very methodical. He had accepted my challenge.

He jumped on the roof and awaited the impact. I hesitated. My big balls shrunk a size as he stood there waiting for me. When it stands there in defiance, you begin to think about your actions. Your mind begins to play tricks with the possibility that the prey might know something you don't. And in my world, that mistake usually left you six feet under.

I remained committed. The semi groaned with strain. I pushed it far past its capacity. The Gambler remained stiff and silent. Eyes bulged from his head.

The impact filled every sense in my body. Forceful. Violent. Destructive. Metal against metal. Explosions flashed from under the rig as I went air borne. We floated across the air in an eerie silence, followed by a bone jarring slam to the earth again. My ribs hit against the steering wheel. I slammed back into the seat. The semi tilted to its side. My body slammed against the driver's door with violent force. Old coffee cups, paper, and glass danced on my skin as it sought out the ground again.

The Gambler hung above me. The seatbelt the only thing that kept him from falling from the top of the truck.

The body of the truck slid against the pavement. The large trailer behind us pushed with the strength of a locomotive. My shoulder only inches away from the ground beneath me. I held tight to the steering wheel. If I let go, I'd be skinned alive.

Before the truck came to a full stop, I reached for the Magnum and crawled free from the belts. Victor lurked somewhere within biting distance. I could feel him more than see him. And with the semi now on its side, the advantage swung back into his favor.

I didn't have to wait long. A pasty white hand smashed through the windshield, dumping a flood of glass on me and the Gambler. Demonic eyes looked back as me. Fangs sharp and ready. Blood slithered down the damaged cheek. "Time to die, Avenger."

As I pulled the trigger, I heard Victor scream. He moved with incredible power and speed. Glass shattered around me. He remained invisible as I spun for a visual. I could hear his footsteps as they moved along the cab. I followed with the Magnum and fired again and again with synchronized explosions. Along the street, I could hear the screams of by-standers, searching for safe haven along the nooks and crannies.

A trickle of blood came from the Gambler's head. It didn't seem like all that deep of a cut, but then again, when compared to mine, most wounds would be about as deadly as paper cuts. For extra kicks and giggles, I pulled the large silver bladed knife from its sheath. Never know when one might have the chance to torture before the kill. "You're going to be alright," I added as I made my way out of the windshield.

I crawled onto the pavement and caught the outline of his shadow above me. Another cockroach myth is that the creatures don't cast shadows or have reflections. Not true. And it gave me a sliver of an advantage. Without the shadow, I'd never had seen him.

Victor jumped from the cab and attempted to land on top of me. I rolled onto my back and held the knife upward toward the monster. The silver blade ripped through his flesh. I could hear the cry of pain as he slid from the blade and landed on the ground. His hands rushed to the wound. I squirmed with pain myself as his elbow caught me right in the chest. It seemed to take forever as I tried to catch my next breath.

I rose to my feet and ignored the pain. Ignored every sight and sound around me except the ugly creature in front of me. I had totaled a man's semi, put not only his life, but the life of many others in danger, and backing away from the fight never crossed my mind. Killing Victor would send a message back to not only Judas and Sasha, but to Kasey as well.

I pushed the knife back into its sheath. Victor stood in the glow of headlights that had long since come to a stop. I could hear the approaching sirens; see the red and blue of the flashing lights. The Magnum raised in an act of self-preservation. Preservation of my species.

Victor stood in defiance. The Magnum I had aimed at his head, didn't seem to intimidate him at all. Perhaps he had seen things my way and wanted to end it all. Push up daisies for real this time. I pulled the trigger. Victor fell on the blind side of the overturned semi. Screams filled the air. Sirens grew closer. I reloaded.

With as much caution as the situation would allow, I moved around the front of the semi. I looked into the eyes of the countless by-standers that gathered along the sidewalk, no more than fifty feet from me. I saw the same looks of horror and disbelief as I saw the night Father Garcia and I killed the fang maggot years earlier. Like the gathering mob that night, I had little doubt this one would find me out of line and see me as nothing more than a cold blooded killing lunatic. Piss off. I didn't care about public opinion. If I had anything to do with it, Victor would die tonight.

I sucked myself against the grill and still glowing headlights of the truck. Magnum ready. Body not so much. I took a breath. Then held it. The wound reminded me I still needed attention.

I swung the Magnum around the corner of the semi, instantly firing a shot. I screamed as I released the bottled up fear. My feet slid about two inches forward as I slipped in oil. I
looked down. It wasn't oil, but blood. Fresh and tasty. Not in an appetizer sort of way, but instead, it gave me hope and promise that Victor might be oozing from more spots than just his face. Usually with the ultra violet bullets, one shot will do the trick, but I have had a few that took on a few more holes before flurrying away.

My movements became spasms. He could be anywhere. With guarded apprehensions, I spun in a circle, looked up and then under the semi. Nothing. I looked in the thousand or so faces that looked back at me with mouths wide open. Nothing. There were no screams. No movement. He had simply vanished.

But he had left me a trail. Looking back down at my feet I saw them. Small, dime sized droplets of blood, leading away from the street. I smiled on the inside. I might get to kill a roach after all.

My feet began to move. The pain in my chest started to dull to a constant throb. The blood, nothing more than tacky, coagulating liquid. It would still be hours before a doctor could put me back together. I'd rather die in the streets tonight than be stitched up and know I had allowed the deaths to accumulate.

"Master Vampire," I heard from behind me. Most of his body still remained hidden behind the wreckage of the semi.

I turned. Magnum in one hand, wooden stake in the other. The cockroach smiled back. Weaker than Victor, but strong enough to take my life. One reason he had been successful in sneaking up on me. I could barely feel his power. Chances were good, this one hadn't been a drinker for very long.

"You smell delicious." He raised his head into the air and took in a deep breath. I laughed. The undead didn't breathe. Then those sinister eyes dropped back on me. "To think I will drink your blood and become master vampire all in one feeding." His smile spread wide.

"You're going to die hungry."

. "Who's to say I haven't already fed." From out of view, the blood tick pulled The Gambler into view.

The Gambler's pale face shined in the numerous lights around us. His face showed the undeniable fear. His pants were wet. His body shook. "Please help me," he cried.

I gave him a weak nod. "I'm going to, Gambler. It's the least I could do for dragging you into all of this." I kept the Magnum on the monster.

"How do you plan to do that?" it asked.

"Gambler, move your head to the right a little please."

He looked at me with confusion.

"Now!"

He moved. I pulled the trigger. Brain, bones, blood and matter exploded into the air. A taste of sulfur filled my mouth. The Gambler dropped to the ground. The body of the roach twitched on the ground. Headless.

"Who are you?" the Gambler asked as he scooted away from me.

"He's one of my anger management patients," a voice answered.

CHAPTER TWENTY-ONE

I turned my head to find the source of the words. It didn't come as a surprise. I did my best to hide the continuous throbs of pain shooting through my body. With the amount of excursion I had done and the fact that I smoked, catching my breath seemed impossible. Having a hole through my shoulder didn't make the act any easier. "Dr. Feelgood," I acknowledged as I kept the Magnum handy. Victor's power had evaporated, but I knew he remained somewhere close by.

Most of her patients called her Dr. Lydia Petty. I had been ordered to see her for my anger issues by *those that run the city*, which is a nice way of saying 'cockroaches'. I took in her short yet wide frame. Glasses at the tip of her nose. Large round eyes peeking through the frames. She had 'nerd' written all over her. Worst of all, Dr. Petty was a roach actrivist, which with my line of work, instantly made us bitter enemies. I knew justifying my actions would be a waste of time. She would only see the mad man behind it all. I simply stood there and waited for that mouth to open with stinging words.

Then things got worse. Dieter stepped out of the crowd next to her and looked down at the cockroach I had turned into a fine ash. "I see it is a busy night for you, Avenger. You lookas if something tried to eat you for dinner." His black pupils seemed to fill in the whites of his eyes. An abyss of darkness tried to dig its way out of his head. As tall as me, Dieter looked like something out of a gothic comic book. Gaunt and sickly. Sunken cheeks that left shadows in his face.

Although dressed in an expensive grey suit, red shirt and very vogue shoes, all I saw equaled pain in the ass. He stood so still, anyone could have mistaken him for a mannequin that had mysteriously been left on the sidewalk. His pale skin caught the neon reflections and caused him to glow in a rainbow of colors.

With what I had done, these two were the last I needed to see tonight. Dr. Feelgood would find a way to make this bite me in the ass, and with the death of a fellow vein muncher, Dieter would testify the killing to be unjustified. I looked around at all the faces in the distant crowd. Tonight's little killing wouldn't be justified from anyone's perspective other than mine. I stood alone against the city at the moment and still had no proof if Victor survived or not.

I looked at the two of them and shook my head. "Don't tell me this is your date for the evening, Feelgood? Even you can do better than this." I lowered the Magnum, but never put it away. Dieter and I had a long history and none of it could be called pleasant. I didn't think he had the guts to try anything here, but taking chances only got you killed. After all, he worked as Quinn's right hand man.

Feelgood refused to answer at first. Again I smiled. The more I could make her hate me, the less time I'd have to spend in her office. "It's so good to see that the therapy is working, Paul. I hardly noticed you among all the destruction, gun fire, and killing. Thanks to you, I feel safe to walk among the living dead." She shook with disgust. Therapy at its best for me. "No worries though. With all the witnesses here tonight, the next time we talk, you'll be behind bars. Where you should have been all along. Even those that were loyal to you won't be able to shovel you out of this."

Dieter placed his arm around Feelgood. I couldn't tell if it had been to protect her or console her. Her hair matted in the thick gel in his hair. A waft of cheap cologne attacked my sense of smell. "Even those that object vampire rights will turn against you. Tonight it was human lives that you placed in harm's way."

"What have you been eating that smells so bad? You smell like ass." I walked up to my two friends, slid between them, and wrapped an arm around each of their shoulders. The blood loss made me a bit dizzy. I used them as crutches as I continued to try and catch my breath. "So what brings you kids down here on such a lovely evening?" The temptation to bang their heads together nearly distracted me.

Feelgood tried to free herself from my hug, I kept firm. But that mouth remained free as a bird. "Oh, I don't know, the usual I guess. We came here looking for a demented idiot that would steal a semi, drive it into a crowd of people, turn it on its side, then get out and kill vampires in cold blood." She looked up at me. "And low and behold, here you are."

Dieter shoved me free of Feelgood and himself. "You have blood all over you. And I find it highly unlikely the doctor would prefer your disgusting hands on her."

She checked her black dress for signs of blood. She tried to do it without me catching her, but no such luck. Telling someone they have blood on them and then thinking they wouldn't look is not human nature. Hell, I even looked.

"She's hanging around with you, Dieter. Something tells me her tolerance level for disgusting things is pretty high. What is it they say, when you sleep with dogs, you wake up with fleas." I pivoted around in search of anything that might be sneaking up on me. "Don't guess you've told her about Judas and all the fun he's been having with human lives have you?"

Dieter tried to hide the smirk on his face but failed. "What Judas has done is no worse than a man that drives a massive vehicle into an innocent crowd."

Along the street I saw the flashing lights of police and rescue vehicles arriving. I had to make this conversation short. I didn't have time to be bogged down with police reports tonight. "There's a new bat boy in town that has kidnapped Detective Kansas' wife, Price's grandson, and my... and Angie." Talk about your Freudian slips. I made a major one.

"*You're* Angie?" Dieter asked. A crooked smile joined his otherwise ugly mug. "Perhaps it is not me that is sleeping with dogs."

"Don't you have to turn into a bat and fly away somewhere?" I hated this cockroach more than any of the others. Not that I saw him as dangerous. Simply that he had achieved the most points for fang ass of the century. Again, I tried to talk to Feelgood. "His name is Judas. He, along with all the other neck biters, have it in their heads that I'm some damn master roach and wants to kill me. Cockroach rights or not, I'm not going to be the biting end of his twisted game." I turned to Dieter, allowing the Magnum to move against his chest. "Where did Victor go?"

"Why would I know, master vampire?"

I started to say something really nasty, when Feelgood spoke up. "According to what I have heard, Detective Price's grandson killed a vampire a couple of nights ago in cold blood. If that is true, he will be tried and punished. As for what you claim this Judas has against you because you are some sort of master vampire seems a bit of a stretch. I've heard you use some incredible excuses for shooting up this town, but this one really takes the cake, so to speak."

Time ticked away. "According to cockroach rules since I have their virus in my blood and have killed Asa, it makes me a master blood sucker. Now Judas, Victor, Sasha among others are trying to kill me to become the next true master of the city. And they are using an innocent man, a pregnant woman and a wolf to do it. It's sick and it's insane." I turned to Dieter. "So if you know where I can find Judas or Victor, you better tell me now. If he kills those people and I find out you and Quinn knew where to find them, I'll be back for you."

Dieter laughed first, but Feelgood spoke. "You? A master vampire? How wonderfully horrible for you."

"First thing we've ever agreed on. Last night he kidnapped Angie while the fur balls left me for dead in an orange grove. Victor is trying to align himself with whoever can gain him the most power. And now Kasey and the wolves are involved."

"If all that you say is true, Avenger, why are you so insistent on killing Victor rather than Judas? Killing Victor will gain you nothing, will it not?" Dieter continued to manipulate the conversation.

"Victor isn't ready to kill me yet. He knows if he does, Judas will come looking for him. He's hoping that I kill Judas and Sasha. He wants to be close by if I do. Then he'll try to kill me and become the new fang king." I surveyed the crowd for Victor again. I gathered my nerve to ask the real question. It would be well thought out and articulate…"And he knows where Angie is." Okay, maybe not.

"What makes you think such a preposterous thing?"

Dieter asked. "You have said yourself that it is Judas that has Angela, not Victor."

"When one of his thugs attacked me in the orange grove I tasted her in his…" I refused to finish that sentence. Inside I kicked myself for saying that much. I started to pace.

"Tasted her what?" Dieter's voice flowed low and hypnotic. He had waited to pounce on me and now he had his chance.

"Nothing."

Feelgood shot a glance to Dieter as he smiled even wider. "You tasted her in his blood did you not?"

I ignored the question and spoke to Feelgood. "If you've heard anything about where these people are or the vein robbers that have them, I'm begging you to tell me. This isn't about roach politics, or even you and me, it's about human lives. Innocent human lives." I went for a real guilt trip. I knew in normal circumstances she wouldn't tell me anything if it meant a coffin napper's death, but put in a pinch of human life and I might get those lips to loosen a little. "My God, Feelgood, there's an unborn baby in harm's way here. If I don't find Judas and end this, I'm afraid a lot of people will die."

"Including you." Feelgood said it as if it were the answer to all the world's problems. She turned to Dieter. "Do you know about this Judas vampire?"

Dieter gave a shrug. "I know of his coven. And the Avenger is right. They are attracted to his power and status. Covet it would be a better choice of word." He looked to me. "Only a true vampire could taste and gain power from lycan blood, so Judas' claim has some merit." Dieter acted as though he had slipped into deep thought. Not something I thought he could do. He glanced at Feelgood, then looked back to me. "The only true solution to this situation is for Paul and Judas to come before a Vampire Council for resolution." His dead eyes looked back at me. I refused to meet the gaze. "But be aware, Avenger, that under Vampire law, what Judas is doing is not only justified, but encouraged. The Council will always want what is best and who is strongest for its territories. I think we both know that in this instance that Judas is far superior to you and will abide by vampire law with far more conviction, making him a far more desirable candidate." He lifted a finger to emphasize his next spew of lies. "Keep in mind, from this day forward, any vampire you kill, will be subject to Council scrutiny and you could possibly be tried by vampire law, not human law. I would suggest you be more frugal in whom you kill from now on. There is already rumor of a pregnant vampire that has been tortured and killed. If this is true by you or one of your vampires, terrible retribution awaits you. Killing such a vampire is considered the greatest crime of all against the species. The Council will show no mercy if found guilty."

"I didn't kill her." Why I answered that to Dieter, I'm not sure. Perhaps I simply needed to hear myself say it out loud. I thought about the baby and what Kansas had done. I had justified my actions, but to Judas, the Council, or even human authority, it might not be as cut and dry. My dance card remained full already, no time for another thing like this to slow me down. I only hoped his wife and unborn son didn't have to pay the price for his stupidity.

The crowd grew thicker by the minute. Seas of cell phones recorded me. I had to go. I looked past Feelgood and Dieter and saw the seven or eight police officers moving in our direction. Hands were already pointed at me. I looked down at the Gambler, still in some state of shock. A small huddle of good Samaritans were tending to him. He'd be okay. I convinced myself of the lie.

I did my best to evaporate through the crowd as Feelgood shouted. She wouldn't cover for me anymore than her dead date. Inside, I grew tired of running from things. And lately, there had been a lot of things to run from.

CHAPTER TWENTY-TWO

It had been nearly twenty-four hours since Judas had taken Angie. Even after a night of torturing everything in Bat Town with fangs as to the whereabouts of Judas and Victor, no one talked. Thanks to me, in more ways than one.

I stood at the precipice of insanity, ready to jump. Madness consumed me. The thought of death seemed like a plausible solution, but suicide solved nothing for me. One, I wouldn't let the blood suckers have that satisfaction, and two, not even hell could keep me from finding Angie and getting her to a safe place. She had put her life on the line for me without thought, and I would do the same.

My strides grew faster as I thought about everything. The police would be looking for me, the roaches would be doing the same. If I wanted to see Angie, Stephanie or Josh alive again I had to catch a break and catch it fast.

Dr. Feelgood had blown my phone up with messages. She really thought she could help me with my irrational hatred of vein lickers. What a load of crock therapy had become. I was in no mood to talk about anything that had to do with cockroaches unless it dealt with a stake through the heart. Misunderstood, my behind. They were nothing short of killing machines.

I needed a good night's sleep. But I couldn't justify it. There were innocent victims being used simply to get me to conform to twisted cockroach pleasure and profit. Staying awake helped me avoid the nightmares that were sure to follow.

As I walked I tried to call Father Garcia once again, only getting his voice mail. Something lingered in the back of my mind to go there, but I couldn't take the chance of bringing all my little demons with me again. Guilt rode me. I had made my choice. Angie over Father Garcia. The ultimate damned if you do, damned if you don't situation.

I pulled the keys to the 'Cuda from my pocket. Above me, nothing but black sky. All had been gobbled up in a blanket of obsidian evil.

My cell phone buzzed again. I looked at it. "Price," I said under my breath. He'd have to wait. Like Feelgood, he had called me relentlessly. I understood the why behind it, but so far I had nothing new to tell him. I let it go to voice mail.

My feet came to a stop. My body froze in place. I had no reason to suddenly grow afraid other than through intuition. And it usually proved to be right.

Two sheets of paper flapped under the windshield wiper of the 'Cuda. One, a pink copy of a ticket, which I half way expected. But the other one made my heart beat fast.

I began to walk again, picking up the pace. Fingers reached for the paper, grasping it as gently as shards of glass. Holding it in my hands, I noticed the crimson corner to be blood. Still wet to the touch. My nose could smell the metallic odor, both enticing and vile.

Experience had taught me to reach for the Magnum, and take a mental inventory of all the killing devices I had on me. A growing obsessive compulsive behavior, but one I hoped I never found a cure for. Squashing such behaviors only would leave me in tiny pieces of skin under a vampire's fingernail.

Images of Angie ran through my head in flashing scenarios. I prayed an agnostic prayer to the Christian God that my initial thoughts weren't correct. Helplessness already filled me even though my eyes hadn't read the note.

Unfolding the paper seemed to take hours, each crease weighed tons, exposed and spilled out fears that were, so far, still in my mind.

The cell phone buzzed. Price again. I cursed him under my breath. I knew I needed to answer the call, but I needed to sort through things I knew I couldn't handle. Again, I let it go to voice mail.

With the note now unfolded in my cradled hands, my eyes read it a thousand times trying to understand what it meant and knowing what it meant all at the same time. My mind raced with thoughts at a rate that I couldn't comprehend. I refused to accept my assumptions as truth. There had to be another explanation.

FORGIVE ME FATHER FOR I HAVE SINNED. The words were written in what appeared to be human blood. My head spun as I fell into the car and started it up. Hands reached for the cell phone that I had ignored. Like a bitter pill, I swallowed the fear and called Price.

"About time you answered your phone," I heard on the other end. His voice agitated and high. A bad sign. "And I already know about the psycho stunt show you put on down in Bat Town so don't bother lying to me about that. God, Paul, I need to talk to you now!"

I closed my eyes and tried to keep the panic attack as far in the back of my throat as I could. "Father Garcia," choked out of my mouth.

A long silence stopped time. "You need to meet me at the station. I can be there in thirty minutes."

"Why?" I asked, knowing it was rhetorical. I needed to hear the words, no matter how hard they would be to take in.

"I'd prefer you be there before I say anything."

"He's dead isn't he?"

Price grunted a couple of times on the phone but never made any words. Another couple of seconds went by in silence before he spoke. "Paul, I'm sorry."

"I did it didn't I?" I pulled out into traffic, unsure of where to go. One minute, I planned to go to the church, the next, going to Bat Town and causing genocide. It seemed so silly to even ask the question. I knew the answer. I had been the one that killed him two nights ago. I knew whether Price confirmed it or denied it, it would change anything.

"Just meet me at the station. We'll get into it there."

"There. Meaning you're at the crime scene. Where are you?"

"You don't want to be here, Paul. Trust me."

"Tell me where you are. If it's a cockroach attack, you know as well as I do that I have to be there."

"We're calling in someone else to…" he hesitated. "Take care of the body."

"The hell you will. Now you tell me where you are. I want to know and I want to know right now. You owe me that much."

Again silence filled the air. "At the cemetery."

"Price, there's a lot of cemeteries. Which one?"

"Your parent's. I'm begging you not to come down here, Paul."

I never answered or said goodbye.

* * * * *

As I parked along the sliver of blacktop, I noticed Kansas sitting in his Explorer. He took a drink from something as my headlights went out. I saw him move in frantic motion under his dome light. I could tell by his body language he would be of little use in this investigation. Talking about falling down, Kansas looked like a tortured soul on its last leg. Usually the most dapper of officers on the scene, he now stood unshaven and frumpy beyond belief. My eyes shot a glance inside the Explorer and saw an open bottle of gin. Most of it gone. I could tell by the look in his eyes, he had had about as much sleep as me. "Thank God you're not dead. I've been looking and asking everyone I know where they might have taken you," he said as he approached me. "You look like hell warmed over. What did they do to you?"

I gave him my signature glare. Even if he had nothing to do with Kasey and the fur balls trying to kill me, he had been the one responsible for putting me within biting range with the roaches. I had reason to believe he did very little to stop the shifters from making me extra bloody.

"I know you won't believe me, but I am sorry for everything. I just wanted my wife and baby back. I did stupid things and hope you can forgive me one day." Bloodshot eyes filled with tears. His words were laced with a slight slur from the alcohol. "You don't think I set you up last night do you?"

"What would have stopped you, Kansas? It wouldn't be the first time." I breathed in the alcohol. "Besides, you're drunk."

"Stay mad at me if you want, but you know as well as I do that if it were you're wife, you'd have done the same thing."

"Do us both a favor and get a hot cup of coffee and get the hell out of here. You smell like booze and I think I can speak for Price when I say you being here isn't going to help anything."

"Paul, I'm sorry." He opened and closed his mouth several times as his thoughts changed gears.

I moved past him and tried to keep the panic in my chest from exploding. The world spun at breakneck speed and confusion clouded what thought process I had left. I remembered the night in the church with Olivia and doubts grew about what really happened. I questioned what had been real and what had been illusion. The fact that I might have had something to do with his death ate at me from the inside out. Again, I prayed it had all been nothing more than blood leech magic.

Ahead of me, I saw the various cops that usually work this type of crime, all looked at me between the flashes of red and blue from the various lights on the ambulance and cruisers. As if I were a true vein weasel, they dropped their glance as I looked them in the eyes. Each hoped to avoid bringing me the inevitable bad news.

Kansas flanked me. "After I got the call about Father Garcia tonight, I got a call from somebody to meet them here about my wife. You know anything about it?"

I scowled at him and never stopped moving. "Ask your fang gang. I'm sure they have all the answers you're looking for. You probably set us up for feeding time." And I meant every word. The man to my right had sold me out before on the empty promise of getting his wife back. Thinking tonight would be any different only made me a bigger target for the things that wanted to eat me or suck me dry. I started to grow more and more aware of my surroundings as we walked.

He tried to stop me with a hand on my shoulder. I gave him a look that made his grip instantly release me. "You can't honestly think I had something to do with this?"

"Why not. Let's see. You gave Price's grandson to the blood munchers even though you knew he was innocent, you led me into the snake pit of master biters without even a single word of warning, and I'll bet you watched as they ran off with me and planted me in the grove. Yeah, Kansas, I think you're capable of just about anything." I tried to stand as straight as I could. The pains in my chest had changed from wound to full on anxiety. The hole seemed to be healing much faster than if I had been absent of all the crud in my veins, but not fast enough to suit me. "And may God have mercy on your pathetic soul if I find you had anything to do with them taking Angie."

"I had nothing to do with them taking Angie and you know that." He looked ahead as he walked beside me. "I still don't see what you see in her. Sure, she's great eye candy, Paul, but she's also a fur ball. She'll kill you one day just like the vampires will try to do."

"Don't talk about anything killing me without putting your own name on that growing list. And if you end up widowed after this, you only have yourself to blame. Don't forget it was you that killed Allana's baby. I'm sure Judas will be more than happy to even the score." I saw the hurt in his eyes and liked it. No matter the reason, he represented the reason I had been caught up in all this in the first place.

And now the party just got creepier.

Dead black eyes, hollow and infinite looked back at me. I made a point not to get caught up in that evil gaze. "I am surprised the police have allowed you to be here tonight. Though I am sure it will be met with sarcastic wisdom, I offer my condolences." Dieter held out his hand and seemed to bow. It didn't matter to me if he had been sincere or not. All I saw before me reminded me of why I hated his kind so much.

I said nothing as I hit him with everything I had. He rocked on his heels but never fell. He stepped backwards to avoid the second swing. Several officers grabbed me around my waist and by the shoulders and pulled me free of my victim. "How's that for sarcasm, shit head." Breaking free from the officers, I pulled the Magnum up and placed it against his forehead. I pulled the trigger only to miss my target as an officer pushed my arm upward.

The cocky son of a bitch never moved. "Violence will not bring him back, Avenger. And I assure you that I am not here to rub salt into your wounds." He gave me a demonic grin. "This is business, not pleasure, Avenger."

"Suck my dick, Dieter. You and Quinn and the rest of the daisy pushing community did this. Don't tell me you didn't.

Every one of you in this God forsaken city will answer to me. Admit you did it and I'll stake you quick and painless. How's that for class?"

"It would do me no good to say such things, even though I assure you neither Quinn nor I have blood on our hands when it comes to this matter." He glanced at the officers around us. "There is a preposterous rumor being spread among the vampire community that it was you that has slain the Father. We have it from Judas' blood host. I would hope you haven't taken your duties as the new master vampire to such heart."

"Let me tell you this only one time, you piece of miserable slime, we are nothing alike. And I'm not here under obligations. I'm here for…" I stopped there. The Magnum dug deep into his skull again. Kansas and two other officers again pushed me away.

"Walk away," Kansas said as he pushed me further from my target.

Several others joined Kansas and the other two officers and pulled me away from Dieter. Still more pushed the dead head away from me. My anger grew so far out of control, I couldn't catch my breath.

Price moved through the crowd, his eyes filled with horror and sympathy. My anger turned to him and I didn't know why. Guilt grabbed me before I said or did something I would regret.

Dieter smiled. "Even the Father betrayed you because of what you are. Deny it all you wish, Avenger, but we are alike in more ways than you wish to believe. The only real difference is that I have come to terms with what I am and you have not."

This time, Kansas grabbed Dieter. "Where's my wife, you dead fuck?"

Dieter turned to Kansas with glass-like eyes. "How is Allana, detective? I hope you have not done something that you shall regret for the rest of your life?"

I started to walk away. "They're all dead, Kansas, thanks to you."

Kansas' hand caught my shoulder and spun me around. "You think I did any of those things because I wanted to? I had no choice in it. You have to tell them that. You're a master vampire, can't you talk to them, negotiate or something?"

"First of all, touch me again, and you'll be pulling back a stub. Second, you had choices. You could have warned me or Price that we were walking into a bee's nest. You chose to not only put your wife and child's lives in danger, but everyone else. I hope we do find your wife alive and healthy, but even if we do, I'll never let this end without you going down for it. You don't deserve to have this all work out nice and tidy. Now if you don't mind, I need to see what your cockroaches have done. Unlike you, Father Garcia didn't deserve to die. As for me being a master roach, if I am, you'll be the first to know."

Kansas looked at Price, then came back to me. "Price already told me that you confessed to this two nights ago. You're no better than me. It's me that should be questioning the motives in all this."

I cold cocked him in the nose. Euphoria filled me as he bounced on the ground, pain showing in his dead face. Price and a few others rushed around me, pinning my arms to my side. I struggled for a few seconds, then tried to regain my composure.

Guilt and grief built up in me. I could almost recite word for word all the angry things I had said to the Father the night I brought Olivia into the church. I had wished him dead for thinking of me as a monster. Now there would be no apologies or forgiveness. It would be an albatross around my neck for the rest of my days.

Price looked down on Kansas. "How dare you show up here after what you've done to all of us. You gave them my grandson. If Paul doesn't put you out of your pathetic misery, I will." I caught him as he pushed Kansas back to the ground. Couldn't blame the old man, but turning Kansas into a punching bag didn't get us any closer to those we loved. Yeah, it would feel great, but we had a bigger, darker issue to address. Price nearly melted Kansas with his stare. "Not to mention, sober up".

Behind me I heard the demonic giggle of Dieter. I turned as he entered our little circle. "Perhaps, Detective Price, you should ask Paul about who he has tried to save and whom he has allowed to simply be sacrificial lambs. There is a certain wolf that has consumed all of the Avenger's attention. If he had met the demands of Judas' coven, I believe your grandson would be safe as we speak."

I saw Price asking the question with his eyes as his grip on me loosened. "What's he mean about a sacrifice, Paul? What's it got to do with Josh?"

I didn't answer. If given the chance, I would have saved Price's grandson. I knew that in my heart. All of my energy might have been spent on finding Angie, but Dieter made things sound far more one sided than they really were. Then again, Dieter hit closer to the target than I wanted to admit. His stirring of the pot caused all the doubts to bubble to the surface.

Before I had a chance to scream more profanities at Dieter, Price pulled me to the side. I turned my head to see eyes begging me to listen. My feet continued toward the crime scene. "We aren't done here. That's why I wanted to see you at the station. You don't want to see this. We haven't gotten him down yet. Dieter couldn't wait for you to get here, just so you'd see the priest. Go home now and don't give that undead son of a bitch the satisfaction of seeing you hurt like this. I'm begging you, Paul, don't do this to yourself."

Now I stopped. "What do you mean, you haven't gotten him down? Down from what?"

Price did his best to pull me back. I held firm. "Let's go get a cup of coffee and talk about it. Away from Dieter and all the other eyes and ears here."

"I'm not thirsty and I hate conversation. Now either you tell me what I'm about to see, or I'll find out for myself."

"I think the Christians called it crucifixion," Dieter added. "Although, Olivia and yourself might have called it elimination."

I looked to Price for an answer. Anything.

Price instantly looked to the ground. I began to shove my way through the crowd faster. My mind empty of thoughts. For some odd reason, I had to see for myself. Knowing I'd regret it as soon as I did. I think Feelgood called it closure. But there wouldn't be any kind of closure from this. I had seen him hanging from the cross at the church. This wouldn't be closure, this would be the beginning of hell.

On the large oak tree that spread across several plots, including my own parents, I saw the most vulgar act against humanity I had ever seen. Father Garcia had been crucified naked and upside down. Nailed to the tree through his kneecaps and wrists. His genitals had been ripped from his body. Trails of dried blood spider webbed across his pale skin. Bite marks filled his torso and neck. There must have been fifty bites. His mouth and eyes wide open in a permanent scream.

Below his body, the horror continued. The tombstone that marked my parents grave had been broken in half. Only jagged edges of stone remained. Dead roses sprayed across the ground like a blanket. I slowly read the words burned into the grass over my mother's and father's graves. FIRST PAYMENT.

My knees gave way under me. I tried to swallow the rage as it flowed into my mouth, but it grew unbearable. Screams filled the air as I pounded the ground with my fist. I stood with so much rage I grew numb. I had done this. Somehow in all the pathetic corners of my mind, I had been able to suppress it, but now the proof starred me in the face. *I had done this.* "I'm going to kill him tonight. I'm going to kill every last one of them." I moved back toward Dieter. He would die first.

Price's big hands tightened on my shoulders. I already knew no amount of time would dull the pain of this. My heart ached with the loss. "Told you, you didn't want to see this."

I looked at Father Garcia again, hoping that somehow I could tell him I'd get his revenge. Price pushed me away from Father Garcia's body. I knew tonight had changed my world. Forever. Again.

CHAPTER TWENTY-THREE

My world spun out of control as I collapsed in the passenger's side of Price's car. My anger and revenge hadn't really hit full throttle yet. Every part of my body grew cold and numb. I had hit a wall.

Price sat across from me and looked about as hollow as I felt. He stared straight ahead for a long time. Finally, a gentle hand rested on my shoulder, followed by a few pats. "Paul, I didn't want you to see him like this. That's why I'm calling a guy from Tampa to come over and…you know." He took a drink of cold coffee.

I looked across the cemetery and thought about nothing. I couldn't. Every human thought in my head had been ripped from their roots, leaving me without emotions of any kind. "Absolutely not. We made a promise to one another that we would end it for one another if the time came."

He shook his head. "I don't think that's such a good idea. But the choice as to what happens here is yours. If you want us to do nothing at all, I won't ask any questions."

My stare shot to his stoic face. "I hope you're not suggesting that I let him rise as a fang head."

The old man shrugged. "I'm just giving you every option I can. I know it would be something I will have to consider if we find Josh like this." I heard the sniff and the shake in his voice. "I can't imagine my life without him, but I'm finally understanding why families hide the bodies from us. I can't imagine living without him. In some twisted way, better a vampire than just dead." He gripped the steering wheel. "It's all my fault he's in this predicament. If I wasn't working the monster districts, he'd probably be okay. I just hope my wife can forgive me for all of this one day. I know I can't. Even if we get him back, I don't think I can do this anymore."

I knew exactly what he meant. "You can't beat yourself up over any of this. I've done nothing but go head to head with these things. It's been a losing battle and I've been too dumb to figure it out. You've lost your grandson because of me and I'm the one that's sorry."

He pushed his glasses back up his nose and cleared his throat. "My father always told me that you should never apologize for doing the right thing. No matter how unpopular you are while doing it. I just don't think he saw this kind of world coming."

I gave out a frustrated laugh. "I've now lost both my parents, Father Garcia, and still have nothing to show for it except more questions and more bitterness. I don't even know who I am anymore. I go through the motions and for what? We will never win this war. We've been kidding ourselves. All I've been doing is signing other people's death warrants." I couldn't get Father Garcia's body out of my mind. My heart ached to the point of crying. I had lost my father a second time. "This is why I've never allowed anyone to get close to me. I knew they would use it against me, just like they have with you and Kansas. Sick bastards will stop at nothing to manipulate and destroy us all."

Price grew silent for the longest time. "Paul, the other night when you said you killed Father Garcia, you said you were with this Olivia. Do you think she's the one that's done this?"

I thought before I spoke. Something I hadn't done very many times. "I'm still not sure I didn't do something. All I know for sure is if we kill Judas, we kill Olivia."

Price gave me a fatherly hug. "Go home, Paul. There's nothing you can do here. As a friend, I'm asking you to not make yourself a part of this. Get some rest. You look like hell." He held a small crucifix that swung from the rear view mirror and fell deep in thought. "I've never been so afraid in my life."

I couldn't bring myself to looking in any direction other than straight ahead. That image consumed me. The wooden stake through my chest could never cause this much pain. "I told him that I hated him and that I could live without him in my life. I saw the hurt in his eyes, but like everyone else that's said something at the spur of the moment, I thought I would have time to patch things up. I was angry and wanted to hurt him verbally. I hate myself for that. I saw that look in his eyes. He was scared of me."

"Why would Father Garcia even think of you as a vampire? He's known you your whole life. Why the doubt in you now?" Price's voice couldn't hide the hesitation in it. A simple and fearful question. I had to remind myself that he didn't see what I saw inside the church.

"It seems as though all of this is because of the roach virus in my veins and because I killed Asa. Now, according to the monsters, that makes me a master roach. Judas is able to somehow feed off of that virus to enter the church. For the first time, Father Garcia saw the monster in me, not the human. If I hadn't brought Olivia in there, Father Garcia would probably be alive. So whether it happened by my hands or the hands of Judas, the result is the same. I fucking killed him."

"But you're not a vampire? How can you be a master vamp when you're...you know, human. Just because they say you're something doesn't mean it's true." Leave it to Price to bring everything back to the simple black and white. There had been many times in our investigations I had accused him of being gray-blind. But perception meant everything to the fang heads. If they saw you as something, changing their minds never became an option.

"I wish in cockroach world it was that simple. I've become tangled in something out of my control. And now people are dying because of it." I wiped away the next flow of tears. My body ached as if I had come down with the flu. Coldness made every muscle shake. "Every daisy pusher with a power fetish will be looking for me."

Price shook me. "You have to stay strong, Paul. I need you now more than I've ever needed you. We have to get all of them back alive. You're the only one I trust and I don't care what's running in your veins. Grow fangs and turn into a bat for all it's worth, but I'm not giving up on you." I saw him wipe away tears of his own. "My family is everything to me and I've placed their very lives in your hands. If that isn't trust, I don't know what is." He tried to smile. "And I'd never do that with a damned vampire."

I placed my head into my hands. The smell of blood still lingered. I shook with disgust. "I appreciate that, Frank. I really do, but trust isn't enough. If the fang heads can ride off of my power and kill anyone they want, or see you and your family as a way to get to me, all I've really done is signed their death papers. You can't put that responsibility on me. I don't know if I trust me right now. I can't ask the same from you."

"I'm an old man, Paul. My time has come and gone. Got a bad heart and living on borrowed time. My grandson hangs in the balance of all this. I can't just sit and do nothing. I'd rather we all die with fangs in our necks from trying than do nothing at all. If you won't kill them, that only leaves me and I'm fat and old."

I opened the door to allow some air to get to me. "I've proven to you and everyone else over the last few days, I can't protect anyone from them if they really want to come after you. I'm done. I'm walking away."

"You can't blame yourself for all of this. Without your presence in all of this, they would have killed more in this city and we both know that." He gave me a grin that made me smile in the midst of everything that had happened. "You can't reason with things that see you as food."

His insight actually made me smile for a quick second. But all good things must come to an end. I saw the shadow and the undead stinging pricked along my face and arms. I looked up. I reached for the Magnum again. Right now, I didn't real picky on which cockroach I wasted.

Dieter stood overhead. Unlike the cocky smirk he usually had on his face, I saw something that almost resembled pity. His eyes traced my hand around the Magnum. "At least allow me to speak before you do something stupid."

"What's so stupid about killing you?" Price added.

The dirt napper handed me a piece of paper, folded in half. "This is for you. I know it will not bring about closure, but I do hope it will help in stopping the one responsible. I did not want protocol to lengthen the matter at hand."

"What's this?" I asked as I unfolded it. I had read enough bad news for one day. I hesitated and looked back to the roach.

It was confirmation that Father Garcia had died a victim of a fang head and had been dealt with in ways favorable to the Council, which in layman terms means Father Garcia could be decapitated. It usually took an act of God to get Dieter to sign one of these things. I stared at him, trying to figure out his motive. I wanted to rip his head off right now. I saw every roach as Father Garcia's killer. But instead of the usual smug look on Dieter's face, I saw pieces of compassion. I'm not sure that didn't make things worse.

Dieter bowed his head in defeat. "I do not wish to bring about more stress and sorrow pertaining to the Father than has already been done. I wish for you to have the proper privacy and time to deal with this matter as you wish."

I closed the paper. I flinched at my own assumptions. I wouldn't allow one random act of kindness change my opinion of him as a person or species. "If you're looking for a thank you, you're not going to get it."

The cockroach nodded. "I would not have thought I would." With that he practically vanished.

CHAPTER TWENTY-FOUR

As I watched Dieter fade into the crowd of officers and paramedics, my eyes focused on the job at hand. Father Garcia hung there like a demented representation of Christ. I swallowed my gorge for the thousandth time. My palms were wet with sweat. My life had become nothing more than tunneled visions of denial. I couldn't believe this great man that had taught me everything I knew about the execution of vein lickers had been killed by them. Once again the monsters had taken something I loved from me.

The crime scene investigators finished up their work, took the last of the gruesome pictures, made notes of their surroundings and decorated everything with yellow tape. Others hustled to take the lifeless body of Father Garcia down. A large part of me wanted to believe it had been out of decency and respect for the man, but the pessimist in me thought differently. That side of me only saw men taking him down quickly so they could see the show. Something they could tell around the dinner table later on.

I rubbed my hands together. Sweat gathered in my palms. Cutting the head off of nameless victims still got to me. I hated it. But now the victim had a name and a history with me. It had become personal.

I waded through the flashing red and blue lights of the various rescue and police vehicles as they pulsed into the dark night sky. My mind raced with grotesque images of things still to come. I breathed deep as I approached the 'Cuda, opened the trunk and retrieved the large ax that would do most of the dirty work. I looked at the stained blood on the metal from acts long ago and shivered. Nothing more than a methodical monster with little too no remorse for what I had to do. In simple terms, I had become what I hunted.

By the time I returned to the site, they had pulled Father Garcia's body from the tree. It now rested on the ground in a flood of fluorescent lighting. Being killed in a cemetery had to be the worst form of irony. Life's little stab at unfunny humor.

I cut through the sea of faceless officers and paramedics and stood over the body. I looked down at the naked body and did my best to control my emotions. Truthfully, it didn't even look like the Father. From behind, I could hear Price scold the officers and onlookers to move back. I never turned to see if they had obeyed. It didn't matter. Nothing did right now.

I crouched beside Father Garcia and touched his face. Even with all the wounds in his body, he looked asleep and at peace. Speckles of gray stubble scratched my fingers. "I'm so sorry for everything," I said, as my eyes filled with water. I clutched the ax handle for support.   All the spiteful words I had said to him, rushed back to me. I did everything I could to block them out, but they leaked through anyway. I blamed myself for this. If I hadn't brought Olivia into the church this wouldn't have happened. But I had made my choices and now faced the grave consequences of my actions.

"We made a promise a very long time ago, that we would protect one another against these things in life and in death. It was an empty promise on my end, Father. I never really believed I would have to be doing this." I wiped away both sweat and tears. They mixed together and dripped through the hairs on my chin. "I did this to you. Please forgive me."

I pulled myself up by the ax handle. My knees were so weak and shook so bad I couldn't keep balance without it. Which led me to my next big fear. What if I didn't have the strength to do the act? Forget having the guts. My hands were so weak right now, I didn't know if I could even lift the tool, much less deliver a final blow. Having to take two swings at this made my head spin with madness.

"May God forgive me and bless you," I started as I did everything in my power to build the nerve and strength needed. Power stung me as the ax swung above me. Horror curled in my veins.

Father Garcia's eyes flicked wide. His mouth opened, exposing large fangs. Skin already rotten and crawling with decay. "Even God will not forgive you for this, Paul!"

I dropped the ax on his neck with a violent impact. Flesh and bone gave way. I stepped back and pulled the stake from my belt and drove it through his chest again and again until every ounce of strength in me had expired.

I lay on top of Father Garcia and wept with exhaustion. I clutched his skin with my fingernails, trying to drive the hurt and anger from me.

"What the hell happened?" Price asked. He reached down and touch my shoulder.

I pushed it away. "Run, Frank. Before I kill you all." My face remained buried in Father Garcia's chest.

"I don't understand?"

"Father Garcia. You saw him come to life. It's because of me. The cockroach in me caused him to rise like that. I'm a master roach. I can do shit like that now." I lifted off of the priest and looked back at Price as I stood. I spread my arms wide. "Do it, Frank. Kill me now before somebody else is lying here. I'm more monster than human. That proved it. Judas rode my power like he did at the church. Shoot me, Frank. I'm a coward and I can't do it myself."

Price's mouth moved but nothing came out of it for what seemed to be ten minutes. "Paul, I don't know what you're talking about. Who came to life?" Confusion colored his face.

"Don't screw with me. You saw his eyes open. You saw those fangs." I stepped back, unsure of reality and the madness playing games inside my head. I had gone insane. Judas' game hadn't been about power and blood, it had been about taking my sanity from me, destroying my credibility and sealing my demise. "I killed him, Frank. At the church that night, I killed him. I told you I did!" I pointed to my chest. "Please, if you have any sympathy for me at all, you'll do it."

Price continued to look at me, shaking his head. "Why don't you come with me? We'll get some air, a hot cup of coffee, a sedative…" He allowed his words to trail off as he tried to put his arm around me again. I could feel the tenseness in his body language. He patronized me, but I didn't have the energy to fight it. Soon I wouldn't be able to play with anything sharper than a crayon.

"Don't tell me you didn't see his eyes open."

He shook his head. "It's been a long night. You need rest. This is unhealthy for you. You shouldn't even be here." He led me away.

Again, I wiped away the combination of sweat and tears. I looked back at the body of Father Garcia again. "Are you telling me you didn't see his eyes and mouth open?"

Frank gave me a blank stare. This time, not even his mouth moved. Then he spoke. "No, Paul. Nothing happened. You need to rest. Call that doctor of yours and see if she can give you something. You shouldn't have been here. I tried to tell you that."

I clutched his shirt. "I'm going insane, Frank!" Nearby officers stopped what they were doing and turned. I had reason to believe they had heard every word and merely pretended to be occupied. I didn't care. Being the freak side show didn't matter right now. I began to question myself. Perhaps I bought into this master cockroach thing a lot more than I wanted to.

I looked at the officers, each turned away as I made eye contact. "You're all right. I am insane. Pathetic and hollow. Take your best shot at me. Put me out of my misery, please. At least be humane enough to do that for me." I looked back to Price. "If you were the friend I thought you were, you'd do it now. Don't let me go so far off the deep end that I start killing more innocent people. There's only so much I can blame on the virus. At some point I've got to start looking at the man in the mirror."

Price's face showed the pity, but if you looked close enough, you could see the frightened man behind it all.

CHAPTER TWENTY-FIVE

We both turned at the same time. A late sixties hearse with headlights that seemed to almost glow with a green tint to them crept through the thick blackness of the night. It chugged along the back of the cemetery. Large lakes of rust ate away at the lower portions of the doors.

"Who's that?" Price said as he stood next to me.

I considered it a rhetorical question and went into defense mode. "Make sure all your men are prepared. Ultra violet bullets and crucifixes mandatory." Around us, every officer had stopped what they were doing to watch the black hearse slowly lurch its way along the thin ribbon of asphalt. Blue smoke bellowed from the tailpipe in ghost-like clouds as it swirled under the moon and hanging moss. I leaned against a police car, drained of energy. Whatever hid inside the hearse could kill me here and now. I didn't have a fight left in me. I threw the ax across the lawn.

"Don't tell me someone's being buried at night?" Kansas asked as he moved to the opposite side of the car. He stayed at arm's length from both myself and Price.

I lit a cigar, but said nothing. I took the first drawl and allowed the tobacco to fill my lungs. Nausea burned in my stomach. The ground spun under me. With Father Garcia dead and Angie, at best, a new enemy of mine, my list of friends and allies had all but disappeared.

"I *am* sorry," Kansas still pleading his case to me.

"It doesn't matter anymore, Zeke. They're all dead. Angie, Josh, Stephanie." I had come to terms with the inevitable. None of us were going to get anybody back alive. Not Josh Price. Not Stephanie Kansas. Not...I couldn't go there.

"For Christ's sake don't say that, Paul. I know you've been through a lot tonight, but we can't give up on them. I need you to snap out of this. We have nothing to prove either Stephanie or Angie are dead." He stood in front of me. His face showed the genuine concern and I couldn't blame him for it. I didn't feel like sugar coating everything. Nothing I did would change the outcome. Even if it could be changed, I wouldn't be a part of it.

"No," I said as I smoked the cigar. My eyes remained on the hearse.

"What do you mean, no? No to what?"

"There is no 'we' in what you're saying. You want help for yourself and Stephanie. If I was of no value in helping you get her back you'd be ignoring me right now. I wish you the best, but I don't care about any of this anymore." I saw the hurt in his eyes and I basked in it. After what he had pulled, I only wish I could drive my hatred for him home a little harder. He deserved to squirm a little.

I pushed off of the police car and started to make my way against the growing sea of officers to my car. Price had been right. I shouldn't have come here.

The hearse stopped about fifty yards from us, the engine purred, headlights burned bright. So bright, they swallowed the black vehicle behind them. Swirls of dust and moths cast shadows in the beams. I shielded my eyes and tried to get a better look at the faceless driver.

I realized that running away wouldn't make my problems go away, but instead prolong them or make things worse. I had to face all this shit head on and I knew it.

I took a wide approach to the hearse. It helped me escape the direct hit of the headlights. I got a better eye on anything that might jump out. The more I thought about Father Garcia the more the revenge boiled inside me. Perhaps killing one more thing before giving up wouldn't hurt things.

Price jogged the few steps to catch my pace. "Wait, I'll go with you."

"No, you stay here. If I know our cockroaches like I think, this is about me." I intentionally slowed my pace. I didn't need him to drop with a heart attack. We were all going to funerals, no need to have one more.

"They have my grandson. I think this has everything to do with me too." Price continued to move with me, as though I hadn't asked him to step back, apparently unaware of my request. He checked his Glock pistol as he walked. Small talk time had ended. We knew something inside that hearse had come here to kill or be killed. If we didn't stop it here and now, it might never be stopped.

The driver's side door opened and a skinny young girl jumped out, no more than twenty. Dressed in gothic attire, pale white skin and several piercings on her lower lip. I knew her and that alone had me a bit uneasy. Camilla. One of Kasey's wolves. Now I grew more confused than ever and thought about switching up guns. I had expected roach, not fur balls.

She made her way around the front of the hearse as it purred in the night air, the headlights illuminated the moss in the large cypress trees that surrounded us. I could feel her animalistic vibrations as they stood the hair on my arm on end, but something else rode on top of it. Something deadly and powerful.

I wasted no time in pulling the Magnum free of the holster. I looked at the wolf, but I smelt bat. With a quick survey, I noticed many of the police officers had moved toward the hearse for a closer look. Bad idea. As fast as this could happen, some of them would be dead before they knew it.

"Stop right there, vampire man. What I have might make things a little better for you," the wolf said with a voice of confidence. Like most of the wolves, she didn't fear me in the least. I hated that fact.

The wolf stopped at the passenger door and opened it with grand drama. I stiffened. Anything could come out of that car and that left us all very vulnerable. If I hadn't seen what they had done to Father Garcia, my answer would have been to run like the devil away from here.

A pale body stood with reluctance. Trails of dried blood marked his back. Deep wounds rested where flesh had once been. Black and blue marks shined against the whiteness of skin around it. His naked skin reflected the moonlight. He had a ball gag shoved in his mouth and a large silver crucifix hung from his neck. Red skin showed where it had burned and scarred.

"What the hell is this?" I said under my breath.

"Better rethink all that, master vampire. You kill him before we work things out here, and we might still never find Angie. This is one of Judas' boys. Kill him and we all lose Angie." I stopped. I had to rethink everything. Camilla had thrown a wrench into everything. What she had done might get Angie killed quicker, not save her life.

In the vampire's hands I noticed a white box, or at one time it had been white. Tattered wrapping paper hugged along most of the box in wrinkled disarray. A large red ribbon had been tied to the box, clean, new and shining in the lights of the hearse.

"Who is this, Paul?" Price asked.

"Frank, I'd like you to meet Camilla. Not sure who the roach is." I kept telling myself to pull the trigger. "Get your men to move back. I don't want you to need more than one body bag." Then I addressed the lovely couple before me. "So what do you want?"

Camilla smiled a grill of glittering teeth. "Olivia told me where to find him and to bring him here as a gift to all of you. Seems he's the one that has been harboring Angie for Judas. " She shoved the roach forward. So far the monster didn't respond, but I knew he wouldn't let me remove his head without a fight. I had little trouble in convincing myself to keep the Magnum handy instead of the 9mm. "Olivia says I need to talk to Detective Kansas first, though."

"What do you want with him?" Price asked taking a step forward.

"I have been asked to give this package to him and to tell the detective that every action is met with an equal and opposite reaction. Olivia has gifts for all of those that have lost something tonight." I didn't like the sound of that. Olivia might not have been a full on roach, but it didn't mean she couldn't play little wicked games with us. Price, Kansas and I had all lost something very valuable to the coffin leeches. It made me nervous. I couldn't stand still.

Out of the corner of my eye, I saw Price pull up his weapon. He had as much vengeance for these things lately as I did. The fang head before us had something very important to him as well. He had as much of a right to take the first shot as I did.

Camilla looked over to the old man. "Don't do it or all deals are off. Olivia has something for you as well. She said you would know it when you saw it."

"Why would Olivia help you and the wolves? If I kill Judas, she dies."

Camilla shrugged her shoulders. "Not for me to say other than she hates him as much as you do. She's a blood host, not a loyal vampire. As far as dying goes, we planned on killing her anyway. Cooperating with us makes it a bit more civilized of a death for her."

I turned my head to see Kansas and about four other officers. I had seen them work various scenes before, but had no idea what their names were. "I'm Kansas. What do you want?" His words were monotone and full of pessimism, but at least the slurs of alcohol were gone. I think he knew nothing inside that box had been sent to make our night better.

Camilla took the box out of the dirt napper's hands and turned to Kansas. He took the box with an unsteady grasp. He looked at Camilla, then to me and Price, eyes asking the million dollar question. What twisted shit hid inside that box.

"You are to open it now." Camilla's words remained shallow.

Kansas sat the box on the hood of the hearse and rubbed the sweat from his hands on his pants. With apprehensive fingers, he untied the bow, allowing it to fall each side of the box, held now only from the bottom. Kansas touched the lid on the box with his fingers and began to weep loudly. He looked at each of us. "I don't know if I can do this." To Camilla, "What the hell is this?"

"Take a step back, guys," Price said, shooing off the police that had gathered for the event.

Kansas returned to the box and swallowed hard. He closed his eyes in a silent prayer and pulled the lid off with methodical care. The lid fell to the ground without ceremony as Kansas looked inside.

"Fuck! Jesus Christ, no!" He threw the box to the ground in disgust and crawled up the hood of the hearse.

The scream I heard chilled bones in me that I never knew I had. His face went instantly pale. Vomit flew from his mouth along the ground and on the fender of the hearse. He cried hard and deep. Kansas' body rolled into the fetal position. He rocked aggressively with immeasurable sorrow. He shook and screamed more. Eyes wide with fear. Skin bleached white.

I moved to him, looked in the box and saw the torn flesh and blood that filled the bottom, wrapped in some sort of plastic. A skinned baby fetus. I melted to the ground as I remember the sights in Allana's eyes. Killing Father Garcia, killing Kansas' baby, I had done it all! It hadn't been the twisted fucking nightmare I tried to make myself believe.

Price's shadow appeared from behind. "Dear, God." He gagged.

My nails dug into my hands as I balled them. Nothing in the nightmare I had could have prepared me for what I saw. I held my breath to keep from passing out. Every voice around me seemed a million miles away. Uncontrollable sweat poured from my head.

In deep labored breaths, Kansas looked at the box again, slid from the hood of the hearse and crawled to it. "My baby!" he cried as he picked the fetus from the box and cradled it. His lungs continued to bellow with the pain I couldn't even fathom. Blood stained his shirt as he rocked the baby gently. I stepped away from the growing crowd of officers. Near a large tree, I vomited and fought the growing rage that clawed to escape. I had killed some of the most horrid creatures known to man, but nothing could have prepared me for this.

"I'll kill him!" I heard Kansas scream behind me. I turned to see him running with incredible force, breaking away from the officers that tried to hold him. His face showed the lost hope inside. He no longer controlled his emotions. Blood from the fetus stained his hands.

"Kansas," I started. I tried to stop him. He pushed by me with such force, I nearly ended up on the ground.

The detective crashed through me and several other officers and raced to Camilla and the bat head. His gun raised high as he hit the open space between them. Camilla rushed between the monster and Kansas.

The detective's gun fired once, missing Camilla and the blood head, but his second shot hit him in the shoulder, spitting blood and muscle across the hood of the hearse. he grabbed Camilla by the neck and tore a large hole. Blood rushed from the wound as she fell limp. Her eyes grew hollow as she teetered for a second before turning to face the vein weasel.

As Camilla fell, her eyes showed the life leaving her body. She looked up at the monster before her with so many questions and sorrow. Judas had meant for his little helper to kill Camilla. His means to getting us all in one location.

Power multiplied through me. My ears rang, my knees folded. Screams of undead souls called out to me. The daisy pusher flew into the air, over the hearse and tried to fade in the blackness. With the aid of the hearse's headlights, everything around it grew dark. I lost him somewhere above us. Kansas and I fired in synchronicity. I could tell by the sound of Kansas' gun, he didn't have the right kind of killing bullets.

Three officers worked their way along the right side, crouching low among a thin line of trees and other grave markers. Others flanked along the road in an ill attempt to capture the fang head. I heard a shot from one of the officers as it hit the side window on the hearse, spraying the ground with shattered glass. A chorus of shouts from the officers filled the air. Sometimes at each other. Their forms lost in the blackness. We would all be lucky if we didn't shoot each other.

From behind, Price ran along the side of the hearse as Camilla leaned against the front bumper. Kansas ran across the darkness shooting at anything in front of him. Madness had kicked in.

Other officers moved off in various directions, but the roach could be anywhere by now. I stayed low next to the hearse, working my way toward the back. My eyes scanned above me. More than likely, he would be found in one of the over-sized trees around us. If we didn't kill him quick, he would be at full power in a matter of minutes.

I looked back to the front of the hearse and saw Camilla slumped over. Dead. I cursed under my breath.

Near the back of the hearse, Kansas stood in the middle of the road, his gun to his head. "NO!" I screamed as I made my way to him. No matter what I thought of him right now, going out this way wouldn't be an option. Against everything I had said, I didn't want him to end this way.

"Take one more step, Paul and I'll kill us both. I'm already dead. There's nothing that can save me." His face showed the madness and hopelessness. I opened and closed my mouth. Words weren't coming as freely as I wanted them to.

In one giant leap Price grabbed him and tackled him, pushing both of them into the back door of the hearse, then to the ground. I saw the hollow face of Ezekiel Kansas that mirrored my own hatred. Price pinned the gun hand to the ground and pulled the weapon free. He pitched it in the grass.

The old man looked at me, panting for breath. "Paul, I'm getting to old for this." He pushed his glasses back up his nose as other officers surrounded us.

I remained still.

Price looked back at me, the half-smile faded. "What is it?"

"I still feel power."

CHAPTER TWENTY-SIX

As the army of police officers swarmed the new crime scene, all with their weapons drawn and shouting orders over top of each other, I did something I didn't think I would ever do, but with the circumstances as they were, I found it to be the only humane thing any of us would probably accomplish on this night. I pulled Kansas from the ground along with two paramedics and walked him to a nearby ambulance. I gave him a hug, knowing that it wouldn't even scratch the surface of what he must be feeling at the moment. Kansas had become nothing more than a living rag doll. He mumbled incoherently as we walked. I had never been good in these situations, but with my personal loss of Father Garcia, we were both too hollow to do more than walk in a zombie-like trance. And as the ambulance door shut, I knew our nightmares were far from being over. Stephanie, like Angie, still remained in the hands of blood leeches. Nausea hit me in the gut as I thought about the possibility that he might have to attend not one, but two funerals. Worst of all, every life that had been taken and those that remained in jeopardy, could be linked back to me. If I didn't exist, or at the very least, hadn't been considered a master roach to Judas and his coven, all our loved ones would be safely tucked away in bed tonight.

Kansas now lay on the small bed in the back of the ambulance, hooked up to various IV's. He hadn't said anything to any of us, simply mumbled Stephanie's name over and over. Without saying a word, I tried to convey my condolences. It didn't matter. Nothing I said could change what had happened tonight.

The small box with the infant disappeared into the crowd of officers. I said a silent prayer in its behalf. Not that it would do any good. In all my anger, hatred and self-indulgence, I would never have wished such a horrid event on anyone. Despite all my anger, I knew Kansas' heart had been in the right place. I would have done the very same thing, had things been reversed. I kept telling myself that. He had simply fallen into the traps that the monsters so lived for. They knew our weakness, what we were willing to live and die for. And they used it against us.

As much as I would have loved to have gone home and licked my wounds, I knew I couldn't. My animosity ran through me. I refused to become like them. My thought and reasoning had shut down. I wanted more than just revenge. I wanted to see them all die a piece at a time. Forget laws and governing powers. I would handle this the old fashion way. I would make it messy and bloody. With all the shadows across my heart, I had to redirect that pain and boil it into a pure anger. I checked the Magnum for bullets.

I turned and walked back across the field of tombstones. Power vibrated in my bones. More than one roach lurked somewhere in the darkness. My mind raced through various thoughts. At the moment, nothing would make me happier than to stake as many of them as I could. But on the other hand, I knew they hadn't come here unless they thought they had an advantage. My heart pumped hard, my fingers stretched. At least I wouldn't have to hunt them down tonight.

As I moved by the hearse, more officers and medics moved Camille's body. A small pool of blood had soaked into the pavement as a reminder of yet another loss of life due to me. The wolf had been betrayed. But like the rest of us, she had no choice in her actions. Pack came first in her world. Now, like the rest of us, the pack had been left with nothing.

I stopped and allowed the power to wash over me. My eyes turned to the back of the hearse. I brushed my hand along the back door and instantly took a step back. The source of the power pushed against my hand. Tingles trickled up my arm, raising the hair as it ascended.

Ahead of me, I could see Price talking to other members of the paranormal unit. He looked tired and defeated. The box had sent a very simple and sobering message to us all. We were all at the mercy of these things. We all had something to lose tonight. With Father Garcia dead, and now the box Kansas received, it only stood to reason that Price thought the worst.

I waited until Price and the others were far enough away that I figured whatever came bouncing out of the back of the hearse couldn't eat them. I, on the other hand, welcomed whatever came out of the hearse. My priorities were very simple. Kill or die trying. I pulled the Magnum free of the holster and took a deep breath.

I held my Magnum in the right hand and reached for the door handle with my left. My hands trembled so badly they were nearly useless. Fatigue had caught up with me as well. Sweat dripped from my forehead. I had no fear. Excitement urged me forward.

As the door gave way, I pulled the Magnum down on the inside of the hearse, but nothing jumped out. Yet.

I searched the interior in all directions, only to find the casket that sat before me. I watched as Price and a couple of officers looked to me and started to move in my direction. I stopped them at a safe distance as I raised my hand.

Large clumps of dirt still held to the casket, smaller balls of mud smashed into the used carpet. It had recently been unearthed. The smell of soil filled the small area, mixed with a moldy odor from origins unknown. Maggots danced along the bottom of the rotting wood of the coffin. I grabbed hold of the end of the casket with my free hand and tried to pull it toward me, only to find it heavier than I expected. I cursed under my breath. To get it out, I would have to set my Magnum down. Something I refused to compromise on.

"Help me pull this thing out," I said to another officer. "Price, get ready for anything that comes out of this thing." He shook his head as he looked to other officers with great reluctance. We all knew if we pulled the thing free, we put ourselves in greater danger, but we really had no other choice. I had thought about setting the hearse on fire and killing whatever waited inside, but I couldn't take the chance. Just because I felt roach power, didn't mean we weren't dealing with another hostage as well. Josh. Angie. Both still unaccounted for. We were dealing with a complete psycho willing to kill an unborn child. No stone could be left unturned in all this now.

Other officers gathered round and we soon became six pall bearers. We lifted the coffin from the hearse and laid it on the ground. Unlike me, the other officers moved back quite a distance. We all watched and waited to see what might come out of the morbid jack-in-the-box. As a precautionary measure, I took a few steps back as well. My hand instantly readied the trigger on the Magnum.

My left hand grabbed the lid, finding it locked. I looked inside the hearse and grabbed a well-used crow bar. My heart continued to beat harder and faster. Anything could be inside this thing. Living and dead. Friend and foe. Reluctantly, I placed the Magnum back in its holster. I looked back to Price. "Shoot the hell out of whatever come out of here."

Another officer appeared with a flashlight and illuminated the top of the box. I wanted to tell him to step back, but I was happy for the company. I pried the crowbar between the lid and body of the mahogany colored casket and pushed down with everything I had. Several officers stood guard from a distance with their weapons drawn, including Price.

On the third bounce, I heard the wood split and the lid begin to give way. I saw white fingers shoot out of the side of the box. I dropped the crow bar and instantly reached for the Magnum with both hands. My feet began to scatter backwards, but something told me not to shoot yet.

As the lid sprang open I heard Price scream. Not out of horror, but desperation. "Don't shoot! Don't shoot!" He came rushing by me, only to be dragged back by a few more officers. I began putting the pieces together. Though I had never seen the man in person, I knew who we were looking at.

Josh Price.

My heart sank. I could feel the power coming off of him. "Get everyone back!" I shouted.

"It's Josh, Paul! It's Josh!" Price repeated again and again as he struggled against the hold of the officers. I saw the look of hope back in his eyes. The glimmer of life returned in him. God, I hated that, knowing what I knew.

"Keep him back!" I shouted to them.

"You don't understand Paul. It ain't no vampire. It's my grandson. Please, let me go!" He continued to squirm against the other officers. I made eye contact with one of them and could tell he knew what I knew. We dropped the glance and weighed our options.

For the millionth time, I began to turn in tight little circles, trying to take in all the things that might be hidden in the darkness. I tensed every time the wind blew through the tree branches. I jumped every time I heard a dog bark in the distance.

I didn't know what to do. I couldn't stake Josh in front of his grandfather. But I knew if I didn't, the newly turned monster would snack on us all. Josh and I looked at one another for a few seconds. A thin smile rose on his lips, but nothing more sinister than that. He stood there waiting for us to make a move. "Get him out of here." I shouted to no one in particular.

Even before killing Josh, the death toll had risen again.

CHAPTER TWENTY-SEVEN

I heard the swoosh of air long before I saw the officer hold his throat. Dark crimson fluid squirted through the gaps in his fingers. His mouth moved but unable to speak. Eyes bulged and threatened to explode. Knees buckled and he fell to the ground.

Josh moved through the sea of officers in a blur of speed. Having recently risen from the dead, hunger drove him toward any available vein. He sped toward the officer in front of Price. The old man stood there watching his grandson commit unspeakable acts. I hadn't been prepared for this.

I raised my Magnum with reluctance. I had psyched myself up to kill as many of these daisy pushers as I could, but not this. Hell no, not this. My skin nearly caught fire as more vein biters ascended on us. Phantom figures moved through the darkness and out of the shadows. They moved through the pocket of officers and paramedics. The lucky ones ran to vehicles to avoid the slaughter. Screams filled the cemetery. Shots rang out in defense.

Two more officers fell to the ground next to me. A cockroach grabbed another from behind and bit into his throat. More screams and shots fired. Pandemonium set in as each person tried to find some sort of sanctuary from the monsters that seemed to come from every direction.

Blood began to puddle in the uneven soil as more humans fell victim to the fangs around them. Two more shots. At least one cockroach flurried into ash. I think I got the other, but in the chaos and darkness, I had no proof. The daisy pushers weren't feeding. They were killing.

I made brief eye contact with Josh as he moved toward

another pocket of officers and drew a bead on his miserable head. Still, my fingers couldn't do it. I dropped my aim. I had to get to the old man and find another way to dispose of his grandson. Even with all the hatred I had for his kind right now, I couldn't kill him in front of Price. I had enough crosses to bare, thank you very much. Again, the little voice inside my head reminded me that all of this had been my fault.

I moved from the shadows of the large trees and kept my head low. Not to avoid the attacking cockroaches, but to keep from being shot by an overzealous police officer. I zig zagged through the maze of headstones, dead bodies and night crawlers in route to Price. He watched with great hesitation as I grabbed his wrist and pulled him against a large cypress tree. "Price you have to get out of here. Josh isn't one of us anymore."

He pulled free and looked at me with thousands of hurtful questions. A light shake of his head, let me know he didn't believe me or ready to cooperate. Even if it meant saving his own life. "No," he finally muttered.

I reloaded the Magnum. "He's a damn roach, Price. I should have ended this when I first picked up on it. He'll kill us all if we don't stop him and the others. I'm sorry, but he's dead." I crumbled with guilt. No way I could look him in the eyes. He had told me earlier that if I wanted Father Garcia to live as a fang head, he wouldn't stop me, but I couldn't return the favor. This had to end and the sooner we got there, the less number of funerals families would have to attend.

He shook his head. His face turned beet red. Before I knew it, I looked down the barrel of his gun. "You're a damned liar, Paul. He ain't one of them and I ain't gonna let you kill him just because you think he is. I'll stop you any way I have to."

I started to speak when Sasha descended on me. Something I hadn't expected. I had been so consumed with Judas that Sasha and his little coven had fallen off of my radar.

Theoretically, my coven, but after tonight, I planned to clean my city of blood licking covens altogether. I pulled the Magnum up and shot. The cockroach twisted in the air, avoided the bullet and stopped short of me. Price fell down the slight embankment behind us.

Sasha smiled. "Hope you haven't forgotten about my

promises to you, Avenger. By the time the sun rises, I will be the new master vampire of the city."

Now things were getting really fun. "Sasha, so good of you to join the party." I pulled the trigger again. Sasha scrambled up a tree and jumped behind me. I heard his feet hit the ground. I pivoted to face him. I glanced to my right as Price came back to his feet. He pointed his weapon in our direction. Sasha and I stood equal odds of being shot.

Before I could get my next shot off, Josh plowed into me from my left. His hot metallic breath filled my nostrils with a whole new flavor of stink. I grabbed him by the hair and flung him against the nearest headstone with all the strength I had. My chest jolted with pain. My old wounds were going to be the death of me one way or the other. I had to compensate against the lack of full strength, but so far bashing Josh's head against the marble proved to be great physical therapy. Razor sharp fingernails dug into me. Again, I kept an eye on Price. My odds of being the one that got shot just increased.

Sasha joined in and hit me chest high. I had taken a step backwards to miss the blow, which helped with the force of the impact, but the heel of my left boot got hung on a tree root, toppling me to the ground.

I had no more than landed, when Sasha attacked again. Stained fangs protruded from ancient lips, destined to bring my life to an end. My elbow lifted as a bar between me and those jaws, catching Sasha in the Adam's apple.

With my free hand, I punched him in the side of the face in order to gain enough of an advantage that I could bring the Magnum up. His strength began to overpower me. My elbow started to give way. Muscles burned with fatigue. I refused to go out this way. "Frank!" I yelled as I saw the old man simply standing with his mouth wide open. He had gone into shock. I knew Josh and Sasha would waste little time in attacking him.

Above me, a shadow grew, moving quickly. Josh started to move past me, toward his grandfather. I had to make a decision fast. I could let him go and keep my distance from Sasha, or use the hand that pounded on Sasha's head to stop the new blood flea.

I grabbed a wooden stake and drove it into Josh's thigh,

sending him off in another chorus of pain.

The added activity allowed Sasha to gain ground on my arteries. He pulled my neck farther back than it had been designed to go. My back popped from the pressure. The Magnum jarred free from my hands. Fangs moved in on me. I tried to pull free, but the roach held tight. My hands pried at his fingers only to find my situation grow more desperate.

Price aimed his pistol at the back of Sasha's head.

Sasha twirled to meet Price. "Go ahead, detective. Shoot me. Pull the trigger and I'll gut your grandson in front of you. He means nothing to me." His red eyes looked back to Price as his hands remained around my throat. Josh limped out of biting range but moved in on his grandfather.

"Kill him, Price. Shoot Sasha. He can't kill Josh without a head." In only a matter of time, the young roach would turn on his grandfather. I needed Sasha dead in order to keep that from happening.

Josh circled around behind Price. The old man couldn't see him from his vantage point. I tried to talk, but my airway had been closed off. I pointed as the monster moved in for the kill. A hand reached around Price's shoulder.

Price panicked. I heard the detective's gun go off. The bullet caught Josh in the chest. Bone pieces flew and stuck to the side of a nearby oak tree. Josh fell to the ground and began to rot to dust.

I pulled up the 9mm from the hip holster and fired at Sasha. The bullet caught him in the side of the head. Gray matter spewed from the side of his face. A nothingness grew on his face as his hands reached for the wound.

Sasha moved with lethargic steps, dark blood rolled down the side of his head. Life escaped his face. He stumbled. His eyes were no longer focused with great intensity. Silver nitrate ate away at his reality and thoughts. By sunup, Sasha would be dead.

A chorus of screams filled the air. Price fell to the ground, holding his chest. Time stood still and raced at breakneck speed, all at the same time. My God, he couldn't die on me too. "Josh!" he cried as his eyes rolled in the back of his head. I cursed under my breath. Why couldn't he have put the bullet in my head? If anything, it gave me an out.

The smell of blood filled the air and the power disintegrated around me. Sasha's blood stained the tombstone near him as his coven descended into the night. Howls of wolves echoed in the darkness.

CHAPTER TWENTY-EIGHT

I ran to Price as fast as I could. Let the roaches and fur balls come all they wanted. Right now, I had to somehow preserve the life of my shrinking list of friends and acquaintances. The more sympathetic side of me thanked God Price hadn't been conscious to see all of this. The realistic side convinced he had had a heart attack. His skin turned a shade of blue. He already looked like a corpse. "Someone help me!"

I cradled him in my arms and shook him. A helpless feeling swept over me. Whether I could find signs of life or not wouldn't change things. I didn't know CPR from a hole in the ground. Panic welled up in me as I watched him slip away. "Somebody please!" Thank God there were paramedics close by, but with all the killing that had taken place, I didn't know if I could find one available. Everything around me looked like a battlefield. There were bodies littered in every direction and I could link them all to my stupidity and denial. Time seemed to move in slow motion. I hadn't had time to process everything that had happened on this night and I knew there would be more deaths before the sun rose. I couldn't allow myself to think about Father Garcia. Every time I did, I found myself blubbering and falling deeper into a dark hole. All of this had been a good distraction from his death, but it came at a grave cost. I thought about Angie and said my goodbyes. If Kansas' unborn son and Price's grandson were dead, I had not reason to believe Angie had remained untouched. After all, she represented the grandest prize. Like with Father Garcia, I pushed the thoughts of her deep inside me and prepared myself for the inevitable.

Each living or dead roach had their own unique force of power. Much like a fingerprint. And that went for their blood hosts as well. I felt it. Without turning, I knew Olivia lurked close by. I turned and prepared to kill her as well. Innocent of her powers or not, she represented everything I hated at this moment. Time had come to take a piece of Judas.

Olivia stood only feet away from me. She looked graceful and pure. It caused me to hesitate long enough to hear her speak. "I am sorry for the cruelty that has happened tonight."

Practically dropping Price, I jumped to my feet. I only had a wooden stake with me. I pointed it at her, as I scanned the area for lost killing tools. The Magnum had been lost somewhere in the grass, out of reach, and I had emptied the 9mm. "Where the hell is he?" She might have been guilty by association, but I wouldn't think twice about pulling the trigger. I did everything I could to see her as a victim in all of this, but deep inside I knew better. Killing her would make me feel better and possibly feed some of the demons inside me, but I knew in the long run it wouldn't do anything to stop Judas.

Olivia looked down at Josh's remains, followed by a quick survey of the other bodies that now littered the ground. "It would appear as though your enemy has underestimated you, Paul Isaac of Orlando." She gave a fake smile. "I do hope you will be able to get your coven under control. It is acts such as this that make a master vampire appear weak and vulnerable." Her eyes moved down to the stake, still pointed at her chest. "And with you killing your own vampires, the Council will be greatly disturbed by your actions."

My right hand wrapped around the wooden stake as I eased over to the Magnum and picked it up. Instead of using it, I placed it back in the holster and kept the stake's pointed end at her chest. I ran the shots through my head. No guarantees I had another bullet in the chamber, which was a bitch. Blowing her head across the cemetery seemed really easy right now. With as much dignity and speed as I could muster, I placed myself between Olivia and Price. "I don't give a damn if you're a blood host, a fang head, a human freak, or any other coffin sleeper terminology, I'm telling you this for the last time, I'm not one of you, not in the least, so if the Council wants to discuss things with me, they will have to wait in line. The coven that attacked me, not the other way around. Maybe they should talk to what's left of Sasha's little gang about treason, if such a thing exists in your little twisted world." Again I could feel the vines of cockroach politics wrapping around my throat. Every action I took seemed to have far more complex reactions that painted me deeper into a corner. I stood there for a few more seconds and waited for a reaction that never came. I retracted the stake. My attention returned to Price. "I need some help over here!" I shouted to the various men and women in the area.

Olivia remained stoic. "Unless your friend receives medical attention soon, it would appear as though you will be keeping the local florist busy. He needs your power."

"What the hell do you mean?"

"Your blood. It will keep him alive."

And now for the question you don't want the answer to, but don't have the ability to keep your mouth shut. "What do you mean my blood will keep him alive?"

A grin sprouted on her face. "I think we both know what I am talking about. Cut your vein and allow the man to drink from it. Do it or he will surely die. It is one of the perks of being a vampire, Paul Isaac of Orlando."

"Go to hell, Olivia," I answered.

She shrugged. "Denial will not make what you are go away." She looked around. "I'm not here to judge you. Vampire or not, your blood will save this man's life. Denying who you are will not change things or make them go away. There will be others. They will never stop. Kill Judas and ten more will take his place."

The thought of it all made me sick to my stomach. It had been one thing to be called a master roach or even be killed because of the technicalities in it, but when it is thrown in your face that you have some sort of undead special powers, it makes you want to puke. I wanted to deny it, but then I looked back down at Price and knew without my help, another innocent person would die because of me. He already looked dead. "Somebody help me!" I shouted again. I began to weigh my options. I looked at her hard. "I can't do it. I can't take the chance. Trusting you and what you represent…This is Judas' idea isn't it?"

"Not this time. Your blood is powerful and is why it is so

attractive to the vampires around you. More will be coming for you, make no mistake. You have only minutes to save the detective. Deny what you are to yourself, but you have the ability to save his life. Your blood is even stronger than that of a true blooded vampire." Her fingernails flashed across my skin. My flesh stung. Blood trickled from the wound.

"You…" I stopped as I watched it flow down my arm. For the first time tonight, I had a chance at saving a life rather than taking one, or seeing it taken from me. The blood trickled down my skin and I realized just how crazy it all sounded. If I fed Price the blood and he died, it might prove I wasn't a dirt napper, but if it saved his life it proved things far more complicated. God, I hated cockroach red tape.

Price had stopped breathing, or it had become so shallow that his chest never expanded. "Feed it to him." Her voice consumed with desire and hunger. Her eyes were glued to the flowing liquid. I grew nervous as I bent down over Price and placed my palm across his gapped mouth.

I pulled it away several times as I ran the scenarios in my head. I looked back down at Price. He was dead. I had no doubt about it. With my hand palm up, I watched the blood drip from my fingers. I had two choices. Either I denied it all and let him die, or save him with my blood.

I stepped back. I couldn't do it. If he died, he died a man. I couldn't take the chance of having him rise as something I hadn't thought of yet. I hadn't come to terms with the virus in my blood and to put it into someone else's body without their permission seemed a bit more than I could do. This blood thing had been the root of all the death anyway. What complicated thing did I release by putting it in Price? When I killed Asa, I did it out of self-defense and look what that got me.

Paramedics arrived in time to see the blood drip from my hand. One of them looked at me. I saw the appalled glare in those eyes. I withdrew my hand and wiped the blood on the grass next to me. "What?" Neither of the two spoke anything coherent, but were afraid to come close to Price. "Damn it, help him!" Both men snapped to attention and began to attend the old man, but between actions, I still caught them taking a peek at the drying blood on my arm. My anger grew at the reflection I saw in the men. At one time, they only saw me as a bitter ax man, but now I morphed closer to monster than anything human. And when humans saw you as the other side, options became scarce.

They loaded Price in the back of the remaining ambulance and drove away. More were on the way. I could hear them in the distance, it probably wouldn't matter. I second guessed myself as I looked to Olivia. She could read my thoughts. But another distraction gathered in the blackness. Different, but as deadly.

Somewhere on the edge of the shadows I heard the sound of a different kind of death. I reloaded the 9mm and shouted to those still alive to find cover, or better yet escape. The howl of a wolf echoed in the distance.

Kasey had arrived.

CHAPTER TWENTY-NINE

Outlined in shadows along the horizon, I could see Kasey as he walked toward us. Decked out in a leather jacket, black t-shirt and worn jeans. Muscles bulged as he and his pack made their way through the moonlight. Even steroids couldn't do the things to muscles that the lycan virus could.

Shifter power differed in feel from roach power, but just as potent as it danced on your skin. As to be expected, it presented itself much more lively and vibrant. I remembered the last time we saw each other. It hadn't been such a pleasant account. I liked to run my mouth with Kasey, but the honest truth... he scared the living hell out of me. That alone made things bad, but he had brought about a dozen of his best biting machines and to top it all off, I stood next to a master roach's blood host. And her live-in sucker wanted me dead. Yeah, things were going well tonight.

I took a deep breath as I watched him make his way toward us. At this time, I had no guarantee he hadn't come here to kill me as well. After all, he had tried to feed me to the bat heads not so long ago. Based on what Camilla had told us right before she died, she had been sent here on Judas' word. The wolf had made a deal with the devil to get Angie back alive and failed. Chances were good that Kasey thought I had been her killer.

I did my best to remain calm and hope for the best. Physically, I had nothing to go on. Dealing with the death of Father Garcia had taken all the fight out of me in some respects, while in others it made me want to sever the heads of anything that sucked blood or turned furry.

I kept an eye on Olivia. If I could ride her energy long enough, I might be able to tell where Judas hid. Guilty or not, I still associated her with Father Garcia's death, but taking her life at the moment didn't buy me anything except more roach politics. For now, I would have to keep all that in mind and show restraint. From what Angie had told me, if I killed Judas, I got a two for one deal, so staking her only fed my self-indulgence.

I already had come to terms that Angie didn't exist anymore. Evidence already showed that Judas had ended other lives connected to me, why not one more. Judas truthfully didn't gain anything from killing Josh or Kansas' child. Neither Frank Price nor Ezekiel Kansas were master roaches. But we all knew that I had a vested interest in Angie. Bleeding her would be pure pleasure for him. It would be his final slap in the face before ending me.

I had asked that the entrances to the cemetery be blocked off and that the approaching ambulances remain out of reach. Bringing them in here now would only lead to more lives we would either see fall or have to rescue. Not to be cold, but the human bodies that littered the cemetery were already dead. I couldn't do anything for them now. I had also asked that every officer leave the cemetery. My being here had already put them in harm's way. I didn't want to compromise my killing by running more rescue missions. Flashing red and blue lights littered the boundaries to the cemetery. None would be able to get to me if things went wrong.

Olivia moved next to me, the power radiating off of her made me take a step to the side. Not her power this time. Something much more powerful. Older. I watched along the tree line and in all the darkest shadow pockets for Judas. Still nothing by vision, but close.

"You had better stop Kasey now before he gets close enough to harm you and the officers," Olivia said as she watched them approach. Like me, she scanned the outskirts of the cemetery where the patrol cars and officers waited.

"We'll have to see who he's here to kill, Olivia. Seems to me that it was you that fed Camilla to Judas, not me. Perhaps it's you that's in for a dog bite." I watched his shadow become larger and more defined. "Tell Judas to join us. He can't hide in the trees all night."

She turned to me with a smile. "Kasey and Judas have an

alliance against you, Paul Isaac. With you dead, our coven will gain the city and Kasey's threat as alpha male will be gone. Judas will be here shortly with Angie as an olive branch to the treaty. Once the alliance has been recognized there will be no need to keep you alive."

Now she had my attention. "Angie's alive?"

A glow filled her face. "Depends on your definition of the word, but in the most extreme sense, yes." She licked her lips. "I hear you tried to turn her before the vampires arrived at the Silver Priapus the other night. Too bad she was so weak, or she might have been able to fight Judas off. With you dead, she would have turned and been much stronger." She watched the pack move through the cemetery. "Judas has fed from her as well as many others. Unless Judas releases her, she will always be his. Much like me. The wolves do not know this."

"What you mean he's tied her to him?"

Olivia smiled, then spoke. "Precisely."

"Judas kidnapped Angie because he knew he would get, not only me, but Kasey and the pack as well?"

Olivia shook her head. I could feel Judas riding on her. He had drawn close.

I stuck the barrel of the 9mm against her throat. "With the two of you dead, she wouldn't be in the jaws of a vampire. Where does he have her?" Before I could pull the trigger, the power thickened.

"Do it and I'll rip you to pieces," Kasey said as he walked up to me. He had gotten to me so quietly and quickly, I jumped. He stood before me, daring me to kill Olivia. Long flowing hair cupped his face. The wolf in him, begging to be set free. It took everything I had not to take a large step backwards.

"Didn't expect to see me make it out of the orange groves did you, Kasey? Once again, you've made deals with the fang bangers and again you're going to leave with nothing."

He grinned as he stopped in front of me, folded his legs and widened his stance. "You should have killed Victor. Of all the times I thought you would kill something, you didn't."

"You know Judas isn't going to keep his word and the peace with you. They've already killed another of your pack. How many more will it take for you to see that you can't trust them, no matter whose life is at stake. Price couldn't stop them, Kansas' son is dead because of his father's trust in them and look at what's happened to me. You really think you're any different? As long as Judas is alive, Angie's tied to him. And if others have fed from her they can be too."

Kasey rolled his eyes to Olivia. "I've done what you asked. Now where's Angie. Double cross me again and my wolves will eat your underbelly."

Olivia moved back a step. "You were not double crossed at the Silver Priapus, alpha wolf. You were lied to. Paul was never the prize that night. I thought you would have seen that by now."

My attention remained in the blackness of the shadows. Olivia wouldn't be the one to make the first move. Killing me gained her nothing. If she killed me, the next in line among my coven would be Master Roach, not Judas.

Olivia looked back to me, my 9mm rested between Kasey and Olivia. I had a bad feeling. None of us were coming out of this a winner. If I didn't convince Kasey to side with me, my options would be between slim and none. "From what I know of the last few nights, it is you that has brought things to this. Helping Sasha gain what is not rightfully his will win you no favors with this coven." She took a deep breath and looked at me. "I am growing board with the games at this point anyway, but you do not want to miss the final act."

Kasey stopped only inches from Olivia's face. "I'm not scared of you, Olivia, or any of your vampires either. I did what I had to do. I gave blood, now I want what I came here for." He looked at me. "Or I kill Paul myself and make things really complicated for you."

My mouth opened and closed several times before the thoughts in my head spilled out. "You sent Camilla to Olivia, knowing that Judas would kill her here tonight didn't you?"

Kasey shook his head. "Not in the way you think. It's a bit complicated."

"So is simple math for you, but why don't you tell me what's going on here, Kasey?"

He looked to Olivia for a few seconds, then to me. "I had received word from the Vampire Council to leave you in the orange grove along with all your weapons. I was told to get in contact with Victor and let him know where you were. The Council wanted Victor dead. Once he was dead, Sasha was to kill you and Judas and become the master vampire of Orlando. Fulfill the Council's request and they would convince Sasha to release Angie to me."

"Makes sense why Sasha made an appearance here tonight."

Kasey nodded, but said nothing.

"Not that I disagree with them about wanting Victor dead, but why?"

"They gained information that Victor planned to kill you and become the new master on his own. The Council knew this would implode the coven between Sasha and Victor and weaken the overall status in the city. The Council knew the longer you remained master vampire the larger the threat of more invasions from out of town covens seeking the territory."

"I was supposed to do the Council's dirty work? Too bad how things worked out. I think Victor's still alive and Sasha's out there somewhere dying of a silver bullet to the head." A laughed at him out of spite. "Not only do I plan on killing a few more roaches tonight, but I've managed to piss off the Council and make you look like the incompetent leader you are as well. Tonight's starting to look up." Then I couldn't resist one more insult on him. "By the end of the night, your pack will probably be begging me to be the new alpha."

An animalistic grin formed. "Don't plan on it, master vampire. You'll be dead before that happens. You being alive complicated things and now that Judas knows he isn't the Council's first choice for master of the city, he might be just a bit unreasonable to everyone."

"Including you." I didn't buy the whole story and it didn't make me more at ease around Kasey. He still saw me as a threat to his pack and his love interest. If we both lived through the night, there would still be scores to settle. "Sorry to have pissed on your parade, Kasey, but keeping their end of the bargain is not something these blood lickers are known for. And if the Council wants a roach dead, they're dead. Why did they go through me?"

He shrugged. "You know as well as I do that it isn't about the end result that they love, it's the games. It's just like with you. They've had plenty of opportunities to kill you, but here you are. It's about seeing how much power and control they can possess." He stopped and looked me from head to toe. "They're just playing with their food. Honestly, I think they were half way hoping Victor would kill you, leaving him for Judas, but it doesn't really matter now."

"And now you're no better than they are. You've dragged in those that you've sworn to protect on the promise the Council will remember who you are once this is over and you've delivered nothing to them. They'll want more from you. This won't go away no matter what you do now."

Kasey looked back along the outlines of the cemetery. Searching for something or possibly surveying where all the nice police officers with their guns were hiding. "I have to do what is best for the pack as a whole and sometimes you have to make difficult choices along the way. I come here alone, but the pack will join me soon."

My disgust with Kasey went up a level. "And your weakness shows through the choices you're making. You're doing this for your own good, not the pack's. Angie's brother would have never let this happen."

"It also got him killed." He looked to Olivia for help. She remained rigid and uncaring. Kasey spoke, "I'm not proud of it, but yes. The Council always settles things in blood as I'm sure you're very aware of by now. I made a deal with the devils and lost. I can only hope that my appearance here tonight will be seen by the Council as an act of solidarity. It might keep Angie alive and less of a target of punishment."

"You're acting as though I'm already dead." Built like a rock, and had the intelligence of one as well, Kasey looked overwhelmed. "You're an idiot, Kasey. They're wrapping you around their fingers just like they've done everybody else. Snap out of it. Angie's dead."

He moved in on me. "Angie's not dead. And I would have given my life for her if I could have. More than I can say about you."

"Sugar coat it all you want, but you're the one with the

blood on his hands. And mark my words, Kasey, you might have to give your life for her." I didn't know Camilla all that well. I didn't have the emotional attachment I had with Angie, but the principal of it all made me want to watch him fall victim to the blood suckers. I looked him in the eyes. "So whose side are you on now, Kasey? Are you here to help Judas kill me? Because if you do, keep in mind that you've killed what they see as a master bat head and if you think things are complicated now, you have no idea what you're in for. Snap out of it and see the real evil that's in front of you."

It took him a long time to speak. "I am here for Angie and I will kill anyone that I have to in order to get her back in one piece. I'm not here to kill you, but if that's what it takes, you're a dead man."

"Just keep in mind, she still won't love you." I started to say more, but a darker power rose out of the mist. Strong and old. Judas.

CHAPTER THIRTY

The death dealer advanced from the distance. He dwarfed me as his shadow crawled along the blanket of grass. His stroll remained methodical and confident. Eyes darker than the pits of hell, skin bleach white, fangs brilliant and menacing. His brown hair flowed across his shoulders in waterfalls of color, washed out by the glow of the moon above. All of this under a charm of Southern hospitality.

He wore a deep blue pin striped Armani suit with a white dress shirt. He could have passed for one of those preachers on television. He overflowed with charisma, full of snake charms, lethal in every way.

Judas' facial expressions changed as he looked past me. He almost looked joyous. "Olivia, my dear, I must say you are the most beautiful thing I have seen tonight." He held out his hand to her. "Please join me for dinner tonight." She moved to his side like a good little blood whore.

I would have already put him out of his misery if it hadn't been for one small detail. Angie came into view. Her eyes glazed with a nothingness, deep in a trance of dirt napping magic. Her usual exotic and sensual body now frail and very sick. Her nude body lacked the normal sexuality I had grown to adore. She had been tethered to Judas with a large leather collar wrapped around her neck. The skin underneath pink from abuse and abrasion. A purple bruise and two small puncture wounds colored her right shoulder. The thought of his fangs feeding into her, once caramel skin, gave me the creeps. Yeah, I was going to enjoy taking his heart out.

He released the leash that held Angie, but she made no attempt to run or even move. She never blinked or responded to anything around her.

Judas looked to Kasey. "So convenient of you to join us here tonight alpha wolf. Now I will not have to hunt you down. Pity things did not work out the way you intended." His hand snaked down the side of Angie's face. "I do believe that you had planned on it being Sasha standing here at this moment if you had had your way. Now others must pay the price for your actions."

"I was under order of the Council," Kasey said as monotone as ever.

Judas played with the large handlebar mustache that rested above his lip with his left hand. His eyes now on the alpha wolf. "The Council? Why would the Council involve you in such matters? They would never call upon you for anything." He moved toward us, Angie in tow. I had already calculated my angles of getting a clear shot in time. Problem was, I didn't even have the Magnum in my hand. I knew I would never get to the gun, pull the trigger and make a successful shot before he had time to rip Angie's throat out. He stopped about ten yards from where we stood. "Who told you of Council business?"

Kasey looked back to me before looking forward again. "Quinn Rubio."

Judas surveyed edge of the tree line. "Quinn Rubio might have been the one that talked to you about Sasha and myself, but I assure you, it was not under the direction of the Council. Either you have been lied to, or you are lying to me."

"Who it came from isn't important, Judas. It was orders from the Council and Angie shouldn't be put in the middle of all of this. I told you I was bringing Paul to the Silver Priapus and that we would make sure Detective Kansas was there as well. I did everything I was supposed to do."

My blood boiled. I never liked Kasey, but I always thought of him as being better than the coffin sleepers. Never in my life did I think he would be this deep in bed with them. "What's in it for you, Kasey?"

All three looked to me. Judas broke into a knowing smile. "The master vampire has a right to know all the details to the puzzle, Kasey. Perhaps we should enlighten not only him, but Angela as well."

Kasey grew agitated. "We had a deal, Judas. I bring you Paul and all the other secrets go away."

Judas continued to smile and pet Angie. She remained as despondent as a doll. "And why is it that this one means so much to you, alpha wolf? Is it because the current master vampire is also lustful of her beauty? Because she is something you cannot have? Or because of something far more sinister, such as guilt?"

Kasey moved in on Judas. "Shut up, Judas. It's all lies."

"How is it that you came to being alpha male of the pack, wolf?" Judas stood his ground. "Not much different of a story than I will have when I take over this territory." He waited. Kasey balled his hands into fists and started to pace. "What happened to Angela's brother the night he was murdered?"

I snapped to attention and looked to Kasey. Not a good idea when face to face with something that had come to town to remove you from your head.

Kasey ignored the question. "It wasn't me that double crossed you on all this. You need to talk to Quinn and the Council about Sasha's plans. Personally I don't care who owns this city. I'm here for Angie." He took a deep breath and looked at me. "I didn't have anyone killed." I became painfully aware that the two had had some sort of conversation about Angie's brother. Information I would tuck away for further use at a later date.

Judas laughed. "Deny it all you wish, alpha, but I know it was you that told Piel where to find Angela's brother that night." He gave a vicious smile. "You see, you are not the only one that has communications with the secrets of this city. I know how you sent the alpha male to the underground Tortured Skin party that night to find Angela. How you already knew she was not there, knew there was no party. Only Piel." The last words lingered in the air.

The name Piel, struck a chord with me. I had killed him. A shape shifter that could turn into anything he wanted. He had a special vendetta against the furries and now I knew more than I should. That part I knew by the look in Kasey's eyes.

"Piel acted on his own. I had nothing to do with it." Again, Kasey answered to me for some reason. I heard a quiver develop in his voice.

"And where is Sasha now, wolf?"

Kasey looked back to Judas. "Dead." Silence blanketed the night for a moment. "I have already lost one wolf tonight because of the Council and your coven. I will not lose another. It's Quinn and the Council that owes you blood now."

The master roach raised his hand. "Tell me, alpha wolf, what would Angela think of you if she knew you had her brother killed. Do you think she could ever love someone that led her flesh and blood to slaughter? I think if she knew the truth either I or Mr. Isaac would have a greater chance at earning her trust and love."

Kasey stumbled on his words. I eased my hand toward the butt of the Magnum. Judas looked to me. I stopped.

Back to Kasey, "I am waiting, wolf? Confess the truth or I will kill her in front of you, now."

"Massey was weak. I knew Piel wouldn't live long enough to matter. It was my time to run the pack. Like with Camilla, it was a necessary sacrifice for the good of all."

I couldn't believe what I heard. A part of me impressed to see Kasey had the balls to do anything, but the overwhelming part of me saw him as nothing more than a cold blooded killer like the roaches. All this time Angie had thought Piel had killed him in nothing more than aggression for the alpha position in the pack. I felt better knowing she would hate us both equally if we got her back alive.

Still, among my limited choices, Kasey remained my best ally. I only hoped he saw it the same way. "If you don't help me end this, Kasey, we will never get Angie back." My fingers inched closer to the Magnum. Judas noticed, but I think he enjoyed our lethal game of cat and mouse.

Kasey swung his glare back to me. "There is no we. I'll get Angie back. You'll be dead."

"Do you really think Judas is going to let you live? He's through using you. As long as he's alive, Angie is tied to him. She will never be yours as long as he's above ground." An inch closer to the gun. "So what if he keeps your secret tonight, kills me and gives you back Angie. There will be a next time and he will continue to use it against you for the rest of your life. If you ever want to have a chance with Angie, you have to help me. She will never be yours as long as he's alive."

Judas' attention swung to me. "You wouldn't be so quick to join forces with the wolf if you knew what he had been hiding from you."

I couldn't help but turn my stare to Kasey.

Kasey remained silent. Judas filled in the missing pieces. "You see master vampire, it was Kasey's wolves that had been harboring Josh and Stephanie for me." He gave a small giggle behind the long drawl of his accent. "Right under your nose, vampire man. Stephanie was at the Silver Priapus the night you were there. You just didn't know it."

"Why?" I asked as I looked Kasey in the eyes.

Those deep blue eyes shifted back to me. "You should know by now, Paul, that in this world, we don't always get to choose what's right. You're not a master vampire, but you'll die because they think of you as one. Angie would've already been dead if I didn't do what they said. We're all nothing more than pawns in their twisted world. You, me, Kansas, Price. It doesn't make a difference who dies tonight and no one will give a damn who lives."

Judas pulled Angie's leash tight enough that her neck snapped close to his lips. "Now that Angela knows the truth, there is no need to keep her alive." The monster opened his mouth.

The air rose with animalistic energy. Kasey started to move into wolf form. He charged toward Judas, claws extending as he picked up speed. Jaws wide. Muscles and bone forming. He hit Judas hard. They rolled across the dew covered grass in a violent dance. Angie spun to the ground at Olivia's feet.

Kasey gained the advantage and attempted to bite deep into the coffin maggot's shoulder. Judas moved behind the wolf in a blur of speed and ripped through Kasey's throat. Blood covered Judas' mouth as he pulled away, dropping the alpha to the ground.

I moved in on Judas. Ready to place every goddamned bullet I had left in his head. My hand reached for the Magnum but it would be too late. The monster pounced on me before I had time to fully turn. He hit me with the force of an army tank, sending me airborne into a nearby cypress tree. My chest still hurt and limited my movements.

His fangs closed in on my neck as he descended. I rolled clear of the attack, stood and grabbed a wooden stake. I brought it down on Judas' back with all the force I had before he had time to stand.

His breath became labored. Blood pooled around the wound in crimson droplets. I kicked him in the jaw, sending him in a backwards flip. It knocked one of his lower fangs free.

I readied the Magnum from the holster, but hesitated. I couldn't breathe or move. His power struck me with such force I couldn't think. I glanced to Kasey. He remained unresponsive, which is always a bad sign.

"Before killing me, Avenger there might be something you want to know." I found it a strange thing to say, since he had the upper hand. In the back of my mind, I already knew he had been planning this little scenario. A trickle of his own blood ran from the corner of his mouth. He grimaced in pain.

"Please pull the trigger," I said to myself. But I couldn't. My fingers betrayed me. Panic set in. I had wanted this so bad and now I hesitated.

"I can help you with the demons in your mind. Give you the answers to questions you have sought for a lifetime." He moved to me. Burning pain raced through me until I couldn't move. His heated breath trickled along me skin. "I know more than just secrets about the wolf. I know who killed your parents."

I swallowed hard and again, tried to pull the trigger. Inside, I knew Judas knew nothing about my parent's murders, but I still couldn't find the strength to pull the trigger.

The true killers of my parents had eluded me my whole life. I looked over to Kasey. Still nothing there. Angie remained lifeless at Olivia's feet to my left. No one could save me but myself. And I didn't seem to be motivated to do it.

"Deep inside, I know it still haunts you. Keeps you awake at night. The never ending pain of not knowing if you have killed the vampire that took their lives. I can give you their names."

"You're full of shit." I pushed against the trigger, hoped it would pull back, hoped it wouldn't.

That smile never left his face. "I have watched over you

and followed you far longer than you would have ever known. Which is why the priest had to die. Dead men tell no tales. You see, it was those closest to you that lied the most. The man you knew as your father killed our kind out of hatred and in cold blood." He paused. "Until he met the lovely Mrs. Isaac. A woman that stole his heart and calmed the killing beast inside him. A woman with ties to the Knights of the Night."

I shrugged. "You're not telling me anything I don't already know." I desperately tried to pull the trigger but I couldn't. I blamed it on Judas' power. It had to be. I prayed that Father Garcia hadn't lost his life over something I already knew.

"And I am sure you know that it was Albert Kincaid, the famous skin trader that was in fact your father, not the man that died that night."

I pulled with everything I had. Nothing. I no longer wanted to hear about who killed my parents. I wanted to shut him up. "There's no proof of that."

"Ah, but there is, Avenger. It is in your blood and we both know it. You only deny the truth."

My world spun out of control. Inside, I begged him to take my life. Whether it had been truth or a lie, he had planted doubt. How had I let him get to me like this?

"Here is something you did not know, Avenger. Your mother was vampire and she took your father's life. She was sent to him, on orders of the Council. Shortly before he was killed, your father found out the truth and planned to not only take your mother's life, but yours as well. Your own mother murdered him as you ran and hid in the shadows."

"Lies."

"Ever wonder why the vampires didn't come after you?"

"Lies."

"Only the love of a mother could do that. She saved your life."

"Pull the trigger, Paul. God, pull the trigger!" I said in my head. "My mother wasn't a vampire. It's impossible for a human and a vampire to conceive." My mind cluttered with his lies. Denial flooded through me as I processed the information. I clung desperately to what remained of my fragile world.

He shook his head. "So everyone thought until you were

born. You see, they have been lying to you. Father Garcia, Quinn Rubio. It is why Quinn, along with all the other vampires are so attracted to your power. He knew you were half vampire, just as the Father knew. He used it against you to kill Maximilian. He told you that you had the poison running through your veins, when in fact you already had it there from birth. A true half breed that all vampires have coveted. Many believe that the blood that runs through your veins is twice as powerful as that of a pure blooded vampire. Now you know why you have been able to gaze into the eyes of other vampires while others cannot. Quinn never poisoned you. Your mother did."

I shook my head. "Not true. You're lying to save your ass. Something that won't happen tonight." I couldn't breathe.

"Test your blood. I can smell it from here, just as all vampires can. Tell me that your mouth does not water when you smell blood. You know it's true." He moved in and out of the shadows. "As for Kincaid, he planned on talking unless the vampire nation funded more of his films. He knew who killed your father and he knew what you were. That is why he was murdered, not the dirty little tales you thought were true. He didn't die over money or power, but over secrets." He sniffed along Angie's neck. "How ironic that the one thing you hate the most, has always run through your veins."

I wanted to ask about my mother's death, but I held my tongue. I tried to convince myself, Judas only dealt in lies. And I wanted it to stop. To come to terms with what I had heard and accept it would be too much to handle. I had to make it all go away.

As I had done when I tried to turn Angie, I dug deep inside me and pulled my own power out. If I had roach blood in my veins, I planned to use it to my advantage. I would call on its strength. "Go to hell." I pulled the trigger. I saw the surprise on his face as he looked over to Olivia. My mind spun in shades of black. In the distance I heard the explosion. A wave of heat washed over me. Smelled the death.

The power evaporated around me as I fell back to the ground. My knees hit with violent force. Pain shot through my head and chest. I gulped air as I rested on the cool ground and saw the ash and wooden spike.

It was over. Finally over.

CHAPTER THIRTY-ONE

My eyes shot open again as fingers touched the side of my face. Warm electricity danced on my skin. I rolled as fast as I could and came face to face with Olivia. I saw a glimmer of something dangerous in her eyes. As an animated parasite, she would die within minutes. I wondered what she thought of me now. Killer or deliverer?

I wanted so badly to see the human side of her and make myself believe that she had been as much of a victim in all of this as anyone else that had been on the biting end of a bat head, but I still couldn't totally get past everything I knew about her. Every instinct I had screamed for me to put her down.

I crawled away from her as I gathered my thoughts. My eyes darted across the cemetery. First to Angie. Then to Kasey. Both remained motionless. "Angie," I whispered. I left the Magnum next to what remained of Judas.

I began to crawl toward her. Her eyes were wide open. The magic still there, along with her hate for me. Something told me not to expect the happy reunion I hoped it would be. Those beautiful eyes looked up to me with the intensity of a hurricane. I tried to touch her, only to hear a dark growl.

Olivia reached out to me. I swatted her hand away. "I still feel his power." With what little energy I had left, I stood.

Angie's eyes shifted to Olivia. Lycan power rose around me and crawled up my body. Intoxicating and hypnotic. Blood rushed from my head and muscles. Fatigue ate away at me as the adrenalin receded.

Olivia caught me as I began to fall again. This time I allowed her to. I no longer had the strength to fight it. The power that prickled along her skin continued to make my own skin dance. Nothing evil or even powerful. Warm and comforting. My body fed from the power. I soaked in it.

"How long do you have?" I asked.

"Forever," she whispered in my ear. I heard distant laughing in my head. Cold air stung my flesh. Every thought in my head sucked out instantly. My mouth went dry. Muscles tensed. Panic hit.

I fought to break free from her grasp. The power reached higher levels. My skin began to burn to the bone even though the air around me grew colder by the second. I pulled away from her enough to see a face no longer filled with timeless beauty. The façade had disappeared. In front of me, I came face to face with the most hideous monster I had ever seen. Rotting skin and maggots danced along a crevasse of death. Eyes barely in their sockets. Large fangs that hadn't been there before. "How do you like me now, Avenger? Some say death becomes me."

My mouth moved, but I couldn't speak. "Who…?"

"I knew you would kill my enemies and remain vulnerable to the truth. Victor licks his wounds somewhere deep in the city and Sasha dies slowly from silver poison rotting in his brain. I have defeated them all and never lifted a finger."

"You? It wasn't Judas that was the master cockroach. It was you?" The Magnum remained too far out of reach.

"I told you before it was a game Judas and I played when we came into cities. Judas was not the master vampire, it was I." Her claw-like hands scratched across my face. "And now I will own you and your territories. I will soon be the most powerful vampire on the face of the earth." Blood and saliva dripped from her rotting lips. "You, on the other hand, will be nothing more than my personal blood supply for all eternity. My own fountain of youth."

I fought to breathe. I had been caught off guard. Focused on the wrong enemy. I clenched my teeth as I connected the dots of stupidity.

I could smell the rotten flesh. Feel the slither of maggots and worms. Dead flesh, cold and rubbery. Decaying tissue. Long, yellow nails grabbed my wrist and dug into my arm. Fangs sank into my throat. I could feel the sucking action taking place, but helpless to do anything about it. Strength overpowered me. I resisted with everything I had, but she remained locked to my vein.

My head began to spin. Ears rang. Euphoria filled my thoughts. *"Look into my eyes and stop the pain, Paul,"* I heard in the distance.

I swallowed hard. My tongue swelled. My gorge moved up my throat. Colors pulsated in my vision. Thirsty. So thirsty.

My knees gave way. Strength now gone. I rested in her arms. Relief replaced the fear of dying. There would be no more pain soon. Death hadn't been the enemy I had thought it would be. Instead, it seemed like a long lost friend that would not only come to my rescue, but ease the pain that no drug or therapy could. "...kill you," I managed to get out.

Olivia laughed inside my head. *"Even if you could, all it would do is make you the master vampire of two covens. Face it, Avenger, you cannot kill me. You cannot win."*

The explosion blasted me out of my trance. Something about feeling the chest of an ancient monster explode does that to you. Power evaporated from around me.

Olivia's eyes turned white. They rolled to the back of her head. Animated life dripped from her pours. Her grip released me. I rolled to the ground, unable to move. Olivia fell to the grass as the wave of burned skin filled my nose.

Angie stood behind her. She held the Magnum in her hands. She watched as the master roach writhed in pain and agony. In her face, no emotion.

"But I can." I looked back at the face of my angel and saw the eyes of a cold demon. The lust that I had grown to know from them now nothing but a memory in my mind's eye. Instead, I saw the predator I knew had been there all along, but tried desperately to overlook.

"Thank you, Angie," I panted. I still couldn't move. I could barely breathe.

That cold, yet beautiful face looked down on me. Her skin started to glow again. The seductive tendencies returned. The bitch had returned. Her matted hair framed her face, thick with blood and sweat. Moonlight caught the copper tones of her nude body. "Thank you for what?"

I tried to smile. "You saved my life."

"Bite me."

Okay, not the answer I was looking for, but then again, after our last encounter, it shouldn't have been that shocking to me. I looked up at her and asked anyway, "What?"

"You heard me, you son of a bitch. Bite me."

This time I remained quiet and tried to think it through.

Angie began to unravel the mystery. "I need you to bite me and make me yours."

"Oh, God, not this again…" I started.

"It's not what you think, you self-serving bastard. Judas drank my blood and practically turned me into his blood host. Now that he's dead and Olivia's dead, any vampire with somewhat power will be able to make me their own and tie me to them. Not that I have any respect for you anymore, Paul, but I trust you more than those other sleaze balls."

Deep down inside I knew what she meant, but I asked the stupid question anyway. "What?" Not intelligently, but I asked.

"You know exactly what I'm talking about. You can deny it all you want, but you're one of us now, baby. You're enough of a vampire that you can tie me to you and keep me out of their mouths and beds. I'm not asking you to protect me or even keep me around, but I swear to God, Paul if you turn your back on me now, I'll never forgive you."

"Angie, I can't…"

Suddenly, I looked down the barrel of my own Magnum. "Give me one good reason why I shouldn't spread your brains all over this hallowed ground." Her hands shook with vengeance. Water filled her eyes with anger, not sorrow. "If it wasn't for you and what you are, those things would never have done what they did to me. I hope you burn in hell." She couldn't have done anything worse to me at the moment. I wanted her to pull the trigger. End it all for me. I would take the coward's way out. "Bite me."

I shook my head. "No. I'm not one of you. My mother wasn't a roach. I'm not a roach, and even if I am, I won't fall into the trappings of one."

She laughed. "You sad little piece of crap. You've already fallen into their trappings. Look around you, Paul.

People died because of your trappings. I was kidnapped and sucked because of your trappings. I'm not asking a lot out of you here. Don't even look at it as a favor. Deny it all you want. If it's not true, you have nothing to lose by doing it."

I took a deep breath. For the first time, she saw me as the monster. "Angie, if you think I'm going to beg you not to kill me, you're sadly mistaken. Right now, I think you'd be doing both of us a hell of a lot of good by pulling the trigger. Unlike me, I hope you have the guts to do it. But I won't take your blood. I'm not one of them and I'm not one of you."

She stood perfectly still for what seemed to be hours. I waited. I even saw her finger twitch on the trigger. Then she pulled it down to her side. "You don't deserve to die." The wolf pitched the Magnum next to me, missing my face by less than an inch. She showed no emotion as she turned away from me and went to Kasey. Her hands moved across his wound. "It would be the easy way out for you, and I won't let you have that."

With the remaining strength I had, I stood and leaned against one of the nearby headstones. "One of these days, you'll look back on all of this and see that I did the right thing. Breaking your heart was the best thing I could have ever done for you. Now you can go back to being what you are and not feel guilty about it."

Angie stormed back to me. "You over confident bastard. I've never felt guilty for anything I've ever done in my life. You actually think I'm going to lose sleep over you don't you? I almost feel sorry for you. It's not me that I see as the monster anymore. It's you. And let's get something else straight. I didn't kill Olivia for you. I don't care if you live or die. I killed her for the pack. If I allowed her to kill you, she would have turned us all into blood hosts." Angie stepped back to Kasey. "Don't confuse love with a bullet to the head, baby."

In the distance I could see the movement of the officers and vehicles as they started to make their way back inside the cemetery. I still had a long night ahead of me. I wasn't up for it.

Angie picked Kasey up. He had survived Judas' attack, but weak. I tried to grab the Magnum with as little notice as I could. "How much did you hear?"

Angie stopped and stared. "Nothing. Why?" She shifted

her weight, lifted Kasey farther up and wrapped his arm around her neck. His eyes rolled to me. He left no doubt that we would talk later. I had only stopped the cockroach threat. The lycan threat remained at full throttle. Kasey held his free hand across his wound. Angie stopped short of me and stared. "Funny how you hurt the ones you love as much as you do the ones you hate." Her lips stopped short of mine. I could feel her breath. Smell her scent. Taste her anger. With a swift kick, her foot connected with my manhood. "Hope I didn't hit anything vital." Instantly, I crumbled back on the cold ground in the fetal position.

I watched as Angie and Kasey faded into the darkness doing my best not to throw up. I looked at what remained of Olivia. I swore I could still see her staring at me, power licking at my flesh. I closed my eyes and passed out again.

CHAPTER THIRTY-TWO

It had been two weeks since Olivia and Judas had been killed. And in that time, I had refused to leave my home. Depression had filled every nook and cranny of my being and I didn't have the will to do anything about it. I had dug this hole. Had been digging it for longer than I wanted to come to terms with. I still couldn't wrap my mind around the reality that Father Garcia was dead. Still woke with nightmares over seeing his body crucified to that tree. I hadn't even gone to his funeral. Something I know in time, I would regret.

Through the grapevine, I had heard that Frank Price had suffered a heart attack and nervous breakdown. He had retired from the force. I hadn't visited him at the hospital or even called him at home to send my condolences. Personally, I didn't think my thoughts would matter to him. I had promised him I would get his grandson back alive and I had failed. Miserably. I hadn't been a very religious man, but I prayed to God that he would somehow be able to get through his tragedy.

Kansas? I hadn't seen him in all the time since the night we were delivered the fetus. I hoped the best for him. And coming from me, after the shenanigans he had pulled, took a lot of doing for me. I knew the lab had ran tests on the fetus to see if it was his son, but I hadn't heard how that had worked out. As for Stephanie, she was found alive, but disoriented a week ago. She remained at the hospital, unable to talk or respond to anyone. Staring into space in some sort of comma state. Those that had visited her, say she looked more dead than alive.

I looked in the mirror and tried to figure out who or what I had become. A stranger and outcast to all those around me. Not human. Not monster...roach or fur ball. Nothing and everything all balled into one. I doubted everything. My real father. My mother. Where I fit in and why?

I had become a stranger to myself. Hollow from lack of eating. Old from lack of sleep. My skin pale, in contrast to the two week old growth on my face. Even my shaved head started to sprout hair. I stank from the lack of showers. Gritty and slimy all at the same time.

I had had enough. I had been caught in a winless war. No appreciation for what I did. Not even from me. God, I knew how to throw a pity party!

I placed the Magnum firmly in my mouth. Pulling the trigger would take very little effort if I hadn't been such a damned coward. Taking my life would prove it in every way. I had no doubt that it would be months before anyone found me. And even then it would be because of the stench and nothing more. I had read on a bathroom wall once, "There is only one 'em in this world and that's screw 'em." It had become my creed.

The doorbell rang.

God, that's how this whole nightmare started. A harmless ringing of a doorbell.

I ignored it. Whatever they wanted, would go unsatisfied.

A second ring.

I cursed under my breath. "What does a man have to do to be able to commit suicide in peace around here," I grumbled. I checked the Magnum for bullets and started out of the bathroom, only to stop again. How ironic that I planned to kill myself, but wanted the Magnum for protection against the monster on the other side of the front door.

But I wanted to be in control of how I cashed my chips in. If luck took pity on me, it would be Quinn or Dieter and I would be able to take them out with me. Yeah, I still needed the Magnum for now.

I opened the door with no hesitation. I expected to find death and fangs waiting on me. But instead, I found a medium sized brown box with my name on it, written with a black magic marker. I looked around for the deliverer, but found nothing but empty darkness. Suspicion began to build. No one dropped off packages at this time of night.

I placed the Magnum back in its holster and with all the

dedication I had, I lifted the box and brought it inside. It had been lighter than I expected, and when I shook it, nothing rattled or growled. I sat it on the floor, pulled my keys from my pocket and cut through the packing tape.

I pulled away the ends of the box to find well packed Styrofoam peanuts and a hand written note on a large white sheet of paper, meticulously folded.

"Best Wishes," I said out loud as I read it.

Again, I looked around. The pessimist in me knew the note could not have been in sincerity. I was the Grinch of the story, not the hero. No one had dropped off one of those jellies of the month gifts. I just had a feeling.

I pulled away a scoop of the peanuts, and jumped. It was a human head. Golden long hair, dyed with a tint of human blood. My heart pounded against my chest as I pulled it from the box.

The head spun in my grasp as I held it by a clump of the long hair, much like a macabre ornament. "Isabella," I whispered. I dropped it back into the box, carried it outside and looked around again. This time far more thorough. Nothing moved except the branches on a nearby oak.

My back rested against the frame of the door as I slid to the floor, still holding the box. A dark shiver rose over me as my fingers played with the butt of the Magnum, still snug in its shoulder holster. "Asa is alive."

About the Author

James C. Gillen is an award winning author in Orlando, Florida. His book, *Tortured Skin* has won the Royal Palm award for Best in Horror for Florida writers and was a Finalist for Horror book of the year in 2009 by USA Book News for American and International authors. He has been a member of the Disney Writers Group as well as O.W.L. (Orlando Writers League). Besides writing, James enjoys days on the back of his Harley, playing bass in a jazz quartet called Standard Blu, and graphic design. James resides with his wife, Mindy, three daughters and American Bulldog, Pursey.